SHIELD OF DRAGONS

(AGE OF THE SORCERERS – BOOK SEVEN)

MORGAN RICE

Morgan Rice

Morgan Rice is the #1 bestselling and USA Today bestselling author of the epic fantasy series THE SORCERER'S RING, comprising seventeen books; of the #1 bestselling series THE VAMPIRE JOURNALS, comprising twelve books; of the #1 bestselling series THE SURVIVAL TRILOGY, a post-apocalyptic thriller comprising three books; of the epic fantasy series KINGS AND SORCERERS, comprising six books; of the epic fantasy series OF CROWNS AND GLORY, comprising eight books; of the epic fantasy series A THRONE FOR SISTERS, comprising eight books; of the new science fiction series THE INVASION CHRONICLES, comprising four books; of the fantasy series OLIVER BLUE AND THE SCHOOL FOR SEERS, comprising four books; of the fantasy series THE WAY OF STEEL, comprising four books; and of the new fantasy series AGE OF THE SORCERERS, comprising eight books. Morgan's books are available in audio and print editions, and translations are available in over 25 languages.

Morgan loves to hear from you, so please feel free to visit www.morganricebooks.com to join the email list, receive a free book, receive free giveaways, download the free app, get the latest exclusive news, connect on Facebook and Twitter, and stay in touch!

Want free books?

Subscribe to Morgan Rice's email list and receive 4 free books, 3 free maps, 1 free app, 1 free game, 1 free graphic novel, and exclusive giveaways! To subscribe, visit: www.morganricebooks.com

Select Acclaim for Morgan Rice

"If you thought that there was no reason left for living after the end of THE SORCERER'S RING series, you were wrong. In RISE OF THE DRAGONS Morgan Rice has come up with what promises to be another brilliant series, immersing us in a fantasy of trolls and dragons, of valor, honor, courage, magic and faith in your destiny. Morgan has managed again to produce a strong set of characters that make us cheer for them on every page....Recommended for the permanent library of all readers that love a well-written fantasy."
--*Books and Movie Reviews*
Roberto Mattos

"An action packed fantasy sure to please fans of Morgan Rice's previous novels, along with fans of works such as THE INHERITANCE CYCLE by Christopher Paolini.... Fans of Young Adult Fiction will devour this latest work by Rice and beg for more."
--*The Wanderer, A Literary Journal* (regarding *Rise of the Dragons*)

"A spirited fantasy that weaves elements of mystery and intrigue into its story line. *A Quest of Heroes* is all about the making of courage and about realizing a life purpose that leads to growth, maturity, and excellence....For those seeking meaty fantasy adventures, the protagonists, devices, and action provide a vigorous set of encounters that focus well on Thor's evolution from a dreamy child to a young adult facing impossible odds for survival....Only the beginning of what promises to be an epic young adult series."
--*Midwest Book Review* (D. Donovan, eBook Reviewer)

"THE SORCERER'S RING has all the ingredients for an instant success: plots, counterplots, mystery, valiant knights, and blossoming relationships replete with broken hearts, deception and betrayal. It will keep you entertained for hours, and will satisfy all ages. Recommended for the permanent library of all fantasy readers."
--*Books and Movie Reviews*, Roberto Mattos

"In this action-packed first book in the epic fantasy Sorcerer's Ring series (which is currently 14 books strong), Rice introduces readers to 14-year-old Thorgrin "Thor" McLeod, whose dream is to join the Silver Legion, the elite knights who serve the king…. Rice's writing is solid and the premise intriguing."
  --*Publishers Weekly*

BOOKS BY MORGAN RICE

AGE OF THE SORCERERS
REALM OF DRAGONS (Book #1)
THRONE OF DRAGONS (Book #2)
BORN OF DRAGONS (Book #3)
RING OF DRAGONS (Book #4)
CROWN OF DRAGONS (Book #5)
DUSK OF DRAGONS (Book #6)
SHIELD OF DRAGONS (Book #7)
DREAM OF DRAGONS (Book #8)

OLIVER BLUE AND THE SCHOOL FOR SEERS
THE MAGIC FACTORY (Book #1)
THE ORB OF KANDRA (Book #2)
THE OBSIDIANS (Book #3)
THE SCEPTOR OF FIRE (Book #4)

THE INVASION CHRONICLES
TRANSMISSION (Book #1)
ARRIVAL (Book #2)
ASCENT (Book #3)
RETURN (Book #4)

THE WAY OF STEEL
ONLY THE WORTHY (Book #1)
ONLY THE VALIANT (Book #2)
ONLY THE DESTINED (Book #3)
ONLY THE BOLD (Book #4)

A THRONE FOR SISTERS
A THRONE FOR SISTERS (Book #1)
A COURT FOR THIEVES (Book #2)
A SONG FOR ORPHANS (Book #3)
A DIRGE FOR PRINCES (Book #4)
A JEWEL FOR ROYALS (BOOK #5)
A KISS FOR QUEENS (BOOK #6)
A CROWN FOR ASSASSINS (Book #7)
A CLASP FOR HEIRS (Book #8)

OF CROWNS AND GLORY
SLAVE, WARRIOR, QUEEN (Book #1)
ROGUE, PRISONER, PRINCESS (Book #2)
KNIGHT, HEIR, PRINCE (Book #3)
REBEL, PAWN, KING (Book #4)
SOLDIER, BROTHER, SORCERER (Book #5)
HERO, TRAITOR, DAUGHTER (Book #6)
RULER, RIVAL, EXILE (Book #7)
VICTOR, VANQUISHED, SON (Book #8)

KINGS AND SORCERERS
RISE OF THE DRAGONS (Book #1)
RISE OF THE VALIANT (Book #2)
THE WEIGHT OF HONOR (Book #3)
A FORGE OF VALOR (Book #4)
A REALM OF SHADOWS (Book #5)
NIGHT OF THE BOLD (Book #6)

THE SORCERER'S RING
A QUEST OF HEROES (Book #1)
A MARCH OF KINGS (Book #2)
A FATE OF DRAGONS (Book #3)
A CRY OF HONOR (Book #4)
A VOW OF GLORY (Book #5)
A CHARGE OF VALOR (Book #6)
A RITE OF SWORDS (Book #7)
A GRANT OF ARMS (Book #8)
A SKY OF SPELLS (Book #9)
A SEA OF SHIELDS (Book #10)
A REIGN OF STEEL (Book #11)
A LAND OF FIRE (Book #12)
A RULE OF QUEENS (Book #13)
AN OATH OF BROTHERS (Book #14)
A DREAM OF MORTALS (Book #15)
A JOUST OF KNIGHTS (Book #16)
THE GIFT OF BATTLE (Book #17)

THE SURVIVAL TRILOGY

ARENA ONE: SLAVERSUNNERS (Book #1)
ARENA TWO (Book #2)
ARENA THREE (Book #3)

VAMPIRE, FALLEN
BEFORE DAWN (Book #1)

THE VAMPIRE JOURNALS
TURNED (Book #1)
LOVED (Book #2)
BETRAYED (Book #3)
DESTINED (Book #4)
DESIRED (Book #5)
BETROTHED (Book #6)
VOWED (Book #7)
FOUND (Book #8)
RESURRECTED (Book #9)
CRAVED (Book #10)
FATED (Book #11)
OBSESSED (Book #12)

CHAPTER ONE

Nicholas St. Geste stepped out alone into the space before the tribal encampment, his scale armor glinting under the billowing, pale silks of his clothing and the dark wash of his long coat. Dust from the fringes of the desert swirled around him, but he was used to that.

Already, men were stepping out to encircle him. What did they see? A boy with bronze skin and dark hair, tall and broad, but not truly a man like them? A warrior clad in armor and carrying a reverse curved sword along with a long dagger? Some city dweller, come to tell them what to do?

It didn't matter. What mattered was unity.

"Oredei Redcloak, step out!" he called.

A man stepped forward from the rest. He was larger than them, carrying a double-headed axe and wearing a cloak of red feathers scavenged from the birds of the lands around.

"You've heard that Ravin has died," he called out. "You've decided to rise up. You've declared yourself the new emperor. Why shouldn't you, when he named no successor, when you still remember the days when the Southern Kingdom was a hundred separate kingdoms?"

"I've done all of those things," the other man said with a sneer. "I don't need to be reminded of it by some boy only just weaned from his mother. Go away, before I—"

"*I* will kill you today," Nicholas said, "and any other man who chooses to stand against me rather than joining my cause. I will cut the head from your body. I will impale you on spikes. I will take all that is yours. Or you can join me, and be on the side of the new ruler of this kingdom."

Of course, Oredei laughed at that. "Another would-be emperor? Boy, tell me your name, so that when I parade your flayed corpse, I can tell people who you were."

Nicholas drew his sword, held his dagger reversed across his chest. "I am Nicholas St. Geste, ruler of Sandport, and rightful lord of these lands. Any man who claims otherwise is a traitor."

1

"Sandport?" the big man said with a laugh. "That pile of dust and heat? Last I heard, the lord there went north with the emperor and got himself killed. Who are you, boy? Some bastard come out of the woodwork?"

"I am his son," Nicholas said, his hand tightening around his sword hilt. Hatred flared in him at the thought of what had happened to his father. It was hatred, not just for Oredei, but for all the northerners who had helped to bring it about.

"Then you are weak," Oredei said.

Nicholas knew that there was only one way this was going to go now, only one way he could *let* it go. "I am the man who will reunite the Southern Kingdom. I am the one who will stand against the storm that will come from the north! If you say that you rule, let us duel for it, here and now. No one else has to die!"

That just earned another laugh from the man there.

"Why should I do that?" Oredei demanded. "When I can just have you dragged down and skinned?"

Nicholas sighed and raised his sword. "It didn't have to come to this."

He brought it down, and around him, men erupted from their hiding spots, while lines of them appeared over the nearest hill. The men of Sandport were *used* to hiding in the dust.

"Kill him!" Oredei bellowed, and his men charged forward.

Nicholas moved to meet the first of them, stepping into the swirl of the battle, moving past him and hacking his blade into the man's spine. He took a blow on his reversed dagger, using it as a shield to deflect and parry even as he kept his main sword moving in sweeping strokes aimed at legs and arms, necks and torsos. The sharpness and the weight of it combined meant that he barely felt it as it passed through flesh, while it rang when he parried blows aimed at his head.

Nicholas felt blows scrape from his armor, but he was always moving even as they connected with the scales of his armor, reducing the impact of the ones that managed to touch him. It was hard, surrounded by so many foes, and the only advantage he had in it was that at least *he* could strike out at anyone there, while they all had to be cautious in case they ended up killing their friends.

It wasn't much of an advantage, when it came to a battle. That was the risk in standing so far out ahead of the rest of his men: he was placing himself in danger, diving into a situation where a sword or a spear could come from any angle.

Nicholas didn't care; he reveled in this, in the beauty and violence of the battle. He didn't even feel the fear of it, not really. Instead, he threw himself into it, feeling his sword connect with a man's skull, hearing a blade whisper close to his own ear as he moved to the side.

He kicked out, connecting with a man's knee, then moved in close, stabbing with his dagger at close range. He felt the jarring impact of a blade against his own, but cut back, slicing open a man's throat. He shoved his dying foe back into another enemy and kept going.

His own men were there then, joining the fight, their swords joining Nicholas's in the fray, so that now the enemy were falling all around him, their blood and screams seeming to fill the world. Already, some of them were moving forward into the encampment, to kill and burn.

Nicholas didn't go with them; all his attention was on the figure of Oredei ahead of him, that great axe poised to strike as he got closer. Nicholas didn't hesitate, but charged instead, blade swinging out for his foe's head even as he stepped aside from that first strike.

Somehow, Oredei managed to parry it, but there was a kind of satisfaction in that, in having an opponent who could actually keep up for a moment or two. Nicholas deflected a swing of the axe, stepped out of the way, and circled his foe.

"You should have just dueled with me," Nicholas said. "Your people wouldn't have to die."

"Why are you doing this?" Oredei demanded. "Do you think a boy like you can really conquer anything?"

He swung an overhand blow at Nicholas, but managed to back away as Nicholas dodged it, fast enough to avoid Nicholas's riposte.

"It's not about conquering," Nicholas said. "It's about unifying."

Unifying in the face of what was coming. The Northern Kingdom had already slaughtered many. Did this fool really think they wouldn't come south to butcher more?

"And you're strong enough to do that?" Oredei demanded. He struck at Nicholas again and again, his strength and his weight thrown behind each blow. Nicholas gave ground in the face of it, while Oredei bellowed at him. "I killed my father for control of my tribe, slew the leaders of a dozen more to forge an army. I am strong in a way you will never be."

Nicholas kept giving ground and then stopped, lifting both his blades and catching the haft of the axe in the cross formed by them.

"*I* was trained in war by my father from the time I could walk," Nicholas said. He felt Oredei strain against him, but it made no difference. "I was told that to rule in Sandport, I would need to be stronger and more cunning than anyone there. One of my first memories is of running from assassins through the streets. I have had foes try to poison my wine, and challenge me to combat with champions taken from everywhere from the city states to the tribes. I have survived battles, and Quiet Men, and my own family trying to kill me. You don't know what strength *is*."

He kicked out as he said it, sending his foe tumbling to the floor, the axe spinning from his hands. Nicholas stalked forward through the battle toward Oredei, blades out. He struck down a man who tried to get in his way, kicked aside another. His foe was trying to crawl away now, shuffling away on his back as if there might be somewhere for him to run.

Nicholas cut down another foe and moved to him, looking down at Oredei with contempt. This man had been trying to rule everything? *This* man thought that he could unify the Southern Kingdom? Men like this were part of the reason Nicholas was doing what he was. *They* didn't deserve to rule.

Nicholas stood over his fallen foe, and Oredei did the one thing he hadn't expected: he started to beg.

"Please, I can still be of use to you. If you just let me live, I can—"

That was when Oredei lunged with a knife, fast as a snake, aiming for Nicholas's heart. A part of Nicholas almost wished that he weren't ready for it, that this kind of betrayal could still surprise him, that he had the kind of innocence that could be caught out like that.

Instead, he swayed aside from the blow, kicked Oredei down into the dirt, and stamped on his arm hard enough that he heard the bones break. His would-be rival screamed in pain, but Nicholas had heard plenty of screams before in his life. This one didn't even begin to touch him.

"You should have taken the offer of a duel," Nicholas said, raising his weapons. "At least you could have died with honor."

He slammed them down into either side of Oredei's neck, severing his head from his body. He lifted it, and around him, his men cheered in celebration of the victory. Nicholas barely reacted. It was just one more among a slew of others, each one grimly necessary, every drop of Southern Kingdom blood spilled a waste. He would do it, though. He would bring the kingdom together to face the north, whatever it took.

CHAPTER TWO

It felt so strange for Lenore to be sitting on a throne that had been her father's, and then that of the invader. Just the thought of that made her feel uncomfortable as she sat at the heart of the great hall of the castle, but she knew she couldn't afford to show that discomfort with so many people watching. Not with what was scheduled to come.

What would those watching see? Just a girl, dark-haired and straight-backed, determined to look like a ruler? Or a queen? She was dressed in a flowing gown of white and blue, the crown seated upon her head, her normally refined features set so that they wouldn't betray what she felt. Even so, would they see their ruler, or just a princess playing at it?

There were hundreds of them. Two days from the battle, and still, they gathered to see her, their new queen. People from all walks of life thronged the throne room, and although Lenore had tried to do away with the careful squares of carpet telling each rank of the population where to stand, most of them seemed to keep to their own groups anyway. Loyal nobles stood near the front, representatives of the Houses behind them, soldiers on one side, and the great mass of the people filling in anywhere they could.

It was for them that Lenore did her best to look like a queen, sitting as poised as she could, her dark hair bound up carefully beneath her crown, her pale skin powdered so that it wouldn't show any of the lingering marks of being in the middle of a battle. Today, Lenore wore a simpler dress than most of those she might have worn for balls or public events before, delicate blue with cream underskirts and no train. She wore a scrap or two of scavenged chainmail at her belt, in a reminder of the armor she'd worn under her dress during the battle, but a full suit of it would have been too uncomfortable to wear throughout an audience.

She knew what was coming, as well. There was a reason so many were here. They wanted to see her brother punished. Lenore would put that off as long as possible, though. Some tasks were too much to ask, even of a queen.

"What do we have to do today?" she asked Greave instead. He stood to her left, a list of carefully organized tasks already waiting in his hand. Her brother was standing tall and elegant in dark traveler's clothes, his expression serious. At least he'd gotten rid of the beard he'd been growing, leaving the smooth, almost delicate youthfulness of the features beneath on show. When they were younger, their brothers had mocked him for looking pretty as a girl. Now, something had hardened in his features, leaving strong, handsome lines there.

"Too many things," Erin said, from her right. She was dressed in armor, of course, leaning on the spear that had slain Ravin and looking out over the crowd as if expecting assassins to leap from it at any moment. She was shorter than Lenore, athletically built, her hair cut short as a boy's so that no one could grab it in a fight. Her expression always held a hint of anger anyway, like she was ready to take on the world, but now, after Odd's death, there was something else there Lenore couldn't place.

"That's probably true," Lenore said. "But we have to start somewhere, and there are people willing to help."

Her eyes flickered out over the crowd, finding Devin first, of course, as he stood by Master Grey. The sorcerer seemed to be whispering to him, but Devin's eyes were still on her, and Lenore felt a flush of heat. She quickly sought out others there she knew, not wanting to risk blushing. She saw Aurelle in the crowd, her red hair making her easy to spot as she stood with Lady Meredith of the House of Sighs. She saw Lord Ness standing at the front of the nobles, Renard approaching them in a way she really hoped didn't signal that he was planning to steal from them when he got close enough.

It was hard not to mark those who weren't there, as well. Some, too many, were dead. Odd's absence was like a missing tooth, impossible to ignore. The monk's funeral had only been the day before, and still, it was hard to believe that he was gone.

Others had fled, and even if Finnal and his father had betrayed Ravin by walking away, that didn't mean that Lenore had forgotten them. It certainly didn't mean that she'd *forgiven* them. There would be justice for what they'd done.

Thoughts of justice brought her attention back to the work of the day. There were a hundred and more things to do today. They needed to organize the rebuilding of Royalsport and its defenses, establish how the bridges to the south were going to be reconstructed, send out

7

messages through the country, ensure that the people did not starve. They needed to establish the truth of the rumors that a dragon had attacked the city before they came to it, and work out what that meant for all of them.

Before all of it though, there was one thing that needed to be done. She couldn't put it off any longer.

"Bring out Vars," Lenore said.

"Are you sure?" Greave asked. "You don't have to decide anything yet if—"

Lenore smiled tightly. "I am queen now. What kind of queen would I be if I avoided the tasks that I didn't want to think about? Bring out Vars."

Giving orders as a queen was a little like one of those games they'd played as children, where you whispered a message to one person, and they gave it to another, until it wasn't quite the same by the time it reached the end of the line. It meant that Lenore had to be extra careful about the instructions she gave.

The instruction passed from her to Erin and on down the line. Eventually, a ripple went out through the crowd, and a space opened up, people moving aside, staring.

Guards flanked Vars, Lenore's brother walking between them with his head down. He didn't look much like the prince who had always insisted on the finest things in life. Instead, he was dirty and dressed in the same simple peasant clothes he'd been wearing when he'd been captured. He had manacles on his wrists, and Lenore felt herself caught between thinking that it was right that they should be there and wanting to shout to the guards to take them off.

No, this was how something like this should be done. After all Vars had done, manacles were the least he deserved. What *else* he deserved… that was the hard part.

The guards brought him to stand in front of Lenore. One of them shoved him down roughly to his knees.

"He can stand," Lenore said. "Stand up, Vars. People should see you."

Her brother did it, and for the longest time, Lenore could only stare at him.

"What are we waiting for?" Erin said. "Have him executed, already."

8

Lenore held up a hand to stop her, still looking at her brother. Her *half*-brother, not that it made any difference. The one who had caused them so much misery.

"You've done... so much, Vars," Lenore said. "You betrayed all of us. You killed our father. You usurped the throne. You let Ravin's army in. You left me to the southerners. You got Rodry *killed*."

He'd done so many things, one stacked atop another like stones on a cairn, and any one of them represented a crushing weight. Any one of them might have been enough to call for his execution. All of them together... could Lenore even think of a punishment bad enough to truly punish him for what he'd done?

"Do you deny any of it?" Lenore asked Vars. She braced herself for the excuses to follow, determined not to give in to them.

"No," Vars said. "I did all of that, and more."

"Can you *explain* any of it?" Lenore asked. "You were always good at that, weren't you, Vars? Explaining how things weren't really your fault."

She saw her brother shrug.

"It is," Vars said. "All of it."

"Are you even sorry for it?" Lenore demanded. "All the misery you've caused, all the lives you've cost? Do you feel any remorse for it at all?"

Vars hesitated, and for a moment or two, Lenore thought that he might start begging, but he glanced around the crowd, seemed to spot someone there, and steeled himself.

"What do you want me to say?" he said. "If I say nothing, it sounds like I'm heartless. If I tell you all how sorry I am, it just sounds like I'm trying to save my own skin."

"And what's the truth?" Lenore asked, leaning forward with her hands on the arms of her throne.

"The truth?" Vars said. He looked away.

Lenore sighed. If he wasn't going to even talk, then there was no point to this.

"The truth?" Vars said. "The truth is that I was scared. All my life, I've been scared. Scared, and jealous, but even the jealousy was a kind of fear, that if other people were doing better, they might be able to hurt me."

"And you think that excuses anything you've done?" Erin shouted from the side. "If you hadn't... Odd might still be alive."

9

"A lot of people might be," Lenore said. "You've done so many things, Vars, and they're all things you might behead someone for. Give me one reason why I shouldn't have you executed."

"There *is* no reason!" Erin insisted. Lenore could hear that she was getting angry now. "You should execute him! If you could kill him a dozen times, it wouldn't be enough."

Lenore looked over at Greave. "And what do you think, brother?"

"I think I've read all the law codes of this kingdom, old and new," Greave said. "By all of them, he should die, even if he is… even if he's our brother. That can't excuse what he's done. The law can't apply to some people, and not our blood."

Lenore knew he had a point; knew that they both did. She looked around the room. "What about everyone else here. What do you all have to say?"

Their voices rang out in a chorus that called for Vars's death. They demanded his execution again and again, in a tide that washed over Lenore and felt as if it might drown her. Yet, in it all, she picked out another voice. A woman was forcing her way to the front. She wore simple peasant clothes, and had bruises on her face that might have been from the fighting. Under those, though, Lenore could tell that she was beautiful. She had a strong look to her, obviously used to hard work, and she used that strength now as she pushed forward.

Lenore held up her hands for silence, beckoning the woman forward.

"You, what's your name?"

"Bethe, your majesty," she said.

"And you have something to say?"

The other woman nodded. "Vars… I found him when he ran from the castle. He stayed in my home, and I got to know him. I saw what he was. He saved my life when Ravin's men came for me, and he helped retake the castle. Without him, you might not be sitting on that throne now."

"And a lot of other people might be alive," Erin snapped. "Kill him already, Lenore."

Lenore looked over at her sister. There was still so much anger in her. Too much. Lenore wanted to imagine that she couldn't ever have that kind of anger in her, but the truth was that it was all too easy to picture it.

"That's enough," she said. "Vars, I'm ready to decide your punishment. You… you are to be exiled."

The room erupted in anger, but Lenore just stood there until it subsided.

"Everyone here is right: you deserve to die. But *I* don't deserve to have to be the one who decides to have her own brother killed. That's not the ruler I want to be."

It wasn't the precedent she wanted to set, either. After this, those on the verge of execution would be able to throw the example of her brother back at her, and Lenore would have to listen. In one decision, she was changing everything that would follow.

She looked over to Bethe. "Do you wish to go with him?"

The woman hesitated, but then shook her head. "No, your majesty."

"Very well. Vars, it seems you're destined to be alone in your exile. So leave. Leave my kingdom, and don't *ever* come back. Take what you need, and then go. If you are found here a week from now, you will be executed."

At a wave from her, they dragged him away, and again the room was in an uproar. Lenore sat there, determined to ride out the storm of disapproval, enduring Erin's eyes on her and the chatter of the people.

She was almost grateful when a messenger burst into the room, stumbling forward until he was in front of the throne. His clothes looked singed, and there was a wild look in his eyes.

"Your majesty," the man said. "Your majesty, there have been dragon attacks across the kingdom. A dragon… a dragon being ridden by a monstrous creature, like a human, but scaled."

The words were enough to silence the room, and Lenore was about to wave Master Grey forward when the messenger kept speaking.

"There's more, your majesty," he said. "The rider, the *creature*… it claimed… it claims that it is Princess Nerra!"

CHAPTER THREE

Nerra clung to Shadr as the great bulk of the black-scaled dragon descended on a rocky outcrop. The sunlight glinted from her own scales, in an iridescent blue that shifted as her muscles did. She *had* muscles now, thanks to the transformation that had changed her from a mere human-thing into something more, something Perfected.

She felt the moment when Shadr landed in the contact with the ground, the rush of air as Shadr used her wings to slow her drop from the sky. Nerra slid down from her back, onto the surface of the hilltop, feeling the solidity of the ground after the pure beauty of soaring through the air. Shadr towered over her now, huge as a house, head large enough to swallow a horse in a couple of bites.

Strangely, it felt higher up here than it had been soaring above the hill, as if there were something more natural about being up there in the sky, whereas this, this more earthly height, was enough to make Nerra gasp with it. Maybe that difference was because *Shadr* thought that flying made more sense. The connection between Nerra and the queen of the dragons meant that it was getting harder and harder to be certain about which thoughts and feelings were her own, and which were Shadr's.

Should it matter? Shadr whispered in her mind. *We are connected, two halves of one whole. Your thoughts are mine, as mine are yours, making us powerful together.*

"I know that," Nerra said. "It's just... I'm more powerful, more *help* to you, if I'm still myself too."

You are perfect, Shadr insisted. *You are Perfected.*

Nerra understood that, because she felt the certainty of it in Shadr's thoughts. She wished that there was as much certainty in her own.

She looked out from the hillside, seeing the columns of smoke in the distance, the flames that still flickered up here and there from the spots where she and Shadr had struck. In the moments when they attacked, Nerra always felt such a rush of power, a savage kind of joy at the violence and the flames that seemed to flood through her, impossible to contain.

12

Looking out from a distance, it was easier to remember the person she had been, the one who had cared about every animal in the forest, about all the plants in the royal gardens.

We must connect with the others, Shadr sent to her. Nerra nodded her assent, although in truth, there was nothing she could have done to stop it.

She felt the moment of broader connection to the dragons who waited in the landscape around Astare. The city was empty of humans now, most of the buildings burned, the rest turned into perches for dragons. The Lesser swarmed it, their twisted, lizard-like forms a blanket of scales across the streets.

Nerra felt the conversation that followed as much as she heard it, the connection between the dragons spilling over into her. She felt the desire of the army of dragons to sweep over the Northern Kingdom and then down across the Slate. She felt Shadr hold them back with her authority, her status as the strongest of all of them. She felt the confidence flow from Shadr to the others, certainty in what would happen, faith in their plan.

The plan was simple enough: they would cause enough destruction to draw out the one with the amulet, just the two of them. The amulet bearer wouldn't be able to resist, because that was their purpose, their place in all this. They would come, sure in their power to control dragons, their ability to stop even Shadr with the magic of the thing.

Nerra would kill them quickly, before they even knew what was happening. That would free the dragons to take back their rightful place in the world, and destroy those humans who would harm them.

The thought of that filled Nerra with hope, but honestly, she couldn't be sure if it was her own hope or not right then. Her thoughts and feelings were all too wrapped up with Shadr's, with the other dragons', right then.

For another instant, just an instant, Nerra saw them waiting, all of them. They let out a burst of flame all at once, the heat of their breath making the air itself ripple. Then she was back there on the hill, collapsing to her knees with the power of everything she'd seen. She felt tears in her eyes, and she couldn't imagine why they were there.

Is everything well, my princess? Shadr asked her.

"I... I don't know," Nerra said.

If you are unwell, I must know, Shadr went on. *You must be strong if you are to kill the one who bears the amulet.*

13

"I know," Nerra replied. "I will be. I'll kill them, whoever they are, and then... what do you do with the amulet afterwards?"

I will drop it in the depths of the ocean, where none can find it to hurt us. There will be pain in handling it, but I will be strong.

"You are the strongest," Nerra agreed, but her voice was slightly flat as she said it.

Are you sure that you are well? Shadr asked.

"I'm... fine," Nerra said, but she knew that they could both feel the lie in that. "I just... I need a little space. Please."

Space? But we are destined to be together, the princess and the queen.

"Please," Nerra repeated.

It was almost a surprise when Shadr inclined her great head, those large yellow eyes blinking at her in consideration.

I will find food. I will not be long, my chosen.

She took to the air in a sweep of wings broad enough to obscure the sun. The downdraft as they beat was almost enough to knock Nerra from her feet, only the greater strength of her new form keeping her upright.

She stood there for the longest time after Shadr left, feeling the fading of the dragon queen's closeness. It was like a great, heavy cloth being lifted from her mind, and Nerra was a little surprised at what she found there beneath it.

The truth was simple: she didn't want people to die, didn't like the idea of the dragons sweeping down over the land, burning everyone who lay before them. She hated the thought of people she knew dying at the hands of the dragons, at the people of Royalsport falling before the Lesser.

Yet it was hard to understand quite *why* she felt that way. She knew now what she was: she was one of the Perfected, when all her life she had been seen as something diseased, something to be ashamed of. She would *not* be ashamed of what she was, not when she was something special, the chosen of the dragon queen herself.

At the same time, the feelings that filled her would not go away. She didn't want the people she knew to be hurt. She didn't want *anyone* to be hurt.

She knew there were people who would need to be hurt, people who would need to die. The amulet bearer would be one; there was no way around that. There might be others too, who couldn't stand the

14

idea of dragons in the world, who couldn't understand their power or their beauty.

Yet, at the same time, Nerra couldn't see why whole cities had to suffer. She had seen Astare on the ground, with the violence and the chaos, the blood and the death. She had seen in through Shadr's connection to the others. Could she stand by and see Geertsport like that, or Royalsport? It had been easy enough to kill soldiers, and those who supplied them, but innocent people?

The further Shadr got from Nerra, the more it was like her own thoughts and feelings came into focus. She felt more certain about her own mind by the moment, but a different kind of certainty was settling over her then and it was bigger than Nerra could have imagined.

In one flash, it was like she understood her place in all of this. She'd thought that it was as something rejected, and then she'd thought that it was as a tool of the dragons, there to bring about the destruction of humanity.

Now, she saw herself as something else, as a still point between the two. She wasn't human, and she could never truly be one of the dragons, but maybe that just meant that she was perfectly placed to mediate between the two.

Nerra had no illusions. She knew that conflict was coming, that the dragons weren't going to be content to simply return to Sarras. Yet there were different ways that such a conflict could go. It could be an all-out extermination, or it could be something else. If Nerra was here for anything, it was to *make* it something else. Shadr would only be able to see the pain that humanity had inflicted on the dragons, the human-things... the *humans* would only be able to see creatures come to destroy them. Nerra would need to be the one charting the course between those two, minimizing the loss of life, finding a way toward peace.

First, though, she would need to kill the amulet bearer, whatever that took.

CHAPTER FOUR

For what seemed like the hundredth time, Anders strained against the space within Master Grey's tower that held him, anger propelling him to try to fight his way free. He would not be caught by the wizard's trap, would not be held there like some petulant child when it was the sorcerer who was the one in the wrong here.

The space Anders was in fit around his body perfectly. He had a memory of Master Grey's magic wrapping around him, absorbing him into the wall the way a vat of tar might have absorbed a stone thrown into it.

Being trapped in a wall was inherently terrifying. Walling up a foe was one of the cruelest things an enemy could do, and Master Grey had to know that. Yet he'd done it anyway. He'd imprisoned Anders without food or water, kept him there unable to move even a little. Anders threw his muscles against it, muscles developed by years of training, but they couldn't seem to get any purchase, only leaving him exhausted.

Except that he *wasn't* tired exactly, and that was its own cruelty. Anders had heard stories of people walled up by tyrants, and their deaths had been horrible enough, brought about by lack of air or water, food or sleep. Yet for all the time he'd been trapped here now, Anders did not grow tired or hungry, and that was terrifying. It meant that, in theory, Master Grey could leave him there forever, and Anders would not die. Instead, he would slowly go mad with the inability to *do* anything.

If anything proved the sorcerer's evil, it was this. This went beyond even the cruel game of having Anders trained as the one chosen to fulfill his precious prophecy, only to have another boy, Devin, there all along to do it instead.

Anders took that anger and used it to fuel his next attempt, this time summoning up the magic that he'd been taught and flinging it at the bonds that held him. They seemed to absorb the power, and if anything, it added to them, Master Grey's workings somehow designed to use what he threw at them.

Anders started to ponder that, trying to look at the workings and understand them, but it was slow, frustrating going. Master Grey's workings were complex, and trying to understand them was pushing the limits of what Anders had learned.

Anders was still working on it when the wall around him started to melt away, his head coming through it as if it were breaking through a falling curtain of water. Even though he'd been able to breathe before, he found himself gasping for air as he looked out into the lower chamber of Master Grey's tower. The room was more ordered than it had been in the aftermath of Anders's fight with Devin, magical paraphernalia arranged on Master Grey's desk, artifacts back in their proper places around the room rather than divided up into the piles Anders had been forming to keep or destroy. The curved walls were now hung with tapestries and ornaments, and that just made Anders more furious, because *he was* being treated like just another of them.

Master Grey stood there, bald and stick thin, clad in robes of white and gold, his fingers pressed together as if in thought, although Anders could feel the magic that he was working there. Devin stood beside him, looking recovered from the bruises of the fight, dressed in simple but rich-looking clothes of green and brown that contained a lean figure made strong through his travels. His dark hair was a tangle, and his expression was anything but happy about being there with Anders.

Of course, he had all the accoutrements that came with being Master Grey's preferred chosen one. He had the sword *Loss* by his side now, while the other he'd made hung on the wall of the tower. His wolf-conduit stood beside him, Devin's hand resting on the mystical symbol grown into its fur. He couldn't have made it clearer if he'd tried that he didn't trust Anders.

"We don't need him," Devin said.

"That," Master Grey said, "is where you're wrong, Devin. Where you're *both* wrong."

He looked over to Anders, the piercing depths of those eyes seeming to see into his soul. Anders wanted to flinch away under the intensity of that look, but he couldn't move even that much.

"You have seen the dragons," Master Grey said. "You have survived one, but only because you worked together."

"Are you saying that us fighting the one that came to the city was destined?" Devin asked. He didn't sound convinced. Anders smiled at that; if Grey couldn't even convince the student he actually *favored*, what did that say about his arguments?

"I'm saying that both of you are part of events bigger than yourselves," the sorcerer said. "Events that have the power to reshape the world."

"And you have already decided how it should be shaped," Anders said. He inclined his head toward Devin. "The way you decided everything else in my entire *life*. With *him* as the one winning the day."

"You're the one who tried to kill me," Devin shot back. "You stole my sword, and you tried to murder me. *I'm* the one who should be angry."

"Anger gets us nowhere," Master Grey said. "The threat of the dragons is too great. Each of you was born on the night of the dragon moon. Each of you has the potential to help with what is needed. For a long time, I'll admit, I thought that meant one of you being a hero and the other failing, but I see things more clearly now."

"Oh, you see things more clearly now," Anders said, letting bitterness drip from the words. "That excuses so much. Like entombing me in a *wall*!"

"That is so I have a chance to explain the importance of this to you," Master Grey insisted. "To you *both*. You have seen the dragons. You have seen how powerful even one of them can be. Now imagine an army of them. Imagine them spreading out across the horizon, wingtip to wingtip, with a horde of their creatures below. Devin, tell Anders what the messenger in the throne room said."

"That there was a dragon," Devin said. "Burning a line across the kingdom. That a creature claiming to be Princess Nerra was with it, transformed into something… something not human."

Anders could guess why Master Grey had told Devin to say it: because in spite of how much he hated what Devin had taken from him, he was more inclined to believe him than the manipulations of the sorcerer.

"She has been transformed into one of the so-called 'Perfected,'" Master Grey said. "I feared this for her. A servant of the dragons. Can you imagine it? Can you imagine what it will be like when the rest of the dragons descend on the kingdom? When they slaughter humanity for ever having risen against them?"

"I… can," Anders admitted. He could imagine their power, and the destruction that they had the potential to cause. An army of dragons could reduce even a powerful kingdom to ash.

"So do you see why I need both of you to work together?" Master Grey said. "The two of you, together, represent the only way humanity can stand against the dangers to come. Do you see that, Anders? Will you stand with us?"

"I see it," Anders said, because what else was he going to say? Was he going to tell the sorcerer that he would see him dead? That seemed like a recipe for remaining stuck within this wall for eternity. "Just let me out of this wall, and I will do what is needed. I will work with Devin to take on the threat that is coming."

He heard Master Grey sigh. "I truly wish that I could believe you, Anders."

"What?" Anders demanded. "I'm telling you the truth!"

He wasn't, but this was no time to let go of the lie. There were moments when the only thing to do was press forward and hope that someone believed a deception through sheer commitment to it. His instructors had taught him that, the same way they'd taught him swordplay and magic.

Apparently, though, they hadn't taught him well enough.

"Think on it, Anders," Master Grey said. "I dare not release you until you are committed to this. Doing so risks your death, or Devin's, and I need both of you. In the meantime, you are safest where you are."

"No!" Anders cried out, as he felt the wall start to shift around him, pulling him back in. "I'll kill you for this, you old—"

The wall swallowed the words as it swallowed him, leaving him seething there in impotent rage. Yet there was more than fury in Anders's thoughts now; he saw an opportunity.

At some point, Master Grey would have to let him go, even if Anders couldn't figure out a way out of this prison for himself. When he did, Anders had a surprise of his own waiting, in the form of the amulet that had seemed to offer so much power back in the city.

Anders had hidden it carefully, well enough that even Master Grey wouldn't find it, and when he got it back the power that it offered would help to more than even the odds. Devin would die, in spite of what Master Grey had been saying, and then the old fool would follow him, and Anders… *he* would be the one to deal with the threat that the oncoming dragons represented.

He would be a hero, would fulfill his destiny, and neither Devin nor the sorcerer would be around to stop him.

CHAPTER FIVE

Lenore retreated from the great hall toward a smaller set of chambers, because with the noise and confusion in the wake of the messenger's announcement, there was no way to hear herself think, let alone decide coherent policies. Greave and Erin followed as she left the great hall, and she beckoned a small number of other figures: Aurelle and a couple of clerks.

She thought about the message as she walked. Could it be true? Could her sister be alive? Could she really have been transformed into something monstrous, something that wasn't human? Lenore didn't know what to think.

Lenore would have asked Master Grey and Devin to join them, but to her disappointment, both had slipped out of the crowd during the shouting. Maybe that was good though; she wasn't sure that she would have been able to concentrate with Devin there.

Lenore picked a room that had been one of her mother's old receiving rooms. It had the advantage over her father's in that it was comfortably furnished, or should have been. Instead, she found that most of the elegant couches had been ripped out and replaced by cushions and rugs, with hard wooden stools in the Southern Kingdom style. She should have guessed that Ravin would have destroyed even this.

Undeterred, Lenore seated herself on one of the piles of cushions, gesturing for the others there to make themselves comfortable. She saw Aurelle grab a stool, Erin stand like a statue beside her, Greave glance toward Aurelle and then move to stand on Lenore's other side with an expression she couldn't read. A part of Lenore wanted to ask what was going on, and she supposed that since she was the queen they wouldn't be able to ignore her, but there were too many other things that needed her attention first.

She turned to the clerks. "I want to get one thing out of the way first. We all know that the ruler can annul a marriage. My, *our,* brother refused to do it for me."

21

"You can say his name," Erin said. "It doesn't change the fact that you let him go."

"Banishing him isn't letting him go," Lenore said. "I'm not going to have him killed, and I don't want anyone here doing it either. Vars might not be better than that, but *we* are." She remembered what she'd been going to say before she made the mistake of mentioning Vars. "The *point* is that since I am now queen, I have the power to annul my marriage to Finnal, and I want it on record that I am doing so, before we do anything else. I do *not* want him showing up trying to claim my kingdom and saying that he is king."

She stared at the clerks until she was sure that they had written it down. She gestured to Erin and Greave.

"I want this moment witnessed," she said. "Will you both do it?"

They nodded and stepped forward, taking quills from the clerks and making their marks on the parchments the men presented. Lenore couldn't begin to explain what she felt in that moment, but there was definitely relief in it, and satisfaction, and a dozen other things as well.

She just wished that she had more time to enjoy it.

"We need to talk about the dragons," Lenore said. "The one that came here, and the one they say is burning the countryside."

"I saw the one in the city," Erin said. "It was huge. To kill something like that… it would be hard."

Of course her sister would think about that. She didn't sound scared by the prospect, either, although she knew by now that Erin didn't sound scared even when she was. Lenore had other concerns, though.

"We need to find out the scale of the threat," Lenore said. "We need to know if this is one dragon, or more, and we need…"

"We need to know if it's true about Nerra," Greave supplied, echoing what Lenore had been thinking.

"It could be a trick," Erin said. "It *has* to be a trick."

"We don't know, though," Lenore said. With Nerra being sent away, how could they know?

"There's no way she can still be alive," Erin insisted. "No way she can have been transformed into some kind of monster."

"There are… hints of it in some of the books," Greave said.

"There are?" Lenore's breath caught at the thought of what that could mean. She shook her head. "No, this could still be a trap."

"That's why someone needs to check," Greave said. "And it needs to be someone who can tell if it's really her. That's why it has to be me."

"You?" Lenore said.

"*You?*" Aurelle echoed at almost the same moment.

"If it *is* her," Greave said, "I need to find her. There… there's something I need to do. And if it is her… she's our sister. It needs to be one of us. It needs to be *me.*"

"It's too dangerous," Lenore insisted. "Greave, you're not—"

"I'm not what I used to be," Greave said. "Please, Lenore. I need to do this. It needs to be one of us, because only one of us can get through to Nerra."

"It could be me," Lenore said. "Or Erin."

"You have to rule," Greave said, and even as he said it, Lenore knew that it was true. As for Erin, she already had a task in mind for her. It was just that she was expecting that Greave would be there, helping to organize things.

"I have to be the one to do this," Greave said. "I can help find out what's happening. I can do this. I'm *going* to do this."

Lenore wasn't used to hearing that kind of determination in her brother's voice. It was enough to persuade her that maybe he *could* cope with this.

"All right," Lenore said. "But I'm sending people with you. I'll probably only be able to spare a couple, but for something like this, you'll need the extra protection."

"I could—" Aurelle began from the side, but Greave was already answering.

"That will be fine," he said. Again, Lenore found herself wondering what was going on between them. "What's next?"

Lenore hesitated for a moment before looking over at Aurelle. "Finnal and Duke Viris. We need to know what they're going to do next. Now that Finnal is not my husband, he can't just claim the throne, but they won't just go away, either."

"They won't," Aurelle agreed. "They will gather their men, wait for you to be weak, and try to find a way to take back a position of power. But, with respect, my queen, you don't need me to spy on Duke Viris and his son."

"You're the best placed to do it," Lenore said. "I know I would be sending you into danger, but—"

"That isn't what I mean," Aurelle replied. "What I mean is that spying isn't enough. You should send me to kill them. I *want* to kill them."

"Assassination?" Lenore said, unable to keep the shock out of her voice. "It… it's not the kind of thing I want to do."

"It's the only way," Aurelle said. "They will be a threat as long as they live. Tell me that you can defeat them in open battle, and I will speak no more of this."

That was the problem: Lenore knew that there was no way her forces could stand up to the full weight of the armies Finnal and his father might be able to muster. So soon after the battle for Royalsport, a fair fight against them would only condemn innocent people on her side to death.

"I… hate this," Lenore said, just the thought of what she was about to order Aurelle to do making her feel faintly nauseous.

"This isn't like Vars," Erin said. "He… he's pathetic. These two can still hurt us."

Lenore looked over to Greave, wanting his opinion, wanting him to talk her out of this, but his face was like a mask.

"She can do it," her brother said.

"I can," Aurelle said. "And you've given me the way to get close. I'll bring them the news of your annulment. Inside information taken by their spy from the court of the usurper queen herself. When I hint at more, there's no way they won't speak to me alone."

"I…" Lenore nodded before she could stop herself. She had to think of the lives this would save, not the ones it would cost. She was the queen now, and she had to think about all her people. "Do it."

"With pleasure," Aurelle said, and there was something about the way she said it that told Lenore this was personal.

To take her mind away from what she'd just commanded someone to do, Lenore turned her attention to the last part of this.

"Erin," Lenore said. "I need you for something else."

"What?" Erin asked. "I need to stay here, don't I? By your side."

Lenore shook her head. "We need someone who can go to the Southern Kingdom."

"You're sending me away?" Erin asked, looking like she couldn't quite believe it. "It's supposed to be Vars you're banishing, not me."

Lenore stood, putting her hands on her sister's shoulders. "I'm sending you because I trust you. I'm not banishing you. We've just killed Ravin, and that will have effects. We need to know what those are. Does it mean that they're going to be peaceful towards us, or will they want to attack to avenge Ravin?"

"No one would do that," Erin said.

"They might," Lenore insisted. "We don't even know if they've heard about his death yet. If they have, we need to know what that means, for us, for them, and for the future."

"You could send an ambassador for this," Erin said.

"And who would I be able to trust?" Lenore shot back. "I need someone who can find out what we need to know, and who will be able to act if it's necessary. Someone who can take a small group and find out the truth. Please, Erin."

She saw her sister hesitating, and that was part of why she'd left this until last. Erin looked around at the others, each with their tasks, and finally she nodded.

"All right," Erin said. "I'll do it. I'll play my part."

"We all will," Lenore said, hugging her. "Just stay safe, all of you."

"I'll be fine," Erin promised her. "*You're* the one who's about to send away all her most important protectors when things are still uncertain."

Lenore hadn't thought about it like that. Even so, she knew that she needed to do this. They all did. They'd won against Ravin, but the fight to secure the kingdom was anything but done.

CHAPTER SIX

Vars did his best to ignore the looks people gave him as he went to his former rooms to pack. He was used to people looking at him with hatred now, used to their derision and their assumption that he was worthless. Frankly, the brief moments when people had looked at him like a hero in the course of retaking the city had been the ones that had come as more of a shock.

There were guards alongside him, of course, and Vars wasn't certain if they were there to ensure that he left, or there to make sure that no one killed him in the time that he was still there. He could imagine plenty of people wanting to try. There had certainly been enough baying for his death down in the great hall. Even Erin had called for him to die.

He reached his rooms, and there were more guards on the door, although in truth, they looked like peasant folk who had simply been promoted to the role. Once, Vars would have seen that as a terrible insult. Now that he'd spent time living among the common folk, Vars didn't mind it so much. Not even when one of them started to give him instructions.

"Queen Lenore has left instructions that you are to take what you want with you," the new guard said. "And she hasn't said how long you're to take, but you shouldn't take too long. I was there when you marched on the castle, but there's plenty of others who want you dead."

Vars looked at the man, wondering if he should be able to remember him. It seemed wrong somehow that he couldn't, and that was strange in itself. He shouldn't have *cared* who some peasant was.

He went into his rooms, and they seemed like the abode of someone else entirely. After so long in Bethe's two-room hovel, they seemed too large for one person, too grand with their gilt and their art, their elegantly carved furniture and their mosaic floors. Some of the riches Vars remembered were gone, taken by Ravin or his people, yet more of them remained than he would have thought, left out of the looting because Ravin had kept Vars as his tame royal, there to humiliate.

Vars went through the room, trying to work out what he should do, what he should take. What would he need for a life beyond the kingdom? What would he need to get him through the rest of his days?

A family, friends, people who cared about him. That thought came to Vars quick as a dagger thrust, and as sharp as one, too. He felt tears sting the corners of his eyes, and it was worse because he knew that *he* was the reason for it all. His cowardice, his weakness, his cruelty.

He had to think practically though. He had some time, but he wouldn't have forever. He needed to get things together. He grabbed a large trunk and some bags, starting to pack.

Vars started with clothes, picking out good-quality traveling clothes in leather and satin. Once, he'd seen them as quite simple compared to his usual attire, only moderately embroidered with silver and gold thread, worked with only a few jewels. Now, they seemed gaudy, but he put them on anyway.

He found a sword, setting it at his side, then took a couple of knives just to be sure. It wasn't that he had any illusions about suddenly being a great fighter, but in the places he might be going to, perhaps looking like one would save him some trouble. Vars stood in front of a mirror, trying to look like a warrior no one would want to cross. In truth, he looked too much like a fop, and could barely imagine now that he'd once dressed like this every day.

Vars kept going, finding a bag and filling it with whatever valuables he could. Perhaps someone else would have taken mementos, but Vars hadn't collected those. He'd acquired everything of value, and nothing, all at once.

He found himself thinking of Lyril, the noblewoman who had wanted him for a husband. What had become of her? Vars knew that Ravin had demanded her for his own, but what then? Vars doubted that he was ever going to get an answer to that question, and in truth, it wasn't as if he longed to see her again. She was vacuous and cruel, shallow and vain, well matched to everything Vars had been. It was simply...

...concern. *That* was a concept that took Vars a little by surprise. He was concerned, and for someone who wasn't *him*. He'd felt that way around only one person, and that was—

"Hello, Vars," Bethe said from the doorway.

Vars spun toward her. She looked as perfect as she always had, and Vars went to her automatically, taking her hands in his, staring into her eyes.

"You saved my life," he said. "No one else spoke up for me, and you did."

"Someone had to," Bethe said. "Besides, there *is* good in you, Vars, whatever everyone else thinks. Whatever *you* think."

Vars resisted the urge to set her straight on that, to explain to her carefully all the ways in which every good thing he'd done had just been an accident, or him acting out of fear. He didn't want her thinking of him like that.

"Why do you think I'm good?" Vars asked her. He had more than enough proof that he wasn't. "Even with the things I've done. I *did* do them, Bethe. I killed my own father, and because of me, my sister was taken by the Southern Kingdom."

"I've seen you without any of this," Bethe said. "I've seen the good you *could* do. That's worth something."

"It's…" Vars wasn't sure that he had the words. "It's more than anyone has ever done for me."

Those words sounded stupid, when he was the son of a king, standing in a room filled with riches that his position had given to him. Yet the truth was that no one had shown him the kindness that Bethe had. When he thought about her, it was different than anyone else. So different that Vars knew he had to ask the next part.

"Will you come with me?"

His sister had already asked it, but that had been in front of everyone, and at a point where it had been the foolish thing for Bethe to do, to attach herself too strongly to Vars. He knew he needed to make his case quickly.

"I know you said no before," he said. "But think about all the things we could do together. There's wealth here that we could take, and the places we could find can be so much better than being stuck in a house, baking bread for—"

"No, Vars," Bethe said, and the words had a leaden finality about them that made it hard to say anything else. Even so, Vars felt as if he had to try.

"Bethe, I… I love you."

Bethe was already shaking her head. "No, you don't, Vars. And I don't love you. We were just stuck together in an intense situation, that's all. Don't get me wrong, I'm fond of you, I even care about you, but that's not enough."

"It could be," Vars insisted.

Bethe shook her head. "To uproot my entire life? My home is here, and my life. Vars, you're just scared, and you're reaching out for something, some*one*, familiar."

The worst part of it was that she was right.

"I *am* scared," Vars admitted. "Where will I go? What will I do? Do I head down to the Southern Kingdom, where they'll hate me for being one of their enemy's family? Do I take a boat to Sarras, and try to explore the third kingdom with whatever group of settlers is heading there?"

"You'll think of something," Bethe said. "Go somewhere *new*, Vars. Go somewhere you can *be* someone new."

She hugged him then, and the hug was a lot, but it was still a long way from all the things that Vars had imagined with her. When she pulled back, it seemed like it left a void inside him.

"I need to go," she said. "I'm sorry, Vars."

Vars watched her go, wishing that he had some way to make her come back, to love him. If this were some bard's tale, that was what would have happened. She would have run back to him, would have kissed him, and they would have run off into the sunset together.

Now, he was alone. He was going to have to walk out into the world without her, without any help, and he was going to have to work out what to do with the rest of his life. It was huge, and terrifying, but he'd been exiled; he had no other choice.

Vars looked around at the trunk he'd filled with belongings. He had everything he was going to need. As much as he was putting this off, he was going to have go soon.

A part of him wanted to go and find his siblings, just to say goodbye, maybe even to try to mend things with them a little. He could go to Greave and talk about their memories of their mother. He could go to Lenore and thank her for sparing his life. He could go to Erin and... no, probably not Erin. She would almost certainly stab him.

In truth, though, what could he say? What would one goodbye do, in the face of all he'd done? Sighing, Vars knew what he had to do. There was nothing left for him here. Grabbing his trunk and his bags, he walked out.

Tears misted his eyes as he walked through the castle, but Vars didn't look back. He couldn't.

CHAPTER SEVEN

Greave went back to his old rooms, grateful that he had a purpose once again, sure that he would be able to finally complete the mission that he'd set for himself when he'd set off from the castle what seemed like a lifetime ago now. He'd gone to find a cure for Nerra, and now… now he would have a chance to give it to her.

His rooms were a mess, the bed disheveled as if someone else had been sleeping in it, but at least most of his things were still there. It seemed that Ravin's lackeys had no more interest in his books and papers than anyone else. They lay scattered to one side, so that Greave found himself compelled to go to them, picking them up and trying to put them in some kind of order even though he would be leaving soon.

At least doing that helped to push thoughts of Aurelle from his mind.

Those thoughts had been a constant presence, ever since he'd learned that she was safe and well within the city. A part of him had been sure that he would never see her again, yet now she was here, and Greave didn't know what to do about that. It was as if everything he felt was tangled up inside him, still as unclear as on the day when he'd set her on a boat, sending her off without him. Just the thought of her brought feelings to him that he'd never felt with anyone else, desire mixed with anger, love mixed with pain, until he wasn't sure what was what.

He'd done everything he could to avoid her since arriving back at the castle, had barely even acknowledged her existence. The truth was that even looking at her brought up too many feelings to deal with, right at the moment when everyone around him needed to be the one who could think about things rationally.

"I thought I would find you here."

And there her voice was, melodious as always, more perfect than any song. Greave swallowed and turned to find her across the room, stepping out from behind a screen, just… looking at him.

He couldn't help staring at her too, taking in the deep red of her hair, the elegant lines of her face, the fullness of her lips. She was

31

wearing traveling clothes in cream and red for what she'd agreed to do next, and Greave couldn't help staring at the way they clung to her.

"I never thought I'd see you again," she said. There was a note of fear and pain in her voice that hurt Greave just to hear it there. "When I saw the docks of Astare burn, I thought... I thought you *died*, Greave."

"I only just survived," Greave said. "It's a long story."

"Then tell me it," Aurelle said. She went to perch on the edge of the bed. "I have time. I could listen to you tell stories forever. I used to love it when you would tell me about some piece of history that only you knew, the way your eyes would come alive with it, and—"

"Stop," Greave said, holding up a hand. "Please, Aurelle."

"So that you can ignore me again?" Aurelle asked. "I've been trying to see you since the moment I saw you."

"How did you even get in here?" Greave countered.

Aurelle laughed at that, and in spite of the brittle bitterness of that laugh, it somehow still managed to be beautiful. "We found a way into the Great Library of Astare. We hid from assassins in the dark. Compared to that, breaking into your bedroom was easy. Besides, it's always simpler with spaces you know."

Such a simple way to remind him of all the time that they'd spent here, wrapped up in these sheets, and in one another. Greave wanted to go to her then, wanted to hold her, and to do so much more. Even so, he held himself back.

"Aurelle, I—" he began, but Aurelle didn't stop.

"I can't just sit and wait while you ignore me," she said. "I can't, not when I'm about to leave Royalsport and I don't know when I'll be back. I need to know how things stand between us, Greave. I need... I need *you*."

And Greave needed her, had been thinking about her almost since the moment he put her on the boat and told the captain to bring her back here. Still, he didn't know what to do next.

"I don't know what to say," he admitted.

"Say what you feel," Aurelle said. She stood and went to him, moving close enough to reach out and touch him, her hand moving to cup his cheek in a delicate touch. "I'll start, if you like. I love you, Greave. I've loved you since... well, probably since before we left for Astare. Certainly after the trip there. I was willing to betray my employers for you, and risk putting myself at odds with some very powerful men."

32

"Who you'd agreed to kill me for," Greave pointed out. Some things weren't so easy to ignore, even when he wanted to.

Aurelle let her arm drop for a moment. "I could never hurt you," she said. "When I thought you were dead, it was as if my whole world fell apart at once. You were the only good thing in my life, and I don't want to let that go again. I want to be with you."

"But how can I know if it's real?" Greave asked.

"I've no reason to trick you," Aurelle said. "I'm not here as a spy, not here to kill you. I could have done that a dozen times. I'm here because you're the kindest, gentlest person I've ever met, because you're the *best* person I've met. And yes, you could tell me no, you could tell me to leave and not come back, but I really, *really* hope that you don't."

Greave felt like a dam filled to the point of bursting, emotions roiling inside him until it seemed like it would be impossible to contain them. He wanted… well, he wanted all the things that Aurelle wanted. He wanted to be with her more than anything. He loved her exactly the way that she said she loved him. That was always the problem, though: he could never quite be certain about it now that he knew that she'd tricked him once.

"Don't those philosophers of yours have something to say about this?" she asked him. "Surely one of them has *something* to say on the subject of love?"

"They're surprisingly quiet about it," Greave said. He smiled wanly. "Like me, I suspect that they spent too much time in libraries, and not enough…"

"Not enough with the people who loved them?" Aurelle asked. "What about your songs and your poems? I guess *they* have more to say about love?"

"They do," Greave admitted, although most of what they had to say was contradictory and hard to pick apart. Some of them spoke about tragedy and pain, others about happiness and everlasting joy. Even with those, though, Greave had his doubts. He suspected that the reason so many characters in the songs experienced true love was because they didn't have all the practical difficulties of the world pressing in on them.

Those difficulties felt only too real right then.

"I… I love you too," Greave said. He put his hands on Aurelle's shoulders. "That has never been the problem. The problem has always been all the other things."

"We can find a way around them," Aurelle said. "The bookish prince and the courtesan who kills people. It could almost be one of your poems."

"It's not, though," Greave said. "And there are so many things… for a start, you *are* going to kill someone. You're going to go out and murder Finnal and Duke Viris."

"To stop a war before it starts," Aurelle said. "And if anyone deserves it, it's them. When I thought that you were dead, I came back here to hunt for them. I wanted to avenge you."

"I don't want to be avenged," Greave said. His hand moved to brush Aurelle's hair. "I want you to be happy."

"I can only be happy with *you,* my prince," she replied. "I just wish you could be happy with me."

Maybe they could be. Maybe there was a way for them to get past everything and just *be* together. For the moment, though, there were so many things still in the way.

"I still have to find Nerra," Greave said. "And you still have to do… what Lenore sent you to do. Even if we want to be together, we have to do those things first."

Aurelle nodded, and then darted a quick smile at him. "It's strange, thinking of you going hunting after dragons."

"They're fascinating creatures," Greave said.

"Ah, *now* it makes more sense. You're going to make detailed notes, aren't you? Detailed notes, and diagrams, and philosophical observations, and—"

Greave silenced her with a kiss. He couldn't *not* kiss her then, and it had to come from him, not her. He kissed her with all the passion that had built up in him over such a long time away. He kissed her the way he'd dreamed of kissing her every time he'd thought about her, and it didn't end for a long time.

"I want more," Aurelle said, pushing him in the direction of the bed.

Greave shook his head. "When we get back, if… if we both still want to then. If it all makes sense."

"You think it won't?" Aurelle said. "I'll still love you then."

"And I'll still love you," Greave said. "But maybe, once I find my sister, and you kill Lenore's enemies… maybe some of the rest of it will make more sense too."

He hoped so. He really hoped so.

"All right," Aurelle said, even though she looked as though it was an effort to pull away from him. "But Greave, I *will* seek you out when I'm done. I'm not going to let anything come between us again."

She kissed him again then, and Greave was grateful for it. It was so much simpler than having to find the words to say goodbye.

CHAPTER EIGHT

Master Grey paced the open space of his workshop, unable to make up his mind what to do. It was a rare experience for him. Normally, he understood his place in all of this, had ever since the moment when his teacher had laid it out for him, as *his* teacher had before him.

"You can't just leave Anders in the wall," Devin said, looking over at him from where he stood with his wolf. "It's not just imprisonment; it's cruel."

"He feels no pain," Master Grey assured him. "He will not hunger or thirst. I could leave him a thousand years like that, and he would not die from it."

"Stuck in a wall unable to move?" Devin said. "It's torture. You want to somehow make him into our ally? This isn't the way to do it."

"Then what is?" Master Grey shot back, and he felt a flicker of power fill his voice. It was rare that he lost control like that. He was *all* control, every facet of his magic tuned to the finest pitch. "What can I say to him that will make him put aside his hatred? No, I'll put it more simply: I'm telling you that you have to work together again for the good of humanity. Why are you agreeing, Devin?"

"Because it *is* for the good of humanity," Devin said. "Maybe just try the truth."

"Truth is a fluid, fickle thing," Master Grey said. "As sorcerers, we look at the truth of a moment. We see it as it is, and because of that, we can manipulate it. Yet look again the next moment, and it has changed."

"This is what I'm talking about," Devin said. "The truth *isn't* complicated; you're just hiding it from us. I... I'm not going to pretend to like Anders, but I can at least understand why he's doing this. He feels tricked. He feels as if all his life you were manipulating him for a prophecy you won't even tell us about."

"Is that how *you* feel?" Master Grey asked. It was bad enough that one of them seemed determined to work against him, but if he alienated the other as well... that could be a disaster for the kingdom.

"I just want to know what's going on," Devin said. "You keep asking us to trust you, but the best way to achieve that is to show us some trust by telling us the truth."

Master Grey paced more as he considered it. There were dangers in such a course, obviously. Giving away knowledge always had the potential to rebound, as others used it for their own ends. A man who controlled what was known was better placed to control what others did on the basis of that knowledge.

Still, this might be one moment to consider doing something… else.

Master Grey waved a hand, and the spell holding Anders released, sending him tumbling out into the room, gasping. Grey stood ready, knowing how dangerous the boy was, ready to send him back in at the first sign of a threat.

"Devin tells me that I should release you," he said.

"And I'm supposed to be grateful to him for that?" Anders asked.

"He also says that I should tell the two of you the truth of what's happening," Grey said. He gestured to chairs set before his desk. "Sit, both of you."

"I'll stand," Anders said.

"You'll sit, and that way I know you won't attack me while I tell you this part," Master Grey said. He gestured again to the chairs, and he saw Anders move reluctantly toward one. Devin went to sit down in the other, the two eyeing one another warily.

"Where do I start with this?" Grey asked. He tried to think. "With the dragons? With the first war against them? No, with the period after it. There was a brief time when humans and dragons coexisted in peace."

"With them as our overlords?" Anders asked.

Grey shook his head. "As equals, as friends."

"Impossible," Anders insisted. "I was told…"

"You were told the truth about the years the dragons reigned," Grey said. "But not about what came after. A thousand years ago, there was a time when a powerful magus lived. Each of us has our talents, the things we are best at. Devin has his skill with star metal, you have yours with weaving magic into combat. This magus could create powerful bonds with creatures. Even when he was young, he could draw birds from the trees."

Grey paused, trying to get his thoughts into some kind of order, trying to remember this the way he'd been told it.

"He wandered until one day he met a dragon. This was in the days when they were hunted, and hunting us in turn. The first rebellion was done, many of the eggs destroyed, but those dragons that remained were still powerful, and dangerous. He should have fought it, should have brought all his magic to bear. Instead... instead, he bonded with it, but this was not like the bonds the dragons formed with their slaves. This was a true connection; an equal one."

"With a dragon?" Anders said, obviously not believing it.

"With respect," Devin said, "I've seen dragons, and they don't seem like they can be just... bonded with."

"And can an ordinary man change the path of a storm? Can he direct the wind, or shape star metal?" Master Grey demanded. "Magic can do much that seems impossible. Why not this?

"They went out," Master Grey continued. "And they showed the world that there was another way to do things. They used their combined powers to keep the peace between men and dragons. They stopped the war between them. They created a time of peace."

"This sounds like a fairy tale," Anders said.

Devin looked almost as unconvinced. Of course he would. They'd both only seen one dragon, and that had been in the middle of destroying a city.

"Nevertheless, it is the truth," Master Grey said. "The world was not what it had been before. Dragons did not rule, but nor did humans hunt them."

He kept going with the story. "The magus grew old, as all of us grow old. Slowly, because sorcerers can live a long time, but still he grew old. He saw the way that conflict between humanity and dragon-kind would resume, saw the dangers there. He sought a way to stop it, seeking visions, casting auguries."

He saw the two young men's eyes go around the room to the equipment Grey had gathered over the years for exactly that kind of thing.

"Yes, I have looked as he looked. Each magus of this realm has, because understanding the prophecy is part of what we need to know."

"And part of why you've held it back," Anders said. "So that neither of us could ever take your place."

"You have your own role," Master Grey said. He sighed. "The prophecy was not what the magus hoped. He thought that there would be an immediate answer, but instead, he learned that another child would be born with the ability to bond with the dragons and keep the peace until the night of the dragon moon, a millennium later."

He looked from one to the other of them.

"Which of us is it?" Devin asked. "We keep fighting over it, but is there a way of telling?"

"It's not so simple," Master Grey said. "It's not one or the other of you. Somehow, it's *both*. Two boys, born at the same moment, with the power split between you. It is why I told each of you that you were chosen: because you *are*. But not alone. I believe that it is only by combining your power that you will be able to do what is needed."

They sat there for several seconds. It was Anders who spoke next.

"So what do you want from us, Sorcerer?" he asked. "Rather than playing games, why not just ask for what you want, so I can tell you no?"

Master Grey considered it, and it was a dangerous path. Each word had the potential to send things in a different direction. Still, he knew that he had to tell them.

"The dragon the magus bonded with also saw the danger. It agreed to let the magus place it into a kind of sleep, frozen in place on an island, under a wall of ice so thick a man might build a city on it. I want you to find that dragon. I want you to go to it, and to bond with it. I believe, as that ancient magus believed, that you can provide the means to end this."

Master Grey looked over to Devin, and to Anders. "Will you do it?"

"Do I get a choice?" Anders asked. That was the danger with this, of course; that Grey had already done too much, already damaged his trust to the point where he would not willingly be a part of this. In that case, would the better course be to wall him up again? To *drag* him to the dragon and hope that it was enough? No, he could only hope.

"You could choose not to do this," Master Grey said, "but I hope that you won't. I believe despite everything, you still want to help humanity, Anders. This is how."

"And what humanity was there in putting me in a wall?" Anders demanded. He was obviously still angry.

"This is not about me, or you," Master Grey said. "It is about the whole world. I know you want revenge for those you lost, and for not being honest with you, but people will die if you do not do this."

"I…" Anders looked away, but then nodded. "You're right; it's more important that humanity is protected. I'll go with Devin to find this dragon. That is, if he'll travel with me."

Grey looked over to Devin, who seemed almost as reluctant as Anders had been.

"I can't trust him," Devin said. "I'll do this, but not with him."

"It *has* to be both of you," Master Grey said. "This needs your combined talents, or it will not work."

"All right," Devin said at last. He turned to Anders. "But I'll be watching you."

"Good," Master Grey said. "Gather whatever supplies you need. Get some rest. You will leave at first light. I suspect that you don't have a lot of time."

They both nodded, and even if they were still looking at one another with wariness, at least they were prepared to do this. Even so, Master Grey knew that he had to play his own part in this. He needed to find the amulet that Renard had brought to the city. If the two boys failed, it might be the only hope humanity had of surviving.

CHAPTER NINE

It was dark when Devin walked to Lenore's rooms, padding his way through the castle with Sigil by his side, past candles burning in their sconces. With each step, he felt nerves rise in him, both because of what he would be leaving to do in the morning, and what he was doing right now. Even with everything that had happened, it still seemed wrong somehow for a former smith from the House of Weapons to be approaching the chambers of the queen.

The guards at the door seemed to think the same thing, even though Devin was pretty sure both of them had been common folk just a day or two before. They crossed their halberds to bar his way, glaring at him as if they suspected that he might be some leftover Quiet Man, there to snatch Lenore away. Perhaps it had something to do with the two swords at Devin's side, or perhaps it was simply the fact that he was approaching at this hour. The looks they gave his wolf were even more pointedly worried.

"Who goes there?" one, a woman with the scars of someone who had fought in the battle for the city, demanded.

"Devin," he replied. "Master Grey's apprentice."

Was he still that, at this point? He supposed that the sorcerer *had* taught him magic, even if there had been no formal learning of spells involved. Instead, he'd forced Devin to see the world as it was again and again, until Devin had found the skills to balance it and adjust that balance. Certainly, being Master Grey's apprentice seemed to impress the guards more than saying that he was a smith might have. It got one of them to duck into the room, while the woman was left behind, staring at Sigil as if afraid he might bite her at any moment.

"He's no threat to you," Devin promised her. Still, she looked at the wolf, and at him, with fear. Was this what it was like for Master Grey, cut off from the people around him by the very power that let him help them? Even Devin looked at the king's... the *queen's* sorcerer, and wondered what he was plotting. Was this what it felt like to be him?

As with most things when it came to Master Grey, Devin suspected that it was a lot more complex than that. In any case, he didn't want to

41

spend his time thinking about the old man when he was standing there in front of Lenore's chambers. He let his mind fill with *her* instead, and had to remind himself that she was queen now, that things might not be the same, that she might not even want to see him.

The moment when she came to the doors of the chamber put that point to rest, at least. She stood there in a simple white dress, looking as pure and elegant as a breath of air. In the great hall, she had been regal and authoritative, there to admire for her strength and composure. Here, like this, it was impossible not to just stand there and drink in her beauty.

"Devin?" she said. "I wasn't expecting you. I mean, I hoped that you would come, but… has Master Grey sent you?"

It seemed strange, hearing her words tangle together like that. Lenore always had a smoother way with words than that, always spoke with the clarity and authority of a queen. It was almost enough to make Devin think… no, he didn't dare to hope that.

"I came myself," he said. "I wanted to see you before I left."

"You're *leaving*?" Lenore said, and there was a kind of shocked sadness to the words that Devin hadn't been expecting.

"I have to," Devin said. "Master Grey has a task for me; one that he says is vital."

"I… will you walk with me?" Lenore asked. Her guards looked a little caught out by that, stepping forward as she moved to Devin's side. "I'll be fine. Orianne, I'm going to walk the castle with Devin."

Devin recognized the woman who stepped out alongside Lenore as her maid.

"Then I'll come too."

"I'll be fine alone," Lenore insisted.

"I'm sure," Orianne said, "but then your sister will gut me for leaving you like that. At least this way, you can leave your guards."

"True," Lenore said, and gestured for the guards to stay where they were as she fell into step with Devin. She took his arm, and Devin felt a thrill of excitement just at that touch.

Her maid fell into place just a step or two behind, apparently waiting in case her queen should require anything. When Devin glanced back, she gave him a knowing smile. Sigil padded along behind all of them, so that the four of them made a strange group as they strolled down through the castle.

42

By night, the castle was mostly a quiet place, although there was still some bustle of activity from guards and servants. Twice, guards called out to them, only to step back when they saw Lenore. Several more times, servants stepped from their path, dropping down into bows or curtseys. On every side, Devin saw the marks of repairs being made, damage from the castle's various battles being repaired, but also simple things like tapestries being put up and monuments to Ravin being taken down.

"What will you do with all the paintings and statues of Ravin?" Devin asked.

"Probably sell them," Lenore said. "Then use whatever we get for them to help pay for food to get the poorest through the winter. There's been so much damage done to the kingdom that it will take people time to recover."

"Most rulers wouldn't do that," Devin said. "They'd probably have a statue of them made instead, or just have everything burned."

"That won't *help* anyone, though," Lenore said, and Devin smiled at that. "What?"

"Just that you don't think like any king or queen I've heard of," Devin said, and then realized what he was saying. "Sorry. I don't mean that to be any kind of insult to your family."

"I know," Lenore said, as they walked down a long gallery where paintings of her ancestors were starting to go back up. There were still plenty of gaps, though, presumably where paintings had already been sold on or destroyed.

"This way," Lenore said, leading the way down a flight of stairs. Devin followed as she opened a small, solid-looking door. He was surprised to find a small, square garden below, hemmed in by walls with vines set against them. Moonlight poured down into it, rendering the whole garden in silver and shadows. It must have been beautiful there once.

It wasn't now, though. Someone had been through there, tearing out plants, apparently for the sake of it, the destruction wanton and unnecessary. Devin heard Lenore gasp at it.

"This... how could they? This was my sister's favorite place, Devin. I wanted to show you it, but like this... it wasn't meant to be like this."

Devin could hear the hurt there, and he wished that there were something he could do. Except... maybe there was. He reached out for

Sigil, and the moment he put his hand in the wolf's fur, he felt the pulsing of the soil beneath, the living growth of the few plants left. He poured his attention into them, looking at them, trying to understand the processes by which they grew and the ways in which they would use the energy of the sun to fuel themselves. In that moment, his need to help Lenore made it simple to balance it all, simple to understand it.

Devin sent out a thread of magic, and around him, the remaining plants bloomed in the dark, bursting open and filling out in ways that should have taken weeks. Devin saw Lenore's eyes light up with sudden joy, and that made it worth it, even as the cost of it sapped his strength, exhausting him.

"Devin, did you… it's beautiful," Lenore said, looking from one flower to the next. She turned to him, and she kissed him then, fast and impulsive as a breath of air. "Thank you."

"You're welcome," Devin said, and he might have said more, except that he staggered then.

Lenore caught his arm, and for a moment, they were close enough to kiss again. Somehow, Devin knew that if they did, it wouldn't stop there. They would tumble to the grass of the garden, and—

"*Ahem!*" Orianne coughed, and both Devin and Lenore looked around at her with a start.

"Oh, yes, sorry," Lenore said, even as Devin was mumbling his own apology. Somehow, they managed to move back from one another.

"It's not that I *want* to interrupt," Orianne said. "It's just that, well, you're queen now."

She didn't explain further than that, but it seemed that Lenore understood everything that meant. Devin heard her sigh.

"I'll miss you when you're gone," she said. "Are you sure you have to go?"

Devin nodded. "Master Grey thinks so. It… he says that it's what I'm fated to do." He managed to bring his thoughts back to what he'd come there to do only with difficulty. "I came here to bring you something."

He took out the first sword he'd made from star metal; not *Loss*, but the one he'd made for Lenore's wedding.

"Rodry and your father both paid me to make this for your wedding," Devin said. "But when I handed it over, I meant it as a gift for *you*, not Finnal. Here, it should be yours."

Lenore took it, weighing it in her hands. "I hope to be the kind of queen who doesn't need to wield a sword," she said. "But I'm grateful for it, Devin. Truly. I will remember you when I look at it."

That made Devin feel weak at the knees again. This time, it had nothing to do with the magic he'd used. "Thank you, my queen."

"Lenore," she insisted. "Only ever just 'Lenore' from you. Please."

"Yes," Devin said.

"You've given me so many things tonight," Lenore said. "The sword, the garden, your kiss. I want to give you something in return."

"You don't have to," Devin said.

"I *want* to." She took a ring from one of her fingers, a simple band of what looked like silver, but Devin knew white gold when he saw it. There were marks inscribed on it, runic letters so small that they were impossible to truly make out by moonlight. His fingertip made them out though, her family name and crest there. "Take this and think of me when you see it."

"I will," Devin promised. "Even without this, I could never forget."

Lenore looked as though she might say more, as though she might *do* more, but she glanced across to her maidservant in that moment, and that glance held so much about the things she and Devin would never truly be free to do.

"I… I should go," Devin said. "I travel early tomorrow."

Lenore nodded. "That… that's probably for the best."

She didn't sound like she meant it any more than Devin did. Even so, Devin turned and forced himself to walk back into the palace without kissing her. No matter how many dragons he had to find, or battles he had to fight, he couldn't imagine any of them being as difficult as that, as simply saying goodbye.

CHAPTER TEN

Erin sat in front of the stables in her armor, her spear across her knees, trying to meditate. She wasn't very good at it, and frankly, she was wondering how Odd had managed to do it quite so often. Still, she was determined to try. She ran a calloused hand through her short-cropped hair. Anything that held the promise of peace within it was worth the attempt.

So she sat there, while around her, the men and women chosen to accompany her southward made their preparations for the journey. She watched them by torchlight, trying to work out how they would act on the journey, who would be trouble and who would help the others, who would have good ideas and who would be a liability.

There was a man named Merl whom Erin was sure she recognized as one of the former bandits who had gone to train with her on the farm. He had a bandage on one of his hands, and a long, single-edged sword hanging at his side. The boy, Villim, stood close by, helping with the stays of a saddle. He'd been eager to come, apparently unwilling to go back to his farm in the wake of the battle.

There was a young man named Dern from the House of Sighs who dressed in fine clothes but on whom knives glinted when he thought no one was watching. A woman named Ceris claimed that she was an archer and a tracker, and currently sat fletching arrows to suit her needs. A bulky guardsman named Ulf stood in stark contrast to her, a great mace strapped across his back. Yannis was a minor cousin to Lord Ness, technically noble, but clearly eager for some kind of adventure to make his own name rather than standing in the shadow of his kinsman. He wore a light dueling blade rather than anything heavier. Erin found herself wondering if he had the skills to use it.

There were another half dozen besides, although Erin didn't know them yet, making for twelve in total. It seemed like a good number. Enough that they could fight their way clear of a skirmish if they had to, but not so many that they would be immediately spotted and attacked. A number like this could hide as a trading convoy, or a traveling family, or any one of a half dozen other things.

It occurred to Erin that she was doing a singularly poor job of clearing her mind right around the moment when one of the others, Erin thought her name was Sarel, touched her on the shoulder. She was dark-haired, dressed in the light armor of a raider, and should have been used to dangerous situations, but even so she leapt back as if expecting Erin to strike out at her for interrupting.

"There's no need to be afraid," Erin said as she stood. "I'm not about to cut someone down for tapping me on the shoulder."

Sarel raised an eyebrow at that. "If you say so. It's just, I've heard the stories. I was even there when you finished off Ravin."

Erin found herself waiting for the burst of anger to rise at the sound of the former emperor's name. Nothing came, though. It was strange how quickly a name could cease to have that kind of power over her. Ravin's actions might deserve her anger, but to give it to him was to hand him a kind of victory.

It seemed like the kind of realization that Odd might have been proud of.

That brought a hint of pain with it.

"Is everyone ready?" Erin asked.

Sarel nodded. "Are you sure about *him*, though?"

She jerked her head in the direction of a man who stood slightly apart from the others, hand on the flank of a pale, lean horse. He carried a light crossbow and an arming sword, and wore the armor of one of Ravin's scouts, for the simple reason that he *had* been one of them. Erin could understand Sarel's reluctance, but still, this was necessary.

"Nadir knows the south," she said. "He says he and his tribe were forced into service, on pain of death."

"He *says*," Sarel replied, making a face.

Erin shrugged. "Should I ask about your time as a mercenary? Or what causes Dern has worked for? Everyone here has a reason not to trust them."

"Not like that," Sarel insisted.

"True, but we need him."

In truth there was only one person Erin truly wished were there: Odd. He would have been the perfect companion for a journey like this, rather than this rag-tag group of soldiers and bandits, farmers and spies. She could have shown him how much she'd learned, how much he meant to her as a teacher and as a friend.

47

It was too late for that now, though. Odd was gone. So many people were gone. Even the people she cared about were scattering again, with Greave going off in an attempt to find dragons even as Erin went off about her own task. And Vars… a part of Erin longed to find him and put her spear through his heart, but more of her knew that he simply wasn't worth it.

So many things weren't.

"Come on," she said. "Let's mount up and get going."

She went to her horse and mounted it in a single, smooth movement. The others did the same with their horses, and those mounts were as varied as they were. Some rode what were obviously battle-trained mounts that had once belonged to knights, others horses salvaged from the battle. One man, Bertram, the son of a merchant who supposedly spoke the different trade tongues of the south, rode a horse finer even than Erin's. She had to remind herself that, for a mission like this, men like that were more valuable even than a company of knights.

Maybe if she kept reminding herself of it, it would all make sense. She had to remember that this wasn't about fighting the south. She had plenty of reasons to hate them, but this wasn't about her anger, or even about finding new places to fight. Now that she'd killed Ravin, what was there even left to prove in those terms? No, this was about accomplishing the task that her sister, her queen, had set for her. She would find out how things stood in the Southern Kingdom, see what needed to be done in order to keep their home safe, and do it.

Put like that, it all sounded so simple. Erin smiled to herself, because there was nothing *simple* about what they were all about to do.

"Come on," she called out, digging her heels into the flank of her horse. "We've got a boat to catch."

*

They mostly rode in silence. Even as hours passed under moonlight, Erin's little group didn't really start speaking to one another. Oh, a couple did, Merl and Villim talking in hushed tones in a way that suggested they knew one another already, Ulf the guard talking to a man in the armor of a royal soldier, whose name might have been Edvard, Edmond… no, it was gone, and Erin suspected that simply pointing at the man and demanding his name wasn't the way a leader was meant to do these things.

48

As for the rest, they mostly kept apart from one another, keeping step as the hours passed, the landscape flowing past in moonlit shadows. It was only to be expected, really, and not just because they were probably all tired from riding by now. They'd all come from such disparate backgrounds, but even so, Erin found it a little disconcerting. When she'd ridden with the Knights of the Spur, they'd joked with one another, told stories and sung songs, even while they'd been alert for every danger. Now, her party slipped through the night like ghosts, the sounds of their hoofbeats the only constants.

Of course, no one came close to talking to Nadir. He rode along in silence, several paces from the rest. It seemed to Erin as if she were the only one there who even acknowledged his existence.

She would be grateful when they finally got to the coast. Already, she could smell it in the brine on the air, but she'd been able to smell that for an hour now, and it didn't make the sea come any closer. Now though, Erin thought that she could see lights on the horizon, and it wasn't just the first glow of dawn threatening to break through. No, these were the lights of a town there for fishermen or those merchants who preferred ship-craft to the now fallen solidity of the bridges.

As they got closer, the small town rose up in a series of flat roofs and low towers, with granaries and warehouses there rather than watchtowers and walls. No one came out to meet them as they entered the town, and Erin couldn't see any sign of guards there. It took her a moment to realize why: so soon after the battle for Royalsport, the local lord's men probably still hadn't returned, but Ravin's would have run, realizing that there was no place left for them. It was enough to make Erin move cautiously as she led the others down toward the docks. In a place like this, attacking strangers might seem like the obvious thing to do.

The docks themselves were anything but inspiring. The light was growing there, but it just meant that Erin had a better view of how small and unsuitable most of the vessels there were. They were mostly fishing boats, with a few merchant vessels mixed in for good measure.

"How do we do this?" Yannis asked. "Do we seek out a captain in a tavern?"

Erin shook her head. That could take hours, and at *this* side of the Slate, at least, she had the luxury of being direct.

49

"I need a ship!" she bellowed, in a voice that could have carried across a battle. A dozen men and more looked round. "A ship to carry me and my companions to the Southern Kingdom!"

Silence rolled out in response. The few men who had looked Erin's way looked away again, even when she lifted up a hefty purse of coins.

"I'm willing to pay handsomely," she said. "Three royals each for the passage."

A laugh came from a stack of crates to Erin's left. "*They'll* not help you."

She looked around to see a man lounging there, an empty wineskin perched precariously on his considerable stomach. His beard reached down almost to his waist, while one of his boots lay in the gutter.

"And why not?" Erin asked him. "Do sailing men not want honest work now?"

The man laughed at that. "When have we ever wanted *honest* work? And to carry people south… those who were willing are already doing it, taking the dregs of Ravin's folk back home, and for more than any three royals each. The going rate was seven when the ships started to run out."

"Seven?" Bertram sputtered, the amount obviously at odds with all his merchant sensibilities.

"I can manage seven," Erin said. "If you have a ship."

"I have a ship," the man replied. "I wouldn't be much of a captain if I didn't. Captain Jamison Harkener, not at your service. Not for seven, at any rate."

"Now you're just trying to extort me," Erin said. Slowly, she let her hand fall to her spear.

"Just saying how things need to be," Captain Harkener said. "It's not like I've a wish to head that way."

"What would it take to persuade you?" Erin asked. Strangely, she didn't feel the urge to threaten this man, when once, it would have seemed like the most obvious thing in the world to do. If anything, she got the feeling that he was hoping for that, so that he could walk away.

"Ten each," he said. "Ten, or I sit here."

Erin could guess what he was hoping for. She would try to haggle, shoot back some still outrageous number, and he would walk away. She didn't have time for that, though.

"All right, I'll pay your ten."

The captain looked at her wide-eyed. It was clear that he hadn't been expecting her to agree. Erin smiled as she looked around at her motley crew of would-be spies.

"Come on," she said, before he could wriggle out of it. "The captain here will show us which ship is ours. We'll have get the horses stabled or sold too. We need to get moving on the tide. It's going to be a long way to the Southern Kingdom."

CHAPTER ELEVEN

Aurelle stilled her horse at the top of one of the hills on the outer edges of Duke Viris's estates. She was already on lands that belonged to him, of course; she had been for hours now. The sheer scale of the holdings that belonged to him and his son were awe-inspiring in their way.

In another, they were just one more reminder of why the two of them had to die.

Aurelle's certainty about that hadn't faded during her ride here. If anything, the need to get this done had only hardened in her, turned into something sharp and painful. She wanted this done with, and not just because of the danger the two represented. The sooner she was done with this, the sooner she would have a chance to seek out Greave.

Greave. Just the thought of him seemed to rend her heart and make it swell all at once. Now that she knew he was alive, Aurelle wanted to be with him every moment of the day, but the task she had to perform meant that she couldn't. She needed to do this, then ride back to him and hope… hope that things could be good between them now that he knew all she was.

That concern filled a small portion of Aurelle's thoughts, but more worries filled the rest as she looked down at Duke Viris's estates. His keep stood at the heart of them, of course, thick walled and with a surrounding affectation: a maze of dark stone that stood in place of an outer curtain wall, clearly designed to slow down anyone who came too close.

Beyond that, there were lines of men, soldiers camped in place, gathered around fires, training and living. That confirmed every fear Aurelle had about what Duke Viris and Finnal intended, because if they'd decided to live in peace, they would have sent their armies back home. This spoke of preparations for an uprising, perhaps even an outright coup.

It also meant that there was no true way to simply sneak in. An average assassin couldn't have done it, but then, Aurelle was anything but average. In any case, her entry to the keep was already in hand.

When there was no way to slip in unnoticed, it made sense to take a more… direct route.

She rode down toward the encampment around Duke Viris's keep, wrapping her cloak around herself. Of course, that meant that when she approached the sentries on the edge of the camp, they challenged her. They couldn't do anything else.

"Halt! Who goes there?"

Aurelle pushed back the hood of her cloak then, and quite enjoyed the way the soldier's eyes lingered on her in shock. She knew the part she was playing now, and she took a moment to smile, with just enough cruelty to make him take a step back.

"Lady Aurelle, here to see Duke Viris. He and I have business to discuss."

The sentry stared at her, then gestured to one of the other men there. He ran ahead, obviously to bring the news of Aurelle's arrival to the duke and his son, but that was fine by her. Sometimes the best place to hide was in plain sight.

Aurelle rode slowly to the edge of the maze, and the thing about looking around imperiously at the camp was that she could take in every detail of the layout, committing it to memory as surely as she knew every contour of Greave's face. No, she couldn't keep thinking about him. She had a job to do, and needed to focus on that. Especially for the next part.

There was a servant waiting at the entrance to the maze, one of Duke Viris's retainers. He was balding and thickset, dressed in black and armed with a short club at his side along with a knife. Aurelle dismounted, and he took out a length of cloth.

"Duke Viris welcomes you… my lady," he said, and his tone told Aurelle that he knew as well as she did that she was not a real noblewoman. "He and his son are happy to meet with you within, but alas, none may see the route through the maze save those who are entrusted with its secrets."

"You expect me to blindfold myself?" Aurelle said.

"Duke Viris commands it," the retainer said. He shrugged. "Or you can turn back. It is your choice."

Aurelle took the blindfold, setting it over her eyes.

"A wise choice," the retainer said. "I was ordered to have you taken if you refused."

"Lead the way," Aurelle said, biting back her anger.

53

The man took her arm, leading her through the maze at a pace obviously designed to confuse. Aurelle had trained for this, though. She counted their steps together, making a mental map of the turnings, noting when they doubled back on themselves and when they changed direction sharply. She would not be so easily confused. All the while, she tried not to think about how easy it would be for this man to stab her.

Eventually, Aurelle felt the quality of the air around her change as they moved from the outside to the inside. Still, the retainer led her, guiding her up a set of stairs, and on through what was obviously the interior of the keep. Finally, he drew her to a halt and let go of her arm.

"You may remove your blindfold, Aurelle," Duke Viris said, his voice authoritative, hard edged, controlling. It reminded Aurelle too much of the times he'd come to her in the house he'd set up in Royalsport, or in the House of Sighs.

Aurelle removed her blindfold and found herself in a small, wood-paneled room. Duke Viris sat there behind a scroll-legged table, making notes on a sheet of paper. He was sharp featured and aging in a way that drew his skin tight over his bones, dressed in clothes so simple and austere that even that screamed their expense. His son stood behind him, tall and slender, so handsome that it almost hurt to look at him, his dark hair curled close to his head, his features fine and strong, his body athletic where it was encased in gray hose and a dark tunic, embroidered with silver.

Aurelle almost struck there and then, but there were a couple more retainers in the room with them, standing ready, and they showed no sign of moving away.

"Why have you come here?" Duke Viris asked.

"I was sent," Aurelle said. "I volunteered. Lenore wanted a messenger to bring you news, and I saw a chance to come here to speak with you."

"What message?" Duke Viris asked.

Aurelle reached into the folds of her gray traveling outfit, deliberately just a little too quickly, watching the reactions of the retainers. Both reached for their knives in the same movement, and they were quick. Clearly, they were dangerous men.

"Do not test my patience," Duke Viris said.

"I am not," Aurelle assured him. She took out the letter she had been given to help her gain entry. "I am here to report to you, your grace. Here is a proclamation by Lenore, who claims to be queen of the Northern Kingdom. It… I am sorry, but it is an annulment of her marriage to Lord Finnal."

She expected… what did she expect, in that moment? For them to be angry, of course, perhaps for them to lash out at her. Certainly for Finnal to curse Lenore and his father to have to calm him. Instead, though, they did none of that. They only laughed, as if this were some small matter, some petty thing that they didn't care about.

That said to Aurelle that either they had spies in court, or they had a plan. Perhaps both.

"I… do not understand, my lords," she said.

"Do you think that this is some great shock to us?" Duke Viris asked. "The girl has hardly made any great secret of her feelings regarding my son now. This was bound to happen at some point."

"And it might even be useful," Finnal said. His father nodded but neither of them elaborated.

Aurelle knew she had to think fast. She would have liked to *act* fast, too, slitting both of their throats and leaving, but that would need her to get them alone and catch them off guard.

"Of course," she said, "carrying the message was not the only reason I came."

That seemed to catch their attention.

"Then what is?" Duke Viris asked.

"My disguise as a noblewoman has held up," Aurelle said. "I have access to the new queen's court; she even sees me as a friend. I take it that you wish to dethrone her?"

Duke Viris nodded carefully. "Since we are in the middle of my keep, I will make no secret of it. And if you can help us with this… well, let's start with that. Why *would* you help with such a thing, if you can pretend to be noble for the rest of your days?"

"Because such a thing cannot last forever," Aurelle said, even while she wished that she were able to feel her knife sliding into his flesh. "And you have the power to make such a thing a reality, when your son becomes king."

"That has potential," Duke Viris said. He looked over to Finnal. "We could do with a helper at court, and it's easy enough to do what we want. Your cousin Feld would give her a title if we had her marry him."

"I doubt that he would complain at it," Finnal said. "She is beautiful enough. But if you truly mean for her to eliminate Lenore... it will need to be carefully plotted."

"I know that," his father said. Duke Viris returned his attention to Aurelle. "In the meantime, you will be given a room to stay in. My retainers will show you. Now, please excuse us, Finnal and I have preparations to make."

It rankled with Aurelle to be so casually dismissed, but it was at least better than Duke Viris trying to take her to his bed. At least this way, she got a room to rest in, and the trust of her foes.

Now, it was just a question of finding the best way to kill them both.

CHAPTER TWELVE

Somehow, Lenore's chambers were full of people, and all those people seemed to be trying to talk all at once.

"...that it's a matter of who has always owned those lands..." one nobleman was saying, gesticulating floridly.

At the same time, a woman who appeared to be some kind of merchant seemed to be extolling the virtues of her goods, trying to get Lenore to accept a gift of them so that she could say they were by royal appointment.

"...and the clasps are so smooth that you'll never feel them, even though..."

It would have helped if, in the chaos, Lenore had the faintest idea what the woman was trying to sell her, or what she was doing there, or who half of these people were. She'd come up here in a kind of retreat from the business of the great hall, and yet it seemed that half the people from there had followed her.

She found herself wishing that Erin were here, to glower at them all until they went away, or Greave were there to insist on the correct order of precedence and tell half of them that their claims made no sense in terms of the laws. As it was, Lenore was alone now, and while she *could* have called for her guards to clear the room, she didn't want to be the kind of ruler who did that. She wanted to listen when her people spoke. It was just that they all seemed to be speaking at once.

Lenore knew that the only way to deal with this was to go through it, but that required some kind of order. What would Erin do if she were here? What would Greave do? To Lenore's surprise, the answers to those questions were both the same.

"Quiet!" she yelled, as loud as her lungs would let her. "Be *quiet*. I cannot hear your requests if you all speak at once. So this is what is going to happen: I am going to walk the castle. You will come to me one by one as I walk, and you will make your requests. Anyone who tries to force their way forward will be dismissed for today, and made to come to the great hall tomorrow. Scribes! Where are my scribes? Where are my guards?"

57

They were there, lost amid the crowd. So was Orianne, and Lenore was grateful for her handmaid's presence beside her as she stood. Together, they started forward, and both the clerks and the guards fell into step around Lenore, forming a kind of shield that felt far too reminiscent of the wall of men who had kept her safe during the battle for the city.

Here, though, at least no one was trying to kill her, only asking her for her support in this legal matter or that, or asking for help with the aftereffects of the war.

"Whatever happens, keep walking," Orianne whispered to her as they walked. "I think if we stop, we'll be trampled by all the ones who just need one more minute of your time."

Lenore nodded, suppressing a smile at the thought. She kept walking, and, slowly, she started a procession out through the castle that wound through its corridors and its galleries, up its stairs and down into its depths. Crucially, it led away from her chambers, drawing the crowd of supplicants with it.

"Hang back and find some guards for the doors to my rooms," Lenore whispered to Orianne. "I don't want this happening again when I get back. Come back to me after."

"As you wish, my queen," she replied with a curtsey, drifting back into the crowd as Lenore led them away like some standard bearer showing a battalion which way to march.

Lenore chose the most convoluted route that she could, partly because it meant that a few of the less serious supplicants dropped off the back of the procession, partly because she'd spent so long sitting in one place that she needed the walk, and partly because she simply wanted to see all of the castle that was now hers. She suspected that most of those there wouldn't have seen all of it, either. The poorest had probably never been there before, or had never gone beyond the servant areas. The nobles had probably never set foot in the kitchens or the cellars.

Lenore walked all of it. She led them through the library and the halls, the galleries and the receiving rooms. She led the way through the middle of a guard barracks, where the men stared at them all in shock, and through the main kitchen, where the cook started shouting something about having to work in such conditions. She led the way across a stretch of open rooftop, with a view out over the city, and down into the dungeons, where some of Ravin's men were being held.

With every new room, almost with every other pace, people came forward to her. Each had their problems, and Lenore found herself shocked by just how *many* problems there were still to sort out. An engineer from the House of Scholars came forward because there were problems with rebuilding the bridges over the Slate. A woman complained that one of Lenore's guards had attacked her in the street. Two nobles both felt that a piece of land belonged to them.

Some questions were bigger still.

"What do you plan to do with Lord Carrick's lands, my queen?" a nobleman asked. "My family has a claim to them by blood."

"*My* claim is better," another man said.

"I was told that Lord Carrick had no heirs," Lenore said. "But if you truly have claims, present them to the royal heraldry master. He will verify that they are true. If they are, you will receive your share of the lands, under the crown. If not, the lands will be administered in the crown's name to provide food for those starving after the war."

"But that's—"

"The heraldry master," Lenore said, hoping all the time that the castle still *had* such a thing. "I will hear *his* recommendations a week from now, not yours today."

Lenore found that a lot of it went like that. The truth was that, as queen, she couldn't solve most people's problems, and certainly couldn't solve them when in the middle of a procession around the castle. The best she could do was refer each person there to the appropriate figure within the castle, issuing commands for this or that official to look into it.

That was how it was *meant* to work. Even if Lenore wished that she could see to everything herself, she knew that there was no way she would be able to manage it. She sent people to those who could help them, or told them to come back tomorrow with proof of what they were demanding.

In some cases, though, Lenore tried to help more directly.

"My family," a woman said, in tears. "They killed my entire family. I have nothing. My house was burned, my children killed…"

Lenore put an arm around her. "We will find you something. I promise. My servants will find you a room, and a place here."

"Why does *she* get a place here?" a man demanded. "I was a soldier. I fought."

59

"Because she needs it," Lenore said. "And if you need help, we'll help you too. We will rebuild this kingdom, and it will be stronger for it."

She kept going, trying to find ways to deal with problem after problem. At some point, Orianne came back by her side, and Lenore was grateful for it, because that meant that her rooms would be safe by now. She would have a place where she could find some peace. In truth, she was more than ready to head back there.

"That's enough," Lenore said. "If there are more problems, you can come to me in the great hall, *not* my rooms, tomorrow, when—"

"What about the Dance of the Suitors?" a voice demanded, carrying over the rest. Lenore looked around and saw an older man in the robes of the House of Scholars moving forward, a younger scholar looking apologetic by his side. "What about the Dance of the Suitors?"

Around him, people were starting to mutter, repeating those same words.

"I'm sorry," Lenore began. "I don't understand."

Except, she *did* understand, because her mother had taught her thoroughly when it came to the customs and the traditions of the court. Memories of it came back to her, little by little.

"No," Lenore breathed.

"Tradition dictates," the scholar said, "that an unmarried queen shall not rule without a king. A widow may, but not a queen alone."

"Master Eam," the younger man said, "I'm sure the queen doesn't want to—"

"Tradition does not care what we want, Jurin," the older one said. "And I am sure the queen will want to follow tradition."

"I *was* married," Lenore pointed out with an indulgent smile. The younger scholar gave her an apologetic look.

"But you *annulled* that," Eam said. "An annulment means that legally, the marriage never happened. The kings who have done so before were quite clear."

"The kings?" Lenore said.

"Well, *obviously* no queen before you has ever done this," Master Eam said, even as Jurin tried to pull him back. "You are an unmarried queen, and so tradition dictates…"

"That I must invite every unmarried man of noble birth who wishes to attend to an event where they may try to court me?" Lenore said, unable to keep the incredulity out of her voice.

"Yes, exactly," the scholar said, "all covered by the peace of the courting, of course, so that none of them may strike at each other, or suffer the violence of your laws if they displease you in their courting."

"I really don't think that this is a good idea right now," Lenore said. Or, frankly, at any point in the future. She *had* someone she loved, and even if Devin wasn't of noble blood, he was hers. She didn't need nobles lining up to try to seduce her for power or status, all because tradition couldn't stomach a royal bloodline that wasn't pure enough.

"But it could be a good thing." That was from Lord Ness, who moved toward the front, young and muscled and clearly thinking of his own role in the Dance of Suitors.

"No," Lenore said. "This is not the time."

She wanted to just turn him down flat, but saying that to one of her most important allies right now would be difficult. Lenore could almost hear her mother's voice telling her that the correct thing to do was postpone things, then quietly let them drop once she had secured her power more.

"If not now, then when?" another lord, Lord Travis, Lenore thought, said. He was at least fifty, with graying hair. Lenore could only hope that he wasn't thinking of himself when it came to the dance. "Tradition must be followed, and the kingdom must have a ruler."

"*I* am its ruler," Lenore snapped.

"Until you marry, of course," Master Eam supplied. "But there really is no tradition of an unwed queen ruling alone. The problems even for the succession…"

Other nobles started to voice their own approval for it, and not just the ones who thought that they might have a chance of being the one chosen. Even some of the common folk joined in. Obviously, they thought that this tradition was a good way to get back to something that they thought of as normal.

Lenore knew that she was trapped. As much as she wanted to tell them all about Devin, she couldn't, and because she couldn't, she was caught by this foolish tradition. If she said no… well, she would almost certainly lose Lord Ness's support, along with that of who knew how many other nobles. After she'd already gone against them by exiling Vars rather than executing him, it could drive them into the arms of the rebel nobles under Duke Viris and Finnal. She couldn't afford that now, couldn't risk it while they still lived, and that meant…

"All right, all right," she said. "Send out word. Let it be known that the Dance of Suitors will take place a week from now."

She said it reluctantly, but even so, the people there still cheered as if she had announced it with all the enthusiasm she could muster. Lenore forced a smile and looked over at Orianne. What had she just gotten herself into?

CHAPTER THIRTEEN

Where, Vars wondered, were you supposed to go to look for a new life? He wasn't sure of the answer to that, so he'd settled on the option that had always appealed to him most: a tavern. Specifically, he'd found a tavern down on the coast, which looked as if someone had upturned a ship and put a door in the side of the hull. The keel of the place ran right overhead, while the scent of salt water clung to it, even over the usual stench of vomit and ale.

At least here, Vars could get a drink while he tried to work out what he was going to do next. Persuading a cart to carry him this far had been easy, mostly just a matter of money. Now, though, it was a question of working out what to do next, and there seemed to be surprisingly few answers at the bottom of his ale. Maybe the next?

The drink helped to wash away memories, and there were more than enough of those to go around. The moment Vars had stabbed his father kept coming back into his mind, and only the sheer volume of other things he'd done kept it from being there permanently. Why hadn't Lenore executed him? *He'd* have executed him. He would have executed her, in a heartbeat, if the situation had been reversed. Vars tried to ignore the guilt he felt about that, and the best way to do *that* was with more ale.

Vars sat on his bulky traveling chest as he drank, since it was more than big enough to use as a seat, and heavy enough that no one was going to just run off with it when he got up to get another drink. Everyone else in the tavern sat on stools that had been carved with scenes of ocean life, seemingly every man who had sat on them adding to the carvings.

Vars sat tracing those of the stool next to him, and as he did so, the sounds of an argument drifted over to him. Not the kind that meant an immediate dash for the door to save his hide, nor even the kind that meant reaching for his sword and trying to look as strong as possible in the hope that it would pass him by. Instead, this one caught his attention, making him look over to the spot where two men in the robes of the scholars seemed to be determined to make more noise than the rest of the tavern put together.

"And I'm telling *you* that your research on the archipelago is nonsense. Everyone knows that there are no lands to the east. There is the Northern Kingdom, the Southern Kingdom, and Sarras. That's it!" That was from a man of perhaps forty, red-faced and portly.

"Rubbish," a younger man said. He might have been twenty, and looked both slender and serious. His face was flat, and his head shaved, which gave an impression of toughness undercut somewhat by his scholar's robes. "Von Drent is quite clear that—"

"Von Drent was a fool!" the older man said. "He made things up because he wanted the recognition. To take his writings seriously is madness!"

"And *I* say that the things he describes are too real to be works of imagination."

"You're putting yourself in danger, Simeon, and for nothing."

"*Not* for nothing," the younger man said. "As you'll see, when I return with complete maps of the archipelago, and documentation of everything that lives there."

The older man sighed in exasperation. "You're a fool. A complete fool."

He turned on his heel and stalked from the tavern, leaving the younger man there alone. Or not quite alone, because he went over to what was obviously a group of sailors, briefly laughing with them before retreating to a table that appeared to be strewn with maps.

Vars knew a chance when he saw one. He stood, moving to the man and seating himself opposite him.

"You're setting off on a voyage of discovery?" he asked.

"I am," the scholar said. "I plan to produce the first complete maps of the Seril Archipelago."

"I haven't heard of it," Vars said.

"I named it myself," Simeon said. "As its discoverer, I will have that honor. Assuming we find it."

"And this will involve a long sea voyage?" Vars said. "A chance to get away from here and start somewhere new?"

"Yes," Simeon agreed.

"Are you looking for any more men?" Vars asked. "I'm not much of a sailor, but I can learn, and something like this… well, I need to leave the kingdom, and this seems like a good way to do it."

If the scholar heard the desperation in his voice, he didn't show it. "Well, I suppose we *could* do with more men. For some reason, sailors have been reluctant to join this expedition."

Probably, Vars guessed, because they liked to know that the places they were about to set out for actually existed.

"I would be happy to join up," Vars said.

"Are you sure?" Simeon asked. "The pay is probably not what a man like you is used to, and it's a long journey."

"Both are fine with me," Vars assured him. Just so long as it got him out of the kingdom before Lenore's patience with him ran out.

"Great," Simeon said. "My ship is the *Azure Hound*. You'll find it on the docks. Be aboard by morning, we're sailing with the tide."

"Yes, Captain," Vars said.

"Oh, I'm not the captain," Simeon said. "That will be Captain Yula. You'll like her, I'm sure."

*

With every step Vars took, his trunk scraped across the ground behind him; step, scrape, step, scrape. The weight of it was exhausting, and the size meant that he had no hope of carrying it alone. It was a trunk meant for traveling with servants, not for escaping a kingdom alone. On the cart here, it wasn't so bad, but now it felt like a reminder of who he had been: someone who had assumed that there would always be a servant there to do everything, someone who had needed that help because he had been so useless by himself.

Vars could see the *Azure Hound* a little way away, moored at the side of the dock, its bright blue hull making it clear that it wasn't like any of the other vessels there. Three masts stood out from its deck, and a gangplank led down to the dock, so steep that it would need to be climbed as much as walked along.

Just the sight of it was enough to make Vars stop and sit on his traveling trunk. He would never get it up that without help. He looked around the dock, trying to work out which of the men there he would ask to help. He actually snapped his fingers at one of them: a young man perhaps his own age, tangle-haired and muscled from his work on the boats, his skin bronzed and weathered by the ocean.

"You there," Vars began.

"What do you want, friend?" the man asked. It was only as he said it that Vars realized what an imperious tone he'd just used.

He realized something else, too: he didn't actually *want* most of the things that were in the trunk, or the bags that he carried. Most of them were things he'd brought with him because he'd thought he ought to, fine clothes and finer ornaments, things he could sell and reminders to anyone watching that Vars was someone important.

Yet when had he been happiest? The answer to that was simple: in Bethe's home, helping her with the simplest of tasks. It wasn't that there was anything noble or wonderful about being in a hovel, baking bread. It was more the fact that it had meant something, when the rest of his life had meant so little. He'd worked, and it had produced something people wanted, and that had been enough.

"Do you need something?" the sailor who had come over asked.

"What's your name?" Vars asked him.

"Cillian," the man answered.

"Well, Cillian," Vars said. "How would you like the entire contents of this chest?"

The other man looked at him suspiciously. "Is this some kind of joke?"

"No joke," Vars said. He had enough to get by in just one of his bags. In fact, with that thought in mind, he threw the second one on top of the chest. "All yours, if you want it."

"Is this some kind of trick?" Cillian asked. "Are the watch coming, and it's going to turn out that all this is stolen?"

"No," Vars said. "Put simply, I've realized that I don't want to drag all of this around with me. I'm trying to change my life, and I can't do that if I have a big chest full of things from my old life."

"I don't know," the sailor said, still looking doubtful. Vars didn't blame him. After all, how often did something like this happen?

"Look at it this way," Vars said. "Even if all this is stolen, are you telling me you couldn't find a way to fence it? Are you telling me that you couldn't deal with that?"

"Maybe," Cillian said.

"It's a chance to change your whole life," Vars said. "Trust me, sometimes a chance comes along to be someone new, and the best thing you can do is take it. Me... I *can't* be that person anymore. I might as well do you some good while I'm doing it."

He could see that the sailor still wasn't quite convinced.

"What's the alternative? Go on being the same person, hoping that things will get better on their own?" He stepped away from the trunk. "Let me put it another way, I'm walking away from this box. Take it, don't take it. It's yours if you want it. I don't, anymore."

Vars turned and walked for the gangplank. It felt so much easier, now that he wasn't trying to drag the entire contents of his past life with him. Maybe it was just the weight of it all, but a part of Vars suspected that it definitely wasn't.

He strolled up the gangplank, ready for his new life, wherever it would begin.

CHAPTER FOURTEEN

Devin mostly kept his eyes on the horizon as he and Anders rode northward, taking in the hedgerows and the trackways, the patches of woodland and the settlements. Every so often, his eyes would dart over to the spot where Anders sat upright in the saddle, riding along apparently untroubled by Devin's presence beside him.

Devin wasn't sure what to think of his presence there. They'd been riding now for more than a day, heading ever northward, crossing the kingdom little by little. In the first hours after they set off, he'd been sure that Anders would ride off, or attack him, or both. The first time they made camp, Devin had sat with his back to a boulder, hardly daring to close his eyes in case Anders cut his throat in the night. Sigil had sat beside him, eyes locked onto Devin's would-be rival.

"We still have a long way to go," Anders said. "If Master Grey is right about the location of this frozen island, our best bet will be to find a boat on the northwest coast and go from there. I know some people."

"Where from?" Devin asked.

"From where I was hunting for the shards," Anders replied. He glanced over to Devin. "You did a good job with the sword. It's finer than anything I could have made."

Devin's hand went automatically to the hilt of *Loss*, checking that it was there. Anders had already stolen it once, after all. Anders laughed at that.

"Oh, you can keep it. I'm happy enough with simple steel for now." He wore a hand and a half sword now at his waist, usable with one hand or two. He'd acquired a number of daggers, strewn across scabbards around the leather and chain armor he wore. "Although it might have been better if we had *both* star metal swords with us."

"The other one wasn't mine to bring," Devin said. Inevitably, he found his thoughts drifting back to Lenore. They rarely strayed far from her at the moment, in any case. He wanted to get this journey done with, wanted to get back to her, wanted to find a way to simply be with her.

"What was it like?" Anders asked.

"What was *what* like?" Devin replied.

"Growing up not knowing that you were supposed to be the chosen one of a prophecy," Anders said. "It must have been... free."

Devin couldn't help laughing at that, and Anders glanced across at him.

"What's so funny?"

"It's not free, growing up poor," he said. "The people I thought were my parents had nothing, including any love for me. I had no one to teach me the things I needed to know, no chance to be anything more than the station I started in. My 'father' sent me to apprentice in the House of Weapons as soon as I was old enough to swing a hammer. I had no real choices, no money or status to do anything different."

"When you're the chosen one, money and status don't bring any kind of freedom," Anders said. "Yes, my family is wealthy, but that never meant that I could do what I wanted. My future was set out for me from the moment I was born. Every instant of my day was planned out, so that none of it would be wasted on anything that wasn't a preparation for who I was to become."

Put like that, it was easy for Devin to see why Anders had been so angry that Devin existed. His whole life had been leading up to one moment, and it must have looked to him as if Devin came swooping in from nowhere to take it from him. At the same time, if he thought that Devin's life had been easy, he hadn't understood what it was to grow up in the poorest areas of Royalsport.

Devin was still thinking about that when the bandits leapt out at them. They came out from behind the hedgerows, from spots behind rocks, even from behind a fallen log that Devin now realized must have been dragged into position. They wore what looked like the remnants of Southern Kingdom uniforms, and Devin guessed that they were men from Ravin's armies who had been sent out into the kingdom to take the smaller settlements, only to find their forces defeated down by Royalsport. Whatever the reason for them being there, they didn't even bother trying to demand coin, instead rushing forward to the attack.

Anders blew back the first wave of them with a ripple of magic that made the hairs on Devin's arms stand on end. It gave Devin time to leap from his horse and draw *Loss*, knowing that he didn't have the training to fight from horseback. A man came at him, and Devin sidestepped a blow, cutting diagonally across his torso to fell him. Sigil leapt at another, bringing him down screaming.

69

Anders dismounted then, moving his own sword in rapid strokes to cut through one enemy, then another. Devin was so caught up in the speed and violence of it for a moment that he almost didn't see the man raising a bow to aim at Anders's back. Not knowing what else to do, Devin reached out with his magic, finding the point where the bow string was weakest, seeing it clearly and applying the lightest of magical touches. He heard the bowman cry out as the string broke, lashing out across his face like a whip.

Someone slammed into Devin from the side, his weight bearing Devin to the ground before he could stop it. Devin managed to spot the sword the man held, and managed to grab his sword arm, but that could only hold him at bay for so long. Devin brought *Loss* around then, thrusting it through his foe's ribs, feeling him go slack atop him.

Even as he rolled the man from him, there was another one there. This one stood over him with a spear in his hands, poised to thrust it down, and Devin knew a moment of terror as he realized that there was no time to roll out of the way, no time to block the blow that threatened to come. Devin found himself thinking of Lenore, and the fact that he would never see her again, found himself wishing that he were there with her, rather than here, about to die…

Then the soldier's head seemed almost to leap from his body as Anders's sword slashed through his neck, sending him tumbling to the ground, already dead. Anders held out a hand, ready to help Devin to his feet. Sigil was there, though, forcing his way between them, growling at Anders.

Devin stood on his own, and found the last of the soldiers turned bandits turning to run. Around him, half a dozen at least lay dead, cut down by him and Anders working in concert.

"Thank you," he said.

"No, thank you," Anders replied. "I felt what you did with the bowstring. We should keep riding, though, before they regroup. Men frighten easily when they see magic, but then they decide that it's probably worth something to try to kill you."

"That sounds like it has happened to you before," Devin guessed.

"Too many times to count. People attack what they're afraid of." Anders mounted his horse, obviously impatient to get going again.

Devin got back into the saddle of his own mount, again wondering what life must have been like for his sometime rival.

"When the man I thought of as my father found out about my magic," Devin said, as they started to ride, "he threw me out of our house and told me never to return."

He saw Anders nod. "I suspect my father always saw me more as a way to bring honor to the family than as a son."

It was strange, how different their experiences could be, and yet how similar. Devin found himself wishing that the two of them could have met in a different way, and that Master Grey had been honest with them both from the start. Perhaps then they might have been friends. At the very least, there would have been one other person in the world who understood what Devin's life was like.

Perhaps there was still a chance for them to build that friendship. It was still a long way to the spot where they might find passage to the island, and longer still until they reached it. Maybe it was time to start trusting Anders a little more.

"Your wolf is fascinating," Anders said, looking over to where Sigil loped between them. "Both a real wolf and a conduit. To find a creature like this, and to bond with it, is very rare. It's enough to make me think that maybe the sorcerer has a point about us having different skills. I have never attracted such a creature. May I touch him?"

"If he'll let you," Devin replied. He saw Anders lean down as if he would pet Sigil, and he wondered what Anders would feel when he did. Would Sigil's touch boost his connection to the world as it did Devin's?

They didn't find out, though, because before Anders could touch Sigil, the wolf snapped at him, growling in a tone that made it clear getting closer would cost him a hand.

"Sigil!" Devin said, and the wolf came closer to him, still looking at Anders though, and still growling. If Sigil had been just a wolf, then Devin might have dismissed that as just anger at the ways Anders had struck out at him in the tower. Sigil wasn't that, though; his very essence was about seeing more. So that left the question of what he saw in Anders, what threat he perceived there that Devin didn't. It might be nothing, but it was also something Devin had to take seriously after everything Anders had done.

Devin would keep going and hope that Anders was his friend, but if he wasn't, if he was just pretending, then Devin would be ready.

CHAPTER FIFTEEN

Renard was quite enjoying being a war hero. It meant that he got to enjoy a more upmarket kind of tavern, for one thing. This one was in the noble district, all plush velvet seating and candlelight, fine wines and discreetly pretty staff. It was a definite improvement on most of the places he usually drank.

He stretched out his muscled frame on the padded bench he occupied, hefted a tankard of apple brandy some stranger had bought for him without the usual intervening step of Renard picking his pocket, and proposed the latest in a long line of toasts.

"To all those who fell, but to those who still live!" he said. "We owe it to them all to live our lives to the fullest, for I tell you, I have seen what the alternative looks like!"

He quaffed some of the ale, not caring if he got some of it in the red of his beard. Beside him, a young woman moved closer, giving Renard the kind of inviting smile that usually promised he would be jumping out of a bedroom window to avoid a suitor or a father come morning. She was, he had to admit, rather lovely, and if his thoughts strayed to what Meredith might say, they didn't do so for long. They were far too... distracted, for that.

"Were you *really* the one who sparked the uprising?" the woman asked.

"Aye, all that," a boy called out. "*And* he fought like a wounded bear in the battle for the streets. Even took on the Hidden themselves!"

The boy was laying it on a bit thick, and Renard made a note to have him tone it down the next time he paid him a small coin for all the supposedly unsolicited praise from the crowd. It would have been easier if Renard could simply sing his own praises, but he'd quickly found that the better sorts of taverns preferred their heroes modest.

"Oh, it wasn't quite like that," Renard assured the watching crowd, in a tone that suggested as delicately as it could that it had been a *bit* like that. "I'm no hero, not really."

"What *was* it like?" a woman from the crowd asked. "Tell us the story of you being made old and young again. There's a fable you tell well."

"It is no mere fable!" Renard said, standing for effect. It also gave him a pretty good view of exactly how many people there were in the crowd, who was likely to be impressed by what kind of story, who was likely to buy drinks or throw coins, who wasn't likely to miss their purse in a hurry after Renard clapped them on the back…

He settled on the story of how he'd run from street to street, spreading the news of Queen Lenore's return. It was a good story, featuring plenty of near misses with guards and falling masonry, but also made the people around him feel like *they* were the real heroes. People seemed to like that, and Renard always gave a crowd what it wanted if it meant he had a chance of coin. He'd worked the story out perfectly now, every line of it refined, every pause for drink timed to let the action build.

So it was rather a disappointment when someone interrupted him before he got to the third line.

"That is my *wife*, you cur!"

The man who stepped from the crowd was impressively big, as broad across the shoulders as Renard himself, with muscles only barely contained by the expensive tunic and undershirt he wore. One glance back at the woman beside him said that it was true, although she didn't look particularly shocked by any of this. If anything, she looked quite amused by this development, like she'd hoped it would happen.

"Now, sir," Renard said. "Nothing untoward is happening. I'm just telling a few stories."

"A few *lies*, you mean," the man snarled.

Something in Renard snarled back. "They are *not* lies."

Renard was well used to the small cruelties of the gods by now. The latest one was both subtle and especially annoying, though: it seemed that the more of the truth of what had happened to him he told, the less inclined people were to believe him. It was almost as if they found the idea of a man being forced into the service of the Hidden, running from dragons, stealing gold from Lord Carrick, and carrying the message of the invasion into Royalsport inherently unbelievable.

"Watch your mouth," the other man said, starting to square up to Renard across the table. Now, Renard loved a good tavern brawl as much as the next man, but this particular opponent looked rich enough

73

that beating him senseless might cause problems. Besides, if he went back to the House of Sighs with more bruises on him, Meredith would only want to know what he'd been doing when he got them.

As such, Renard was almost grateful when the unnatural feeling of silence and stillness settled over the place. The hubbub of voices seemed to fade into the background, while the various patrons simply seemed to stop in place, watching as a single figure made his way through the crowd.

Renard recognized the slender, aged, bald figure of Master Grey immediately. He walked to Renard's table and, completely ignoring the man who was currently raising his fist to throw a punch at Renard, started to speak.

"I require you to come with me," he said.

Renard thought about telling him what he could do with that requirement, but even by his standards that didn't seem wise. In any case, if he stayed here, he was liable to catch a beating, so maybe following the magus was the best course.

"Excuse me," he said, to the various people looking on openmouthed. "It looks like I have to leave."

He followed the sorcerer out onto the street. Master Grey led him perhaps another twenty paces, around a corner, out of sight of those who might have been tempted to gawp from the inn. There, he turned to Renard, gimlet eyes pinning him in place.

"Where is the amulet that the Hidden sought?" the sorcerer demanded.

Renard paused for several seconds, unsure what to say. "Ah," he managed at last, "that."

"Yes, that," Master Grey said. "You have felt the power it has. It is a crucial weapon in what is to come. We must have it."

"Ah," Renard said again. "There's... kind of an issue there. You see, I don't have it."

"You don't *have* it?" Master Grey shot back. "You *lost* it?"

"More hid it, and *then* lost it," Renard said.

"You..." The magus was renowned for his self-control, but now he seemed to be struggling with it. "Renard, do you have any idea how powerful that amulet could be in the wrong hands?"

"Well, when the Hidden almost got it, I got a pretty good idea," Renard said.

"That's not even *close* to the full danger it represents," Master Grey said. "We have to get it back."

Renard was shaking his head even before the sorcerer had finished speaking. "We? Why do I have to be a part of this again? That thing almost killed me the last time I carried it."

"But that's the point," Master Grey replied. "It didn't, and I think I know why. Tell me, do you know the story of the magus who forged peace between humans and dragons?"

Renard shook his head.

"He is the one who crafted the amulet. Initially, it was as a weapon, but then it became a tool to allow others to forge links with dragons, the way he could naturally. He made it dangerous, though, so that those who were unworthy could not seek such power. They would wither and die when they touched it."

"Like me," Renard tried, even though he knew what the magus would say next.

"*Not* like you. You are more able to resist it than anyone else I have seen. The magus made it so that only those with the touch of his power would be able to use it."

"He assumed that all sorcerers were good and wise?" Renard only just resisted the urge to laugh out loud at that. "Wait, does this mean that I'm meant to be—"

"You are *not* a magus," Master Grey said. He sighed. "For which I'm sure we are all immensely grateful. My current theory is that you merely share the blood of the magus who made the amulet. Enough that it recognizes you as *him*."

It took a few seconds for the sheer enormity of that to sink in. Even by their usual standards, this was the gods messing with him on a grand scale. He was meant to be essentially the same as a man who was simultaneously responsible for peace with the dragons and for large parts of slaughtering them? If the magus were to be believed, and that was a big if, he shared the blood of a man who had changed the whole world?

He could guess what Master Grey wanted now, and it was… well, it was *big*.

"So what?" Renard said. "You want me to help you find the amulet again, and then somehow wield it against any dragons who come along?"

"It's what you're destined to do," the magus said.

Destiny, because he had the right blood? He was meant to somehow live up to the legacy of a man who had helped the world fend off war with dragons?

Renard *did* laugh then. "I'm destined, at most, to spend my days drinking bad wine, seducing worse women, breaking into song only when I can't steal enough to get by and generally trying not to make any mark on the world. You've got the wrong man."

"The amulet is—"

"I don't *care* about the amulet!" Renard bellowed. "It's caused me nothing but trouble. I want to be done with it! I want to go back to my old life! So no, I'm not going to help you. And yes, I'm sure you could do something horrible and magical to me for not helping, but it can't be worse than what will happen if I do."

Master Grey gave him a cold look then, one that seemed to point out all the ways he could turn Renard inside out just by looking at him. Then he did the one thing Renard didn't expect, and turned on his heel.

"As you wish."

"As I wish?" Renard said, as the magus started to walk off. "Just like that?"

"What do you expect me to do? Take over your mind? I'm not entirely sure that I could find it through the haze of alcohol."

The magus kept walking, and Renard could only stare at him. It took him several seconds to realize that he was free of him, actually free. There would be no more magic in his life, no more strange prophecies, no more Hidden. He could get back to a life where he had nothing more complicated to worry about than running fast enough when the watch came.

Renard dared a sigh of relief. Life was going to be *good*.

CHAPTER SIXTEEN

Erin stood on the command deck of the ship she'd managed to charter against its captain's wishes, ignoring the way Captain Harkener glared over at her every so often as she leaned against the railings. Once, that kind of look would have made her angry, or given her a kind of feeling of satisfaction that she could have that effect on someone. Now, she found that it didn't bother her.

Instead, she was *enjoying* the journey south, even enjoying the fact that it meant being on a ship, having to watch the captain at every moment to ensure that he didn't order a change of course. It wasn't so bad if she just kept an eye on the location of the sun.

Some of her dozen weren't faring so well. One of them, a cunning man named Gress, was doing his best to provide tinctures and potions that would stop the sickness that came with the oceans, but still, half of those with Erin were leaning over the side at regular intervals to throw up anything they dared eat. A man in broken plate armor whose name Erin thought was Orglan seemed to be having particular problems with it, but Sarel, Merl, Bertram, and Yannis were all affected.

The others were playing with dice in a corner that kept them out of the crew's way; all except for Nadir, who sat alone and ignored by them. It seemed that the others were no closer to accepting one of Ravin's former soldiers as one of their own.

Erin would have gone down to the main deck to see how they were doing, but it seemed that there was another problem that needed her attention.

"We're not going to get close to the Southern Kingdom's coast," Captain Harkener declared, apparently out of nowhere.

"What?" Erin demanded. "I'm paying you to *take* us there, not give us a nice view of it and then bring us back."

"And I'm telling you that my crew won't stand for it," the sailor said. He leaned against the ship's wheel and looked back at her. "We've just been at war with the Southern Kingdom. If we come even within bowshot, they'll probably attack us."

"We made a deal," Erin said. Currently, the long head of her short spear was sheathed, so that it looked like a staff, but the temptation to unsheathe it was there.

"Aye, and I'm starting to think that I should have asked twenty royals each, not ten," the captain replied.

"I'd have paid it," Erin said with a shrug.

"Damn it to the depths." The captain looked away. "I still can't get that close to the shore. The best I can do is to come in close enough to lower a boat and let your lot row their way to shore. My men will mutiny if I ask more than that."

Erin considered her options. It sounded like it was the best offer she was going to get, yet even so, it wasn't what she'd been hoping for. It meant that there would be no boat waiting for them when they wanted to come back. They would have to find their own way.

"Very well," she said. "Now, I'm going to speak to my people. If I see the course change, I'll want to know why."

She went down onto the main deck, moving to her squad. She went to the ones who were dicing first, because that seemed like the best way to raise morale.

"Who's winning?" she asked.

"Dern," Ceris complained. "Always Dern."

"That's what you get for dicing with someone from the House of Sighs," Erin said with a laugh. The others scowled at Dern, who held up his hands and then effortlessly rolled a couple of sixes. Erin resolved to have him show her the trick.

She went over to Nadir next, where he sat with his back against a mast.

"Are you all right here?" she asked. "I could have a word with the others."

"And what would that do?" he countered. "Would it make me less of a man who had served the emperor? Would it make me seem less their enemy? Or would it just give them one more reason to dislike me?"

Erin had to admit that he had a point.

"I imagine even you don't fully trust me," he said. He ran a hand through the dark strands of his hair, tangled by sea water. "Oh, I'm sure you try to, but you look at me, and you wonder 'is he a Quiet Man, waiting to kill me'?"

Erin snorted. "It would take more than one to kill me."

"There is that," Nadir said, resting his head against the mast and half closing his eyes.

Erin suspected that she wasn't going to get much more conversation from him, so she went over to where Gress was trying to help Orglan, who looked distinctly green.

"Is he doing any better?" Erin asked.

"A bit," Gress said. "The sailors say this sickness will pass, but hopefully by then we'll have made land anyway, so... look out, Princess!"

He pushed her aside, and Erin had a shocked moment to try to register what was happening as a figure stepped into the spot where she had just been, swinging a blade. Erin saw a sailor slam into Gress, and heard the healer gasp as the knife went into him. Even while Erin was reaching for her spear, the sailor was already pulling out the knife, grabbing for Orglan, slamming the blade into him through a gap in his armor. The former knight cried out and started to fall.

"Quiet Man!" someone yelled.

There was no more time to fumble about trying to draw her weapon. Instead, Erin used it like a staff, slamming into the sailor's knee and hearing bone break. He tried to slash at her even then, and Erin brought up the staff to parry the blow, then smashed the tip of it into the man's throat. She heard cartilage crunch, and the sailor toppled back over the side.

Erin quickly turned her attention to the men the sailor had stabbed. Orglan seemed to be gasping for air, unable to get any. Even as Erin watched, he slumped to the deck and lay still. Gress might have been able to do something to help him, but the healer sat in obvious agony, his hands closed over the wound the sailor had made in him as if he could keep his blood inside him through an effort of will. The sheer speed with which it had all just happened made Erin spin round, looking for more danger, trying to make some sense of it all.

She saw Edvard approaching, the former soldier obviously ready to try to help. For a moment or two, his presence was all Erin could see, stepping toward her, holding out a hand as if he might—

Almost in slow motion, Nadir stepped up behind him and cut his head from his shoulders with the sweep of a sword. Edvard took an age to fall, the red of his blood mingling with the white of the sea spray as his body crumpled. It hit the deck with a thud, and *now* Erin had her spear head unsheathed, ready to exact revenge on his murderer.

79

Half of her squad seemed to have the same idea, encircling Nadir with an assortment of weapons even as he dropped his own onto the deck and spread his hands.

"Look at his hand," Nadir shouted, and it took Erin a second to realize that he was shouting it at her. "Look at his *hand*, Princess."

Not understanding, Erin looked down at Edvard, at the hand he'd been reaching out to her, and then at the other. When she saw the flash of steel there, she thought she understood. A knife sat there, held reversed against his forearm, out of sight and ready to strike even as he grabbed Erin. Erin gasped at the thought of that, and then held up her hands to stop the others from attacking.

"Nadir isn't the enemy!" she called out. "Edvard was! *He* was a Quiet Man."

"It's one of their tricks," Nadir said, his hands still spread. "They send one obvious man to strike, and then, in the confusion, the second one makes the real attack."

Erin looked down at the bodies on the deck, at Edvard and Orglan, and now at Gress, whose attempts to save himself had given way to an awful stillness.

"This attack was more than real enough," Erin said. She looked over to the others, who still had their weapons drawn as if unsure if they should be attacking or not. "Nadir just saved my life. He is our ally. Put your weapons *away*." Except that they couldn't, could they, not yet? "No, wait. Captain Harkener! Get down here."

It seemed an age before the captain did as Erin commanded, stepping into the circle of her followers' blades with obvious trepidation.

"I knew nothing of this attack," he said, without being prompted.

"And what about the man who did it?" Erin demanded. "What did you know of *him*?"

The captain shrugged. "I wasn't planning to sail. When I agreed to your money, I had to scrape together what men I could."

"Meaning you can't vouch for any of them?" Erin demanded. "Meaning that any of them could be a Quiet Man, left over from the ones who retreated through the port?"

"Well…"

"Shut them in the hold," Erin ordered her people. "Even if they're not Quiet Men, we have no way of knowing, and they're already refusing to finish the journey."

80

"Shut them… are you mad?" Captain Harkener demanded.

"No," Erin said. "Just practical."

"What's *practical* about this?" the captain shot back. "How are you going to finish this voyage with my crew locked away?"

Erin smiled grimly at that. "That's easy, Captain. *We're* going to sail the ship."

"But that… that's *impossible*."

"I'm sure it will be fine," she said. "We'll have *you* to teach us, after all."

CHAPTER SEVENTEEN

Greave had two companions with him out on the road as he rode in the direction of the sites that had been burned. He still wasn't sure what to make of them, or even if he truly *needed* companions. He'd traveled to Royalsport alone, after all. Still, Lenore had insisted, and so Greave was determined to get used to their presence.

Peris was a slender, sandy-haired swordsman who had originally trained under the Knights of the Spur but not met their standards, before heading to the House of Weapons to learn from their weapon masters. He carried a basket-hilted broadsword, along with a buckler, and wore light chain armor that didn't seem like much protection compared to the plate of knights. He rode high in the saddle, a crossbow resting across it, ready for use.

Meagan was his opposite in a lot of ways. She was a plump, broad-shouldered peasant woman who carried an axe and a bow to fight with, and claimed to know people in every village from here to the northernmost coast of the kingdom. She kept her brown hair shaved into patterns on one side and hanging loose on the other. For armor, she wore layers of what seemed like any clothes she could find, providing as much padding as possible.

So far on the journey, Greave's main job had been to keep the two of them from arguing with one another, but they both seemed to be committed to helping him in his quest to find out the truth of the dragon attacks.

"How much further before the village?" Peris asked.

Meagan looked around. "Shouldn't be much further. We'll be able to see it over the next rise."

Greave took out his maps, which he'd had bound into a journal so that there was less chance of losing them, but also so that he could annotate them more easily with charcoal. He marked their probable position on one of the maps, and kept riding. The three of them made their way up over the rise, their horses finding a small sheep track leading to the top.

When they reached it, though, the horses shied and whinnied, crabbing sideways in fear at the scents rising from below. Greave's horse started to rear, and he had to jump down from it, holding to it and stroking its nose to try to overcome the fear it clearly felt.

"I know, boy, I know," he whispered. He couldn't blame the horse for being terrified, because the sight below was enough to make anyone afraid.

At its center, there were not so much the remains of a village as blackened stains in the soil, the heat of the fire that had consumed the buildings there so great that it hadn't even left charred posts or stones. There were simply wide, black char marks where the fire had been.

Further out, it was somehow worse, because that was where the fires hadn't obliterated things utterly. There, Greave could see the shells of buildings, with blackened stones and the stick-like skeletons of wooden homes. He could see more than that, though, with the charred remains of what had once been people there, bodies contorted in death, turned into blackened statues by the heat. Even now, a small handful of peasants were moving through the carnage, dragging the bodies away for burial.

There were injured too. Greave could see men and women with bandaged limbs and blood-darkened clothes, could see others limping or with burns on their faces and limbs. Empathy for the wounded and the dead made Greave want to break down and weep for them, but he knew that he couldn't. He wasn't there to help pick up the pieces after the attacks, but to find their cause.

That meant that he couldn't keep hanging back; he had to move forward into all this.

"Come on," he said to the others. "If we're going to find out about the dragon attacks, we need to talk to them."

He led his horse forward, then tied it in place after a few paces when it refused to come any closer to the destruction the dragon had wrought. Greave wondered if that was down to some lingering scent of such a large predator in the air, or if it had more to do with the smell of burning. That clung in Greave's nostrils, making it impossible to ignore the scale of the damage, or the heat that must once have been there.

"My lord," a peasant man said, coming up to them. "My lord, you shouldn't be here."

"It's all right," Meagan said. "This is Prince Greave. He's here to find out what happened."

"A dragon is what happened!" the man snapped back, then looked to Greave. "Sorry, your highness. But the dragon destroyed everything. Big and black it was, the size of a house, spewing shadow alongside the flames. I didn't even know that they could do that, did you?"

Greave took in that nugget of information. It fit with some of the stories of dragons breathing lightning or frost in place of fire. Some scholars had assumed that it must be down to different sub-breeds of them, but if this one could breathe both, that lent credence to the theory from Nararch that dragons were natural manipulators of magic, able to produce powerful effects with their breath on a whim.

He held back from saying any of that, though. He knew that it was the last thing a man like this would want to hear while he was grieving.

"I have been sent by Queen Lenore to investigate the attacks," Greave said.

"She sent her own brother?" the peasant said.

Greave nodded. He wanted people to understand how seriously they were taking this. He knew it would help to spread the sense of Lenore's authority if people understood that his sister cared about what was happening to them. He turned to Peris and Meagan.

"Go among the others," he said. "Find out what you can."

They nodded, and set off among the villagers. Greave kept his attention on the man in front of him.

"I need to know as much as you can tell me about the attacks," he said. "Were you here when they happened?"

The peasant nodded. "Don't know that I can say much more, though. The dragon came in, burned everything. Then it landed, and this *thing* got down off its back, killed people. Told them that it was Princess Nerra and flew off again. Don't know why it would say something like that."

Greave swallowed at the sound of his sister's name. It was her name that had brought him out on this journey, trying to find the truth of things, her name that kept him hoping that he might be able to do some good here.

"Describe this creature," he said. "I need to know... I need to know what we're facing." He needed to know if this was actually his sister, but he couldn't say that, couldn't let people know that it might really be Nerra responsible for... for *this*.

"It was the size of a man," the peasant said, "but scaled like a dragon, blue scales like the sky. It had a lizard-like face, but there was

84

something *human* about it too. It was wearing a kind of robe, or dress, maybe, and its voice... the voice was the strangest part."

"What was strange about it?" Greave asked.

"It just sounded *normal*, like a girl, not a monster," the peasant said.

Until that point, Greave had been ready to assume that this wasn't his sister after all, but the voice... why a young woman's voice, and why did the creature claim to be Nerra? Why would anyone do that if it weren't true?

Yet would Nerra do something like *this*? His sister, who loved all living things and wanted to help people where she could? Yet, as Greave looked around, he could see the people who had survived, and could see the places on the outskirts of the village that had been left alone by the dragon's attack. Why had the whole place not been burned, and every person killed? Had this creature claiming to be his sister been holding the dragon back somehow, persuading it not to simply slaughter everyone?

That seemed more like the kind of thing Nerra might do, and for a brief moment, Greave felt hope. He dared to hope that it *might* really be her, and that he might have a chance to use the cure that he'd crafted for her. To do that, though, he had to find her, had to catch up to her.

"Which direction did the dragon come from?" Greave asked. The peasant frowned and then pointed. "And which direction was it flying when it left?"

Greave nodded as the man pointed again, then went to find Peris and Meagan, leading them back to the horses. Greave took out his maps again.

"Which way?" he asked, the way he'd asked at the last attack site, and the one before that.

They both pointed, and Greave nodded, because it agreed with what he'd gotten from the peasant he'd spoken to. That was the important thing: to get a direction from as many people as possible. One person could misremember or mislead. Multiple people were more likely to get it right.

Greave marked the direction on his map, adding it to the other marks he'd plotted on it. He stared at those marks, trying to make sense of them as he had so many times before. Each place, he realized, was one that had the potential to help an army, whether it was through food or weapons, men or horses. Several places had been ones where clusters of Ravin's soldiers remained.

85

A line of attacks led from Astare in the northeast toward the southwest. Greave knew what sat there, because there was only one place this could be heading: Geertsport.

They could find the dragon, find Nerra. They just had to get there first.

CHAPTER EIGHTEEN

Aurelle walked Duke Viris's keep, trying to hide her frustration. From the outside, she probably presented a serene picture of a noble lady enjoying this or that view from the windows, pausing to admire hunting trophies taken by an ancestor of the duke or sitting to examine the exquisite work of a tapestry depicting the joining together of the kingdom. Inside, though, she seethed.

The simple fact was that she should have killed Duke Viris and his son by now. Yet somehow, it hadn't happened. It didn't help that they were always accompanied by guards, or at least servants, usually two or three, too many to be certain of killing them both in a simple rush. Worse, they mostly seemed to be ignoring her, leaving her alone without so much as a message sent through a servant.

It wasn't that they were treating her with anything less than courtesy. The room they had given her was furnished as richly as any for a true noble would have been, the bed exquisitely carved, the furniture elegantly worked with silver and velvet. Dresses had been brought that could have graced the court of the queen herself, and Aurelle had no doubt that they would fit perfectly, if only as a reminder on Duke Viris's part of exactly how well he knew her body.

Still, they ignored her. Aurelle wasn't used to that. By now, she would have thought that Duke Viris would have summoned her to his bed at least, simply because he could. Even with Finnal, she would have thought she could persuade him to want her, to want to be *alone* with her. Yet there had been no request for her presence, no unscheduled, secretive visit by either of them that she could use to her advantage.

A part of Aurelle thought that was just as well. Once, she might have been willing to do whatever it took to get close to someone, to fully live up to the House of Sighs' training, but now... now all she could think about was Greave, and what he would think of her. He thought badly enough of her as it was, and Aurelle didn't want to risk pushing him any further away.

Still, if she could at least give them the *illusion* that she was available to them, maybe that would give her a way to get close...

No, she couldn't risk it. If Greave found out, even that much would cause him pain, and Aurelle wouldn't do that. She loved him too much for it. In any case, to succeed in even that kind of prelude to seduction, Aurelle would first have to get close enough for them to at least *look* at her. So far, even that didn't seem possible. She would have to find another way.

What other way, though? Aurelle continued to walk the keep, making it look as if she were out for no more than a simple stroll along the corridors, the galleries, the rooms of state, yet every time she paused to admire a painting or a fresco, her eyes strayed to locks and doors, defenses and guard patterns.

Every system had weaknesses. Guards who moved in set ways could be predicted and avoided. Locks could be picked. Walls could be climbed. There had to be a way. Aurelle leaned against a window, looking out at the army surrounding the keep. She would have to *find* that way, or all the men below her might descend on Royalsport, undoing everything that Greave and Lenore had achieved.

What options were there? Aurelle had been trained for this, damn it. She needed to think. She looked down at the ranks of soldiers. Could she go among those armed men and strike with a blade from nowhere when Duke Viris and Finnal inspected them? No, that would mean fabricating a reason to leave the castle, getting a disguise, and hoping that both of them would approach together. Even then, she would be cut down. It was a foolish plan.

What about striking in the midst of dinner in the keep's main hall? Again, there was no guarantee that both her targets would show up, especially when Aurelle's meals had so far been brought to her room by servants. More than that, there was still the risk of being killed while she did it. Perhaps once, she wouldn't have cared, but now... now she needed to live and escape, in order to get back to Greave.

Aurelle smiled in a way that was sweet and bitter all at once. All the love that she felt for her prince had made a coward of her. She had been trained to do what was needed, and now she couldn't, because that meant she would never taste Greave's lips on hers again. She couldn't just *strike*, when striking and escaping seemed equally important now.

How then? That question didn't go away. Sneaking into their chambers at night? So far, the route through the guards and the locks by night eluded her. Send a message suggesting that she longed for each of them? Even if she hadn't already ruled that out Aurelle knew that Duke Viris and his son were both too clever for that. Duke Viris knew that the times she'd let him bed her had been about duty, not desire. He'd *enjoyed* that fact.

One by one, Aurelle ruled out methods. Poison at a meal meant getting close to food at the right moment. An arrow from the dark required a crossbow she didn't have. There had to be *something,* though. Aurelle paused in front of a picture of rolling hills, considering the possibilities of strangulation. She was still doing it when a servant came to her.

"Your presence is required, my lady," the young man said to her. "Duke Viris awaits you."

Aurelle nodded, trying not to show too much of the hope she felt. Maybe *this* was finally her chance. "Lead the way."

The servant did, down a staircase, along a walkway, then through a chamber that seemed to be arranged solely to allow half a dozen clerks to work on whatever tasks Duke Viris had set them. Large wooden doors stood at the other side of the chamber, with a guard there who swung them open as Aurelle approached.

If she'd been hoping for some quiet little chamber for just the two of them, though, she was sorely disappointed. Instead, the doors led through to the great hall of the keep, in which Duke Viris seemed to be meeting with at least a dozen other people, ranging from soldiers to men who were clearly minor nobles.

The great hall was smaller by far than the one in Royalsport's castle, clearly designed for a coterie of trusted nobles to meet rather than just anyone who wanted to be there. The walls were relatively plain, except for a series of suits of armor set around them, each one obviously fitted to some previous occupant of Duke Viris's position. Rather than occupying some kind of ducal throne, he sat in a chair at the head of a long table, with advisors and nobles either seated around it or standing behind them. Duke Viris gestured to an empty seat near him, and Aurelle took it.

From here, it would have been so easy to reach out and cut his throat. Two things stopped her: first, she would be doing it in front of a room full of people who would then cut her down. Second, and more importantly…

"Will Lord Finnal not be joining us?" she asked. The other nobles there and the guards didn't matter, only the fact that his son wasn't there in the room too.

"Events have called him away, Lady Aurelle," Duke Viris said. Aurelle noted the honorific, obviously designed to be a reminder of the offer he had made to her.

"What events?" Aurelle asked, unable to think of a way to put it more subtly.

"We have received news that Lenore has given notice of the Dance of the Suitors," Duke Viris said. "What better chance is there for Finnal to get close to her, and to remind her nobles of our family's power? What better chance is there to take control from under her?"

"But I thought that *I* would be the one to deal with Lenore?" Aurelle said, cursing inside at Finnal's absence. She also found herself astonished that Lenore would agree to such a thing. Didn't she understand the dangers it created?

Duke Viris spread his hands. "Of course, if this eventuality should not bring the effects I require, we still have your talents as an option. And I will fully honor our deal. So stay in my home for now, Lady Aurelle. We were just going to discuss the best ways to use our forces in the coming days. I'm sure your insights will prove... invaluable."

Again, Aurelle found herself cursing inside, and not just because since Duke Viris was the only one of her targets who was in reach, she couldn't risk making any kind of move just yet. No, what made it worse was that she was actually going to have to *help* him. Doing anything else risked her position here. It was too easy for them to find her out if she lied, or for them to decide that she wasn't helpful enough to keep around.

She could just leave. She could kill Viris and try to find a way out through the maze. That would mean getting past an army, though, and hunting Finnal in Royalsport, where he might slip away. Better to take them both together. For now, at least, she was going to have to actually be the thing she was pretending to be. She was going to have to betray her friends, and wait, and hope that Finnal returned soon.

When he did, though, this would end. Aurelle would spend every moment until then working out her options, so that when he came back, there would be no failure. She would kill him, and his father, then escape before anyone realized it was her.

It was the only way to get back to Greave.

CHAPTER NINETEEN

The people of the small coastal town of Arnspur looked at Devin with obvious fear as he and Anders rode into town. He suspected that a part of that was the presence of Sigil walking beside him, because this was the kind of place where farmers would have to deal with wolves trying to get at their flocks.

More of it, though, was probably just that they were strangers. In these times, any armed man was a potential threat, while he and Anders both looked strange enough that it was obvious that they weren't with the royal army. They were probably trying to work out who or what the two of them were.

Whatever the reason, men and women looked at the two of them with suspicion, as if they might be raiders or murderers. The richness of their clothes marked the two of them out as different, as did the mystical charms woven into Anders's hair and even Sigil's presence. Small children glanced at the two of them as they passed, and Devin felt eyes on him from every window.

"Ignore them," Anders said. "I've had people staring at me my whole life."

Devin tried to imagine what that would be like, and realized that he didn't *have* to imagine. He could remember all the looks his supposed parents had given him, worried and fearful, as if waiting for the moment when he would turn out to be a danger. He hadn't known what those looks had meant at the time, but he'd felt the effects.

"It must be difficult, being different," Devin said.

Anders shrugged. "They treated me well enough. To be the chosen one… it was an honor, but an honor that set me apart. People treated me like I was special, but there were always the looks in the background. My teachers would put their all into showing me what I needed to know, but then leave as quickly as they could."

Devin found himself feeling a hint of sympathy at that as he and Anders dismounted from their horses and tied them up in the village square.

"How much further?" he asked.

"I'd guess not far now," Anders said. "According to the maps, another few leagues, and we'll find a route out to the place where the dragon lies dormant."

He took out the map in question, holding it out for Devin to examine. Looking at it, Devin could see the small island there, but also a strange pale line leading from it to the mainland.

"What's this line?" Devin asked. "Is it connected to the land, or do you think we'll need to find a boat?"

Anders shrugged. "We won't know until we look, but it's getting late. I say we stop here for the night and try to reach it in the morning."

Devin nodded. Whatever they were going to face, it would probably be better to do it in daylight, rather than in the shadows of the night, when dangers could simply sneak up on them.

"All right," he said. "I think I saw an inn over that way."

They started to walk toward it, Sigil between them as if to protect Devin from Anders's presence. Around them, the sounds of the small town started to return to normal, with people working and calling out their wares. A town crier was calling out news above it all, and one piece of it stood out above the rest.

"Queen Lenore has announced the Dance of Suitors!" the crier called out. "Any man of noble birth may attend the castle in Royalsport, protected from harm by the peace of the dance. At the end of it, the queen, with the advice of her nobles, will pick a husband to rule alongside her as king."

The crier's words hit Devin like a hammer blow. Lenore... Lenore was going to marry? She was going to pick some noble to be her husband? But that meant... no, she couldn't be doing this.

"Say that again!" he told the crier, and it was only as he did it that Devin realized that he had drawn *Loss*.

"I... Queen Lenore has declared the Dance of Suitors, and will be choosing a husband?" the man said, obviously taken aback by the sudden presence of a blade near his throat.

"Devin, what is it?" Anders said. He reached up toward Devin's arm, but stopped when Sigil growled.

Devin realized how strange this must look, him threatening a town crier like this, simply because of the news he had delivered. Devin stepped back and sheathed his blade, staring at the man for several seconds.

"I... I'm sorry," he said, and turned to walk off, not willing to stand there and be told that Lenore was going to choose some other man over him like this.

That was what it came down to. By declaring this search for a husband, she was saying all the things that Devin had been afraid might be true: that he wasn't good enough for her, that he could never be with her, that anything he felt for her could never truly be reciprocated, because why would someone like *her* truly love *him*?

Devin felt Anders's hand on his shoulder.

"Are you all right?" Anders asked.

Devin shook his head. "I... no."

"Come on," Anders said. "I'll buy you an ale, and you can tell me about it."

Devin wanted to tell him that he didn't want to talk about it, and that they weren't friends, yet right then, he *did* need someone he could tell about all this. He nodded, and Anders led the way to the small town's inn, a sleepy, wooden-walled place with small, round tables dotted around the floor. Devin took a seat at one of them while Anders went and fetched ale. Sigil curled up by Devin's foot, looking round at all the few other patrons there. None of it distracted Devin from the sudden, total hit of what he'd just heard from the town crier.

"I've rented us rooms as well," Anders said when he got back, setting down the tankards of ale on the table. "Now, tell me what affected you so much about hearing that Queen Lenore is searching for a husband."

Devin swallowed back his anger, and also a fair amount of suspicion. Why would Anders want to know this if not to find a way to use it against him? At the same time, though, he needed to tell this to *someone*.

"I thought... I thought she loved me," Devin said, and the pain of that was raw and harsh. "From the moment I saw her, I cared about her, I wanted to be near her."

"Well, she is very beautiful, and noble," Anders said.

"It's not just that," Devin insisted. "I love her."

"Are you sure?" Anders asked. "How much time have you actually spent with her?"

"I..." The truth of what Anders was saying hit home too deeply inside Devin. It was all too easy, with what he was saying, to realize that he *hadn't* had any real time with Lenore. He'd had one moment in

93

the gardens of the castle, shared a couple of kisses with her, and that was it.

Looked at like that, could he really expect that she was in love with him, the way he thought he was with her? Did it make any kind of sense? *Could* it, given who she was, and who he was?

"I know what I feel," Devin insisted.

Anders shrugged in response to that. "I'm not going to try to tell you different. Do you know what she feels, though?"

"She's said... she's said that she loves me," Devin said, and that brought a fresh wave of pain with it.

"People say all kinds of things," Anders said. "They say them to manipulate people, or because they think it's expected, or because they want to believe that it's true. But it's also tricky being noble born."

"Trickier than never having enough money, and wondering if there's going to be enough food for the table?" Devin countered. He found himself wondering how hard it could be to be noble, when that meant having money, power, respect, and all the possibilities in the world.

"Tricky because you don't have as much power as you think you do," Anders said. "Every moment comes with expectations, and if you do the wrong thing, it costs your family allies, or power. You have power, but you can only use it certain ways. You have enemies, just by existing."

"Maybe," Devin said. "Even so, for Lenore to just decide she's going to get a king..."

"It's probably a good way to bring people together," Anders said. "Love for nobles is... difficult. You can feel what you want, go out and have fun with who you want, if you're discreet. But marriage is different. Marriage is about making decisions that affect dynasties and political alliances. It doesn't have any room for feelings. I mean, look at Lenore's marriage to Duke Viris's son."

The truth of that was like a knife to Devin's heart. Of course, Lenore would want to use marriage as a tool to secure her kingdom's stability. Of course, she wouldn't waste it on someone like him, who could never be worthy of her.

"I'm sorry," Anders said. He sipped his drink.

"You don't need to be." Devin tried to hide his feelings, and just how much it all hurt. "I just... we need to focus on the task Master Grey gave us. We need to find the dragon, and find a way to stop the threat that's coming. Nothing else matters. Not me, not Lenore, not any of it."

He said it with as much confidence as he could. He wished, really wished, that he could actually believe it. He sat there drinking with Anders, and he was surprised to find how well the other young man understood him. Just a short while ago, they'd been trying to kill one another, and now, they were, if not friends, then at least allies.

Tomorrow, they would need to depend on that alliance. They had a dragon to find, and Devin suspected that it would take both of their skills.

CHAPTER TWENTY

Vars clambered up the rigging of the *Azure Hound*, surprised to find that he enjoyed the effort of clinging to it, and that the sight of the waves far below him didn't terrify him the way it should have.

"Which rope do I pull on?" Vars called down to where Moray the bosun was standing.

"They're not ropes, they're sheets and lines, new hand!" the bosun bellowed back up. "And ye're not to pull on any of them. Ye're disentangling that one. No, not that one, *that* one!"

Vars did his best to work out the one the bosun meant, saw where it was tangled up in another piece of the rigging, and set about unknotting it. It gave way suddenly, and Vars yelped as it burned across his hand. He barely kept his grip on the rigging.

"Don't just hang there!" the bosun yelled. "Tie it off!"

A part of Vars wanted to tell the man that he had been a king once, and could have had him executed. That part of his life was long done, though, so instead, he tied off the rope and paused for a moment before he had to head back down toward the deck.

The sea spread out around him in a carpet of blue and green, gray and white, each delicate shift in color seeming to mean something to the sailors who crewed the boat. They worked among the rigging or hauled ropes—lines, Vars corrected himself—below, singing as they worked to ensure that they all did it in the same rhythm. Simeon of the House of Scholars stood at the prow, taking readings with an apparatus of his own devising, while Captain Yula stood aft, large and imposing for a woman, dressed in breeches and tunic, a curved sword by her side.

"Stop lazing about up there and get down here!" the bosun yelled to Vars.

Vars clambered down, ignoring the sting of the rope burn across his palm. Already, he had more calluses than he'd ever thought he could get. He felt the movement of the deck beneath his feet, and he was surprised by how quickly his balance had adapted to it. For the first time in a long time, he felt as if he might be able to do anything he set his mind to.

He started about his next task, hauling on the ropes for the mainsail with the rest of the crew. Vars quickly fell into the rhythm of it, his eyes on the horizon, dreaming of everything he might find there. Maybe there was somewhere out there where he could find a new life, start to carve out a place for himself in the world again, actually rise to prominence.

Vars tried to imagine what that would be like. Of course, wherever he ended up, he would find a way to rise to be an important man. He'd managed it in Royalsport's slums, hadn't he? He'd been the one to lead them in their attack on the castle. He'd been the one, when it came down to it, who had ensured that Lenore had a throne to sit on at all.

Wherever he ended up, he would find a way to earn a living. Maybe he would stay as a sailor, wandering the seas. Maybe he would find something else he loved doing more. Maybe there would be women waiting for him in every port, or maybe he would settle down with just one. Briefly, his mind flew back to thoughts of Bethe, but now that he was out here on the waves, Vars could see that he hadn't really been destined to be with her. If he'd brought her along for this, would he even have been able to fit into the crew so well?

"Oi, new hand! Get yourself below deck. Bring us all up water!" a sailor snapped at Vars, bringing him out of his daydream. Vars thought about snapping back that the sailor should go get it himself, but this was the new him, and he was determined to be better than the old version. In any case, it meant a break from the hard work of hauling.

He headed below, into the hold, with its low ceiling and its endless boxes and crates, stacked in ways that looked haphazard but that must have been carefully thought out just to fit. There, at the center of it all, the water barrels lay. It hadn't occurred to Vars until he came aboard that they would need to bring barrel after barrel of water with them, enough to last through the journey to the archipelago and back, although they all hoped that they would be able to refill the barrels there. It was just one part of the running of a ship that he'd known nothing about when he came aboard.

Vars thought about how much he'd learned in such a short time. It was a whole other world out here, and it was one where he felt surprisingly safe, in spite of the dangers of the sea. He got the water and started back up toward the deck, blinking in the sunlight, briefly blind with it as he emerged into the fresh air once more.

Someone hit him in that moment, hard enough that Vars stumbled, dropping his gathered water.

"What's wrong, King Vars?" a voice asked, in the instant before a foot thudded into his ribs. "Not got your sea legs?"

Vars groaned and rolled over, blinking and trying to see properly. "I'm not—"

Another kick slammed into him.

"Don't try to deny it! I know who you are! I was a servant at the castle before I was a sailor!"

Vars tried to struggle to his feet, blinking all the time as his vision slowly came back to him. The man in front of him was... no one, really, just an ordinary-looking man, with sea-weathered features, lean muscles, and a look of pure hatred on his face. In Vars's life, that could be anyone.

"I don't know you," Vars said.

"Of course you don't," the man replied. "Because you never cared enough to look at a servant unless it was some pretty girl you could bed. But I know you. I was one of the ones you humiliated every day, just because you could. You took my sister to your bed and then had her thrown out of the castle. I was there when you became king. I was there when you gave over the castle to the Southerners. I saw the things that happened to everyone because of you!"

When the sailor threw the next punch, Vars knew that he should fight back. He knew that he shouldn't just stand there and take it, feeling the impact and seeing stars explode around him. He did though. He deserved it.

He deserved the next blow, and the next, fists and feet falling on him while other sailors stood around Vars, watching the beating. Probably, they would watch if the other man killed him and threw him over the side. Vars found himself wondering if he would fight back *then*, although by now, he was so bruised and dazed that he wasn't even sure if he would be able to do so.

Worse, his attacker only seemed to be getting angrier.

"Why won't you fight back, Vars?" the man demanded.

"I'm not... that man... anymore," Vars said, looking up at him from the deck of the ship.

"Not that man?" The sailor kicked him yet again, hard enough to make Vars retch this time. "You think you just get to decide that your crimes don't apply to you?"

He stepped back and drew a long knife, curved and wickedly sharp looking. It caught the gleam of the sunlight perfectly, the edge of it mirror bright and deadly.

"Stand up and fight me," he said. "I'm going to gut you for all you've done."

"I won't fight you," Vars said. He could have, could have drawn his sword, could probably even have killed this man. He'd had *some* training with a sword, after all.

"Coward!" the sailor shouted. "It's all you've ever been. Well, I'm going to give you what you deserve, you—"

"That's enough." Captain Yula was there then, her hand closing around the sailor's wrist. The sailor tried to wrench free, but the ship's captain was strong, and when her grip tightened, Vars saw the man's face blanch with pain.

"But Captain, you don't know—"

"I said, enough," Captain Yula said, and she hit the man in the same motion, sending him stumbling to the deck. "That's for making a member of my crew waste fresh water, knocking him over like that. Do you want to see what happens if you disobey your captain?"

Vars saw her hand drift to the hilt of her sword. The sailor looked from her, to Vars, and back again.

"No, Captain."

"Good answer," she said. She looked around to the crew, and to Vars. "Do you think I don't know who that is? Do you think I don't know who Simeon has brought onto my crew? But here's the thing: I don't *care*!" She jabbed a finger in Vars's direction. "So he used to be scum? Half of *you* used to be scum, and the other half still are! No one would be a sailor if they weren't trying to run away from something. So here's what's going to happen: you're going to do your jobs, and stop bellyaching about who we've got on the crew. Vars there is one of us now. He's part of this crew, and if he's a useless dog, that just makes him the same as the rest of you. Get used to it."

The crew started to mutter, and slowly drifted back to their duties. Even the sailor who had attacked Vars did so, although he gave him a venomous look first. Vars dusted himself off, tested the worst of his bruises, and winced as they turned out to be worse than he'd thought.

"Thank you, Captain," he said, taking a step toward Captain Yula.

"What are you thanking me for?" she countered. "If this weren't happening on my boat, I'd have let them gut you."

"Oh," Vars said, face falling.

"Now, get back to work. You're part of this crew, and that means you're as liable to be flogged if you shirk your duties as the rest of them."

CHAPTER TWENTY ONE

Lenore sat on her throne, the great hall around her decked out in the kind of finery that hadn't been there since... well, since the preparations for her first wedding. There were as many people in the great hall as there had ever been, while outside, it seemed that the whole city was starting to give itself over to the event, treating it like it was a way to celebrate Lenore's victory. Even to her, the scale of it all was a little overwhelming.

There were paper decorations hung on strings, each inscribed with a message from some well-wisher from the city below. There were tapestries and banners from all the lords present, each declaring himself and his deeds. There were benches set with food, swans and suckling pigs roasted by the castle kitchens especially for the occasion. A great space had been cleared for dancing, with pipers, drummers, and lutenists already warming up at the side. For her part, Lenore was dressed in one of her finest gowns, layers of blue and white silk cascading until it seemed to her as if she were some semi-mobile cloud, corseted and powdered into perfection. All that was missing from the Dance of Suitors were the suitors.

"Let them in," she said to Orianne. "If we're going to do this, we might as well get it over with."

"I could tell them that you're not feeling well, if you like," her maidservant suggested. Lenore shook her head. Doing that would only delay this; she was as trapped by tradition as she had ever been as a girl, the weight of what was expected of the perfect princess turned into the traditions that limited the options of a queen.

"No, let them in," she said, and Orianne gave the instructions. Around the hall, horns blew, and the doors opened to admit the nobles.

Lenore went to meet them, drawing folk onto the dance floor, turning this into a celebration rather than a formal audience. The peace of the dance meant that everyone was free to be a little wild without the risk of repercussions; no duels would be fought over imagined slights today, no ambushes set for long-term rivals. Lenore was determined to

101

enjoy that freedom as much as the rest of them. If noblemen meant to seduce her, let them come to her on her own terms.

They did come, of course, entering the hall singly, without their usual retinues, dressed in all their richest clothes so that they seemed like baubles that might be used to decorate the walls. They *carried* baubles, too, each one of them seeming to hold some gift that they thought would woo her.

Lord Ness was one of the first to step out onto the dance floor, of course. Lenore had been expecting that, ever since the moment that he'd been one of those pushing for this, almost ever since the moment that she'd asked for his help. Some of the others had helped in taking the kingdom back for honor, or because they expected favors later, or because they simply thought that it was the right thing, but Lenore had seen the way that Lord Ness had looked at her. He'd assumed that this moment would come from the start.

"Your majesty," he said, stepping out onto the dance floor with her with the confidence of a man who knew no one would gainsay him. "You look more lovely than all the flowers of the royal gardens together."

That reminded Lenore uncomfortably of the way she'd parted from Devin. Why couldn't *he* be here? The answer to that was obvious: sorcerer's apprentice or not, he wasn't nobly born.

"Is that what you see of worth in me?" Lenore asked him. "Loveliness?"

"Should a man not hope for loveliness in a woman he hopes to wed?" Lord Ness asked.

"And if I were to praise you as handsome, rather than mentioning your skills as a warrior or a lord?" Lenore countered. He *was* handsome, in his way, muscled and square jawed, almost heroic in his looks.

"I would be honored that you think me so," Lord Ness said. He took out a diadem of elegantly worked gold, set with jewels. "A gift, that you might take what I offer more seriously. And I pray that you will remember the way I aided in the battle, and the authority that I can bring to your side as your king."

"You are too kind," Lenore said, handing the gift off delicately to Orianne, since it was clear that Lord Ness expected to dance. They did so briefly, but already another would-be suitor was there, pressing for her attention.

"My queen," he said, "for I hope you will be *my* queen, I bring you greetings, and gifts."

One by one, they came to her, all dressed in clothes designed to show how much more they were than ordinary folk, all praising her beauty above any other quality, as if it were the only one that mattered in a queen. They all brought gifts, pretty, useless things, which Orianne seemed to be taking delight in stacking on a table in an inelegant pile, as if to highlight how little it all meant. Lenore would have preferred it if one, just one of them, said that he was going to give alms to the poor, or help in the rebuilding of the city.

Lenore danced and danced, while around her the noblemen looked on like she was a prize to be won, and the common folk seemed to be treating the whole thing as a grand entertainment, the pageantry seeming to be more important than any sense of what was actually happening here.

"...and my holdings stretch from Pear Marsh to the Lower Farms," a balding lord in his forties said as he danced. He was a terrible dancer, and he sweated as he danced, so that Lenore had to be careful to pick those dance steps that kept her as far as possible from him.

Another nobleman walked out onto the dance floor, and Lenore had to admit that this one was more handsome than most. He was as muscled as any of the warriors there, but seemed to move with more grace than any of them. His skin was bronzed from the sun, and it was obvious that his dark hair had been cut short immediately before the dance. His clothes were rich, deep purple and blue, edged with silver, faintly familiar looking for some reason. He caught Lenore's eye not just because of that familiarity, but because he was currently juggling three chicken legs the way a tumbler might juggle clubs, making the poor folk at the side laugh.

"Forgive me," Lenore said, walking over. "I don't believe I know you, my lord."

He caught the chicken legs with surprising skill and offered her a low bow. "Hal. And from what I hear, *you're* the one with the power to forgive or not. You're the queen, after all."

Lenore smiled at that. He was just about the only one who seemed to remember that being queen came with actual power.

"Where are you lord of, Lord Hal?" she asked.

"Oh, Enfar," he said, waving a hand vaguely, "it's in the far north of the kingdom. Hardly a place at all, really."

103

"You must have ridden hard to be here in time," Lenore said.

"I've always been more of a man for boats, myself," Lord Hal said. "But I did have to move quickly, and now I realize that everyone else has come with baubles for you." He smiled and held out the chicken legs he was holding. "The best I can do, I'm afraid."

Lenore laughed, suddenly charmed by this man, and took the chicken. "This may be the most *useful* thing I've been given all day."

She took a bite, realizing only then just how hungry she was. The others had expected her to dance and dance, and that took an effort.

"Then will you accept another gift?" Hal said. "A short space, free from the dance?"

"All too willingly," Lenore said. She let Hal take her hand as he walked over in the direction of the table where the stack of gifts stood. Very deliberately, he set down the remaining chicken leg there, and Lenore laughed at it.

"Now, clearly I have the best gift," Hal said. "But which of these is next best? *Can* a man hope to buy the heart of a woman who can conquer a kingdom for herself?"

Lenore found herself glancing back at her throne. The sword Devin had given back to her sat there, resting against it. That was the best she'd been given in the last few days, and it was the one gift among all of it that couldn't count.

"You know, not one of the men here has asked that?" Lenore said.

"You see," Hal said. "I think you're not someone who can be seduced with baubles. You'll look at a man's actions."

"Ah, so you're seducing me," Lenore said.

"Possibly. You'll have to tell me if it's working," Hal said. He looked around. "I think I'm going to have to fade back into the crowd soon. A man like me needs to maintain an air of mystery."

"Of course," Lenore replied, although she couldn't help a hint of disappointment as she did so. "I hope that I will see you again."

She was surprised to find that she meant it.

"I hope so too," Hal said, and drifted back into the crowd. That left Lenore standing there, feeling a little bereft. She went back to her throne, sitting there, her hand on the hilt of the sword Devin had made for her, thinking of the only other person who had made her feel like something more than the position she held.

That was the heart of all this: no one there saw her for who she was. Marriage to her was a chance to possess her. The man to succeed in the

104

Dance of Suitors would be king, and he would be the one with power. Lenore's only duty would go back to being that of producing an heir. All that she had accomplished in conquering the kingdom would count for nothing. Of all of them Hal had been the only one who had seemed to *see* her.

Then Lenore's heart froze in her chest as *she* saw someone, someone who should never have been there. He walked into the room, dressed in black and silver, looking as beautiful as he ever had as he went from noble to noble, talking to them, making his offers, sowing his dissent.

Lenore couldn't stand for it. She stood up, took a grip on her sword, and raised her voice until it seemed to shatter the music of the dance.

"Finnal! How *dare* you come here?"

CHAPTER TWENTY TWO

Erin braced as the small boat she and the others were in scraped up against the coast, feeling the wood meet the rocks. She felt anticipation mixed in with joy that they'd made it, fear about what might happen, uncertainty about what they would do to find out the state of things here.

Away in the distance, Captain Harkener's ship was already turning, ready to sail back. No doubt he'd gone to free his men as soon as Erin and the others had disembarked in the longboat. They were alone here now, with only their own skills and wits to keep them alive. Erin wasn't sure whether to be worried by that fact or to enjoy it. For now, though, there was no time for either.

"Everybody out!" Erin instructed. "Get the boat up onto dry land and hide it. Quickly now. We need to be away from here if anyone comes looking to see who's landed on their coast."

"Who would do that?" Villim asked, the former peasant boy clearly not understanding.

"Anyone looking for smugglers," Bertram said. It made Erin wonder exactly what business his father the merchant was in.

Erin and the others moved quickly. They had cloaks to cover themselves, and Nadir corrected the way that she wrapped hers around herself.

"Like this. That's the way nomad traders wrap them. People let them pass more than other folk, and forgive them if they act... strangely."

"It's everything in this gods-forsaken land that's strange," Ulf muttered, but Erin saw him adjust his cloak anyway. Since the attack on the ship, her crew had treated Nadir with, if not acceptance, then at least a kind of grudging respect.

The nine of them moved out across the barren shoreline until they found a trackway up into the lands beyond. Erin was surprised to find it all green and lush, lined with hedgerows and trees that reminded her more of her own kingdom.

"Is it all like this?" Yannis asked. "It reminds me of our estates."

"Parts are like this," Nadir said. "Parts are desert, or swamp, or grassland. The Southern Kingdom is not one place. It is a hundred or more smaller ones, joined together by force and cunning."

"I need to see those places," Erin said. "I need to hear what's actually going on. What people think, and if there are any more threats to the Northern Kingdom. Can nomad traders do *that*?"

"Yes," Nadir said.

They set off, each hefting packs laden with food and supplies. Erin had made sure that she had sufficient coin to pay for whatever they needed, but she'd also made sure that they had small quantities of trade goods, things that people might expect of travelers passing through.

They started to head out into the kingdom, bypassing the first village they came to, but stopping at the second. Bertram proved to be as good with languages as he claimed, while Dern could feign an accent from most parts of the Southern Kingdom while speaking trade tongue, and Nadir was more than useful. The others mostly kept quiet, kept listening, and moved together.

They traded for horses at the third village they came to, and for a small cart that would let them play the part of traders better. Villim or Merl mostly drove it, and Erin sometimes sat on the back, watching the landscape. Eventually, they came to an inn, and it looked like the kind of place that people would come to from a dozen different directions, so that Erin and her band wouldn't look too strange there.

The inn wasn't *exactly* like the ones Erin knew from home. It was cleaner than most, for one thing, with a great central firepit, and tables set around it like the spokes of a wheel. The owner eyed them with initial suspicion, but when Erin put money on the bar, that seemed to dissipate like mist. Erin leaned against the bar, accepting spiced wine, while her people set out to mingle among the travelers there.

"Trade looks slow," Erin said, although in truth she didn't know if this was brisk or slow for the Southern Kingdom.

The innkeeper shrugged. "Could always be better. You heading along the roads south?"

"Could be," Erin said, not wanting to commit to anything.

"Things are tricky. There's folk saying that Emperor Ravin might be dead."

Erin made what she hoped was a slightly surprised sound. "Think that's true?"

"I don't know," the innkeeper said. "Some are saying that some girl up north rose up and killed him, defeated his armies. Some are saying he was poisoned. Others are saying it's all some grand test."

"And you don't want to guess which?" Erin said. "I heard he *was* killed, and that it's Lenore, Godwin's daughter, who beat him in battle."

"*Her?*" The innkeeper laughed so hard that Erin thought he might hurt himself. "How is some pitiable little girl supposed to have beaten the emperor?"

Once upon a time, Erin would have struck him for that comment. Now though, she stood there and shrugged. Odd might have approved.

"Better to know how things are," she said. "Especially if we're going to go traveling through the kingdom."

"Maybe," the innkeeper said. Again, Erin had the sense of him being careful. She realized that he was looking around, and it took her a second to guess why.

"I'm no Quiet Man," Erin said.

"And I'd have no problem if you were," the innkeeper said. He raised his voice slightly. "I have no quarrel with Quiet Men. I welcome everyone under my roof."

"I'm really not," Erin insisted. "I'm just trying to work out what I'm walking into when I go trading. Don't want to say the wrong thing in the wrong place. Especially not if the wrong person's listening."

A part of her said that it would be easier to just threaten this man, but this way seemed better, seemed *easier*. It was a revelation, in its way. It seemed like the sort of thing Odd would do, or her sister, or something. The coin she slid across the bar probably helped a little too.

"They say things are fragmented further south," the innkeeper said. "It's not so bad up here, where we have *always been loyal*." Again, he raised his voice slightly, before lowering it again. "There, all the rumors that Ravin has died mean that everyone he kept in line with threats and force have started to carve out their own places."

"So... bandits?" Erin guessed.

The innkeeper looked at her as if trying to decide if she were joking. "And tribes that were only ever conquered by force, city states that don't like being joined to neighbors they've always hated, lords who don't like being taxed, mercenary bands pretending to be traders..."

He gave Erin a pointed look, and Erin glared back at him.

The innkeeper shrugged. "There are whole new kingdoms springing up under half a dozen men who reckon they're the next Ravin."

"Who's the smart money on?" Erin asked. When the innkeeper started to shake his head, she grabbed him by the front of the apron he wore. "I'm not a Quiet Man, I have coin for you, and I want information. Now, I'm *trying* to be a less violent person."

"And doing an admirable job, if I do say so," the innkeeper managed to gasp out.

Erin let him go and just *looked* at him.

"There was money on a priest-king in the east for a while," the innkeeper said. "Then on a couple of tribesmen. Now, the smart bets seem to be on a man named Nicholas St. Geste. Already he's bested two challengers and brought half a dozen tribes under his city state. They say if anyone can be the new Ravin, it's him."

"There," Erin said. "That wasn't so hard. Now, my people need rooms, food, and wine."

She handed over slightly more coin than was necessary, then took wine back to her crew. They seemed to be waiting for her.

"All the talk is of one man," Dern said, juggling a knife between his fingers.

"Nicholas St. Geste?" Erin asked, and the young man from the House of Sighs looked a little crestfallen. "The innkeeper said the same thing."

"So what do we do next?" Ceris asked. "Do we keep traveling and looking for more rumors?"

That was the question, wasn't it? In theory, Erin was there in the south just to find out what was going on. Her sister had assumed that things would fall apart in the wake of Ravin's death, and now it seemed that she'd been proven right. The only question was what they did about it.

"Do we go hunting?" Sarel asked. "A man who's attracting that much attention will need supplies. Traders could get close."

She seemed to understand what Erin was thinking, or maybe it was just that she'd been a mercenary, and so she understood the direct option best.

"We need to know more about him," Erin said. "I need to know if this man is really a threat. Nadir?"

"I have not heard of this man," the southerner said, "but they say he is from Sandport, and I know where that is, on the cusp of the desert, in a meeting place for the tribes."

"You can get us there?" Erin asked. He nodded.

That was where they would go, then. Instinctively, Erin could imagine what kind of man this would be. He would be a brute who slew his foes as cruelly as possible, or murdered them in their beds. He would stand at the head of a string of enslaved enemies, reveling in their cries of woe. He would be Ravin, returned in all but name, because what other kind of man could rule a place like this?

Even Odd would agree with what they would do now. They would find him, because a man like that would be only too easy to find. After that... well, a spear in the throat had done for the first Ravin easily enough. There was no reason why it shouldn't deal with the second one as well.

CHAPTER TWENTY THREE

Aurelle was trapped, caught between the thing she needed to do and the impossibility of doing it. She couldn't leave, because that would mean her chance to kill Duke Viris would be lost, yet every moment that she stayed was another moment in which she was apart from Greave.

Aurelle thought that she had a plan, at least, and as usual, the simplest methods were best. If she could find a way to isolate Duke Viris and his son, even for a moment, then she could kill them with a knife. All other approaches were too complex, or had too great a chance of her dying before she could get back to Greave. Actually isolating them was more difficult, but Aurelle had decided that she could do it if she declared that she had information about a way to kill Lenore.

Finnal's absence made the whole thing more complex, though. It forced her to wait, and to hope that nothing would happen in the meantime. It did have some positives. Aurelle had always been able to move quietly and to listen well, so that now she padded from door to door, gathering what small snippets she could. Already, a small tome in her quarters was acquiring line after line of carefully written code detailing the relationships between the various nobles who had sided with Duke Viris, the small secrets of the retainers there, anything that might be used to force them to cooperate.

It would have been better still if she could have sent the things she found out back to the capital, but there would have been too much risk in finding a messenger willing to take the information from within the keep, and trying to slip out to find one beyond would have been complicated by the protective labyrinth. Aurelle thought that she was starting to unpick the route there, but she still wouldn't like to bet on her ability to get through quickly.

Aurelle was still thinking about the problems with it when one of Duke Viris's retainers came to her, giving her a curt little nod rather than a full bow.

"Lady, Duke Viris requires your presence," the man said.

"Where?" Aurelle asked.

"He has a bower, in the maze," the man said. "He keeps it as a place for… assignations."

Aurelle swallowed her disgust at what the man was suggesting. She'd wondered before why Duke Viris hadn't called her to him for this, given how casually he'd done it back at the House of Sighs. Perhaps it had only been Finnal's presence that had been holding him back. Now, he wasn't there for any sense of propriety to prevail, and it seemed that he meant to have Aurelle.

Well, she would give him more than he hoped for.

"Do I have time to change into something more suitable?" Aurelle asked.

The retainer gave a quick shake of his head. "It is better not to keep the duke waiting. In any case, I am sure that milady is more than lovely enough as she is."

That was annoying, because Aurelle would have liked to get her things together, ready for a quick escape. When she did this, she would likely have to leave in a hurry, unable to risk going back into the castle. She and Duke Viris would simply disappear in the maze, and the only difference was that she would be seen again.

She understood then how she was going to do this. Aurelle knew that Finnal was in Royalsport. She would go to him, and tell him that she had news of his father's death. *That* moment would make it easy for her to strike.

"I'm ready," Aurelle said. "Take me to him."

The retainer nodded and led her down through the keep, to a side door that still led out into the maze, but seemed to lead to a different portion of it than the main entrance. The retainer led Aurelle through it, and instinctively, Aurelle tried to memorize the twists and turns, adding them to the map she was drawing in her head that she hoped would let her find her way through.

"It is an honor to be invited here," the retainer said. "His Grace made this bower for his wife, and has only invited a few women to it."

"I'm sure she would be proud of the use he puts it to," Aurelle said, not caring about the look that the retainer gave her. She wondered if this man cared about what he was helping his lord with, bringing a young woman to a place she effectively couldn't leave if she didn't know the maze, with the expectation that she would sleep with a much more powerful man, essentially given no choice in it.

112

There was a time when Aurelle would simply have gone along with it, *had* simply gone along with it. That was what much of the House of Sighs was, after all. Duke Viris expected that he could bed her because he *had* bedded her. The only thing that had changed was…

…was *her.*

She'd met Greave, and that had changed something in her. It had made her care, not just about him, but about herself. He'd looked at her like she was worth something, and she'd come to see herself as worth something.

It meant that Viris wasn't going to get what he wanted today, but Aurelle at least had enough knives on her that she could give him what he deserved.

The retainer led her to an open space in the maze where trees stood, providing shade over a small awning. A bed lay there beneath it, along with a table on which wine and food were set. A servant stood by that table, and Duke Viris reclined on a couch there.

"Aurelle," he said, waving a hand at the table. "Take a drink, join me."

Aurelle knew this mood, open and welcoming, but with an edge under it that meant she shouldn't risk disobeying him. She took a goblet of wine, sipping it.

"Will the servant be standing there for all of this?" she asked. "It might be better if we had some privacy."

"True," Duke Viris said. "You have wine now, and you can get food if you want it. I have no need of them."

He dismissed the servant, and Aurelle waited for the retainer there to go as well. The moment he did, Aurelle would make her move. A knife slipped silently into her hand.

"What about him?" Aurelle asked.

"Oh, *he* is there to catch you when the poison in the wine starts to affect you," Duke Viris said.

Panic flashed through Aurelle, and she looked around for a way out.

"You made a mistake," Duke Viris said. "You brought me Lenore's annulment. You thought that would raise my trust, but you forgot who had *witnessed* that annulment. Prince Greave, the man I sent you to kill; the man you said you *had* killed for me."

Aurelle realized two things in that moment: the first was just how precarious her position was. She'd thought that she was perfectly safe, protected by the role that she'd built up as Duke Viris's confidante.

113

She'd thought that she was the hunter, but now it turned out that she was the prey.

The second was that her legs were starting to go numb.

Instinctively, she turned to flee, determined to throw herself deep into the maze and lose herself there. The retainer was there in front of her, and Aurelle was already slashing at him with the knife she held in her hand before he could even reach for her. She opened his throat and ran out into the maze, taking turnings, not even trying to keep track of them. There was no point trying to do that when she hadn't had a chance to memorize this part of the maze.

She guessed that part was deliberate. Duke Viris was cunning enough to take away every advantage she possessed.

He could do that, but he couldn't take away the skills she'd learned. Aurelle still possessed the knowledge of how to hide and how to kill from the shadows, how to move in silence and how to survive against the most dangerous killers. She'd played this game once in the Library of Astare, but here, she didn't have Greave to help, and she had limbs that were steadily weakening from the poison as well.

She kept going, determined that she would draw away Duke Viris's hunters and lose them in the maze. She would wait out the effects of whatever poison this was. She would come back to him, and she would cut his throat. Aurelle forced her way on, ignoring the way her steps were slowing, her vision was clouding.

Hands grabbed for her and Aurelle lashed out blindly. She felt her knife sink home, and heard a man cry out. She lashed out again and hit nothing but air. Then she felt her arms caught by strong hands, twisted behind her as she was dragged to the ground. She felt herself tied, half carried, half dragged back to the spot where Duke Viris sat waiting.

He looked at her, and now there was only cruelty in his expression.

"We will not kill you straight away," he said. "You are too valuable for that."

"I'll tell you nothing," Aurelle insisted, her words coming out slurred, as if she'd drunk too much.

"Of course you will. You will scream out every secret you have ever known, and still that won't stop us from hurting you," Duke Viris said. "But you will not die. That will not be permitted. You will be kept alive until every scrap of usefulness has been wrung from you, and Lenore is defeated. Then, if you are lucky, you will be granted a swift death."

The part that made it horrific was the flatness of his tone. He said it, not as a threat, but simply as something that *would* happen. That was worse; that was so much worse.

They started to drag Aurelle away, and even though she fought, it made no difference.

CHAPTER TWENTY FOUR

Master Grey walked the streets of Royalsport, carrying the equipment he needed with him. If people thought it was strange that he stopped every few paces to set up an apparatus that looked like a cross between a brass tripod and an astrolabe, they were used to the king's sorcerer being strange.

He manipulated the brass and copper components of the device, focusing on his magic, focusing on sensing what he was looking for. The signature of the amulet was a thing that could be felt, and that meant that it was a thing that could be located, tracked, *found*.

Just not here, because there was no trace of it. No, that wasn't quite true. There *was* a trace, but it was more like an echo, a thing that had been once, but was no more.

Master Grey traced those echoes, step by painstaking step, setting up his device every few streets, adjusting it, and taking a reading. He took out a map of the city, not current, of course, perhaps a hundred years out of date, and he made a marking upon it. Mark after mark, each signifying direction and strength.

The problem was that such signs could only give so many answers when something had moved. They pointed to one spot, and then to another. One strongly, the other less so.

Master Grey hunted down the first of those points, circling it, finding the direction and the distance, closing in on it the way a hunting dog might track some small animal. He found a building that had clearly been destroyed in the dragon attack, or perhaps the retaking of the city. There had been so many events that had left scars on Royalsport that it was hard to tell which had been caused by what events.

He stared at the building, considering his options. Perhaps a spell to force the fragments apart? A way to make it all drift out of his way like sand before a strong wind? Part of what made a magician powerful, though, was knowing when to use magic and when to use... simpler means.

"Coin to anyone who helps dig through the rubble!" Master Grey called out, and watched all those with nowhere else to go descend on the building, starting to clear the debris away. Magic was powerful, but coin, authority, people all had their own powers. One of the things that separated the king's sorcerer from a common hedge magician was that understanding.

Master Grey stood there, watching the people he now employed picking apart the remains of the house, moving aside fallen bricks and beams, revealing the space beneath.

There was nothing there, certainly no sign of the amulet. Eventually, Master Grey had to call a halt to the searching, handing out coins and sending people on their way.

He started his search again with the device, and now it seemed to be pointing him back toward the castle. This would be so much simpler if Renard were here. At the very least, he would be able to tell Grey exactly where he had left the amulet. It irritated Grey that the thief had walked away, but at the same time, he hadn't been entirely surprised.

Grey paused for a moment, considering all the pieces that were in motion. Renard had been one of them, but there were so many others. Part of what he did was to ensure that there were always enough pieces in motion, that things played out as they must.

The loss of the amulet did not fit with that. There were so many moving pieces to this, but there were also still points, things that remained key to the fight against the dragons regardless of what happened. The amulet was one such. Grey had to find it, had to ensure that it remained in play for their side and hadn't been taken by another.

Who *could* have taken it? The Hidden clearly wanted it, and they must have some means of containing it or they wouldn't have sought it in the first place, yet Master Grey didn't think that this was them.

He followed the lines set out by his device, back in the direction of the castle. He frowned as he did that, because he was fairly sure that he hadn't brought the amulet into the castle, not in a *long* time.

Still, he went there, following the faint traces of the magic, trying to make sense of it as he went.

No one could have taken it. They *couldn't* have taken it, because tales of people withering and dying would have been all over the city. Even Renard, descended from the blood of the magician who made it, had found himself drained by it.

Maybe it *was* the Hidden. There were only two remaining now, but maybe between them, they could have concocted something to contain the powers of the amulet. Maybe they had found some other descendant of the first magician to do their bidding. After all, they'd only picked Renard in the first place so that he could help them to get past any defenses that protected the amulet. A man who had any normal number of children would have hundreds of descendants in just a few generations.

Yet to find such a thing with any certainty was more difficult than it sounded. Master Grey had conducted his own such searches, to find the young men born on the dragon moon, and even that had been difficult. It had taken all the skills he had developed, and nothing made him think that Void or Verdant would have such abilities.

What then? What had happened to the amulet?

He went back to his tower, sitting there in his rooms while somewhere below in the castle music pointed to the Dance of the Suitors. Master Grey smiled at that, not because he had any time for such pageantry, but because he suspected how it was going to go. He'd known the people involved for long enough that at least *they* were predictable.

Or were they? If he couldn't accurately predict the location of the amulet, what made him think that he could truly predict anything else? All his plans had been based on his understanding of the prophecies involved, on prediction after prediction, overlapping until Master Grey knew all the key moments of his life, the things he had to say, and do, and provide. If this one simple thing wasn't right, what did it say for the complexity of the rest of it?

Master Grey sighed and set out items he would need to track the amulet from further afield. The magic of the thing wouldn't let it be found directly, but the very energies that masked it and sucked life out of the world around it could be tracked by someone attuned to them.

The map was first, that of the kingdom set out over his table. Master Grey set out candles, and drew lines between them in a mixture of chalk dust and powdered gold. He drew on the magic around him, aligning it, trying to create a still space on which it could move freely.

Actually forming a link to the amulet was harder. His equipment could allow him to trace its residue, but that wasn't the same thing as a stable, trackable connection. The best Grey could do was to try to approximate it, using the residual energy of the amulet, amplifying it

118

and binding it into the spell. Carefully, Grey dipped a gilded quill in ink and whispered words to link it to the rest of the magic.

Instantly, he felt the pull of its power trying to tear at the edges of his life force. Even as the quill danced into life above the parchment of the map, Grey felt it leeching away his vitality, agony flooding him as the energies of the amulet fought off what they saw as an invading touch. He gritted his teeth as the quill drew a line out from Royalsport, fighting against the urge to give in to the amulet's power.

After just a few seconds, Master Grey could stand it no longer. He released the spell with a curse, and the backlash from the sudden undoing of so many energies all but threw him back in his seat. He had to sit there for several seconds, vision swimming with the effort of it all, before he could look at what his magic had wrought.

A single line led out from Royalsport to the coast, jagged and seemingly random. Grey might have dismissed it as no more than a failure of the spell, except that he *knew* the spot that it was pointing toward. He'd been the one, after all, to send Devin and Anders in the direction of exactly that spot.

Realization flooded through Master Grey then, and he understood just how badly he might have misjudged things. The evidence was clear. The amulet was missing, and that could only have happened if someone had picked it up, yet there was no trail of bodies showing where it had passed from hand to hand, no evidence of the Hidden at work in this. What did that leave?

Someone else picking it up; someone the amulet judged worthy. Someone who could fill the role its creator had. What if someone who could hold it had found it? Someone who had been his enemy one moment, and then suddenly seen the value in going to speak with a dragon?

Too late, Master Grey realized the truth of it: Anders had the amulet that would let him control dragons, and he was away in the wilds, searching for just such a dragon with Devin.

CHAPTER TWENTY FIVE

Lenore stared at Finnal, anger rising in her at the sight of the man who had mistreated her so cruelly, who had seduced her, used her as a way to get close to the throne, and treated her coldly.

"Kill him," she said to Orianne. "The House of Sighs taught you, right? Kill him right now."

"That would break the peace of the dance, my queen," Orianne pointed out.

"I don't care," Lenore said, forcing the words out between gritted teeth.

"I think that you do, my queen," Orianne said. "Or at least, you care about how the nobles here will react to you breaking tradition. Tell me another time to kill him and I'll walk over there and do it, I'll enjoy it after what he did to me, but please *think* first."

Lenore thought, and the more she thought, the more she knew that her maidservant had a point. The whole Dance of Suitors had so much weight and anxiety behind it already that one misstep might send the whole thing spiraling into argument. To break its rules even for Finnal would be to show everyone watching that she was the kind of queen who simply didn't care about the laws. It would give the nobles license to do as they wished, and an excuse to some of them to rebel.

She couldn't kill him, however much she wanted to.

"Welcome, Finnal, son of Viris." She deliberately didn't use either of their titles. It was a small thing, but it was a reminder of what this could cost them. "As you are of noble birth, the peace of the dance protects you while you are here."

Again, she chose her words carefully, making no promises about what would happen to him once all this was done.

"Thank you for your welcome," Finnal said, just as courteously, although Lenore noted that he didn't use her title. "I am sure that I shall enjoy myself while I am here."

The dance continued around her, couples whirling, the music restarting. Lenore sat there on her throne, watching it all, watching *him*. He moved around the room, and Lenore could only imagine the things he was saying to the nobles there, promoting his cause, making his case, buying friendships in compliments and gold. There were plenty there slapping him on the back or taking his hand, too. It took Lenore a moment to realize why.

"They think he's a *hero*," Lenore said to Orianne. "They're treating him like he did something noble by not fighting at Ravin's side. They think it was some move to save the kingdom on his part, something *honest*."

"The truth of him will come through," Orianne insisted.

"I hope so," Lenore said.

It was hard to believe that she had once thought herself in love with him. Once, Lenore had watched him on this dance floor, and she hadn't been able to take her eyes off how beautiful he was. Now, she looked at him and all she could see were the schemes and the coldness, the lies he'd told and the ways he'd betrayed her.

Then he was coming toward her, one hand held out, and Lenore knew before he said it what he was going to ask.

"Queen Lenore, will you honor the tradition of the Dance of Suitors by dancing with me? I'm told you've done so with every noble here."

"Maybe you're the exception to the rule," Lenore snapped.

"If you truly believed that, you would not have held this event, wife."

"I am *not* your wife," Lenore retorted, standing as she did it. Finnal's hand was still out waiting for her, and he swept her into the first steps of the next dance.

Lenore tensed as he did it, sure that he would slip a knife into her ribs with the first whirl. Or maybe he would poison her. Perhaps he already was, with some venom spread through touch that he was guarded against. Perhaps every noble here who sought to side with Lenore would fall, leaving him behind standing at the center of an empty room.

"You think far more than you used to," Finnal said. "It has ruined your dancing."

"Maybe it's the thought of being murdered by you," Lenore said.

"A king does not murder. A king has people executed," Finnal said. He spun Lenore into a whirling step, so that she felt as off balance from that as from his words.

"You are *not* a king," Lenore said. "I annulled our marriage, and in any case, you are a traitor to the throne, who sided with our enemies."

121

"Ah yes, your so-called annulment," Finnal said. "An annulment you did not have the power to grant. Our marriage stood at the moment you gained the throne, which means I became king in that moment. You did not have the power to command me, or to set aside our marriage."

Fear filled Lenore at Finnal's words. In a lot of ways, it was a more dangerous threat than that of him murdering her in cold blood. Finnal was too much of a coward to do this himself, and leave himself standing in the middle of a city where he might be taken or killed. Trying to steal the throne from under her was much more his style.

"I've danced with you," Lenore said to Finnal. She stepped back sharply from him, breaking his grip. "I've done what's required. This is done."

"This is not done," Finnal said. "You will announce that your annulment has no power."

"Why would I ever do that?" Lenore demanded. "Who would even believe it?"

"Perhaps you are right," Finnal said. "So let's do this a different way. Pick me from all the suitors who have come. Let us be married again in front of everyone."

"No," Lenore said. That was the part of it that made her stop short of doing more to Finnal. She didn't have to, when she could stop him simply by refusing him and sending him back to his father.

"We'll see," Finnal said, and set out into the room once more to receive his plaudits for something he hadn't done.

It left Lenore to return to her throne. Her hand rested on the hilt of the sword that Devin had made. A part of her longed to draw it and simply cut Finnal down, but that was too much like the kind of thing Erin would have done. Lenore reminded herself that she was queen, and that she had to behave like one.

So she did. She started to move around the room, talking to one noble after another. She went to Lord Ness first.

"How are you enjoying the dance, my lord?" she asked.

"Obviously, I wish that there were fewer people here vying for your hand," he said. "And Lord Finnal being here... complicates things."

"It does not," Lenore said. "He is not my husband, and is not the king, whatever he claims."

122

"That is… good to know," Lord Ness said, sighing as if he'd been genuinely worried that his chance had gone. As if he truly had a chance. "But he *is* a hero of the—"

"You were *in* the battle!" Lenore all but shouted. "You know he wasn't there. All he did was run away to save his own skin and see who was going to win."

What hope did she have of overcoming Finnal's lies when even someone who had been there to see the truth found himself repeating them blindly? Finnal seemed to have worked out that simply saying a thing enough turned it into a kind of truth, and countering that meant playing catch-up, always one step behind what he said next.

Lenore felt her frustration growing, and she found herself looking around for Lord Hal. Of all those there, he had been the only one whose presence had actually lightened her mood. Sadly, though, he seemed to have drifted away through the party, as if deciding that being there too long would render him less interesting or refreshing. Lenore hoped that he hadn't gone completely. He was, at least, a very charming man.

Lenore was left looking at Finnal, unable to stop him from spreading his lies, unable to eject him from the proceedings. If she could have done that, she would have done it, and far more. She was still contemplating what she could do to try to stop him when the messenger came in.

He wore the silver and black of one of Duke Viris's retainers, and the fact that he wore no blade at his side was the only thing that stopped Lenore from assuming that he was an assassin. The guards seemed to share her worries, because they moved in toward him, surrounding him while a space cleared on the dance floor. He reached into his tunic, and swords cleared their sheaths with a ring of steel.

"Careful," Lenore said.

The man carefully withdrew a folded piece of parchment, sealed with Duke Viris's mark. Lenore looked around as she took it, her eyes automatically finding Finnal among the rest of those there. She could see the amusement in his eyes there, and she knew that whatever this was, it wouldn't be good.

She opened the message.

We have your assassin. You will accept Finnal's offer, or she will be publicly executed, but not before she has confessed to being sent by you to murder one of your loyal lords.

Lenore's breath caught as she read that. They'd captured Aurelle. She knew that a more hard-hearted queen would say that was the risk she had accepted, and that she was a servant to be sent into danger in any case, but Lenore couldn't feel that way. It wasn't just that Aurelle was someone she'd gotten to know at the court, or who clearly cared about her brother. It was that Lenore had been the one to send her there, into danger. She owed her more than that.

She sat there for the longest time, considering her options. Duke Viris and Finnal probably thought that she didn't have any, that they'd trapped her neatly so that she could either be responsible for the death of a woman her brother clearly loved, or she could give in. Perhaps once, those would have been her only options. They still saw her as the girl who could not be ruthless, even after all this.

She wasn't that girl anymore.

"I have a reply for your lord," Lenore said. "He has Aurelle? Well, I have his *son*. I will trade one for the other. Come to me, bring her, or peace of the dance or not, I will cut Finnal's head from his body and send it to him."

CHAPTER TWENTY SIX

The landscape grew hotter as Erin and the others headed further south. The lush greenery gave way to dry grassland, and that became interspersed by patches of sand, which became larger and larger until they flowed together in an endless sea of it that stretched to the horizon.

"We'll need water if we're going to cross it," Nadir said. "We'll need supplies, and maps of the oases."

Erin nodded. "Is there anywhere to *get* all that?"

"There should be a trade spot a little way *that* way," the tribesman said, pointing. Their group followed the line of it, through a line of low dunes whose sand shifted even as they walked on it.

Erin paused atop one of them, and saw brightly colored tents spread out beneath. They stretched out broadly, in a sequence of spiraling curves that seemed to have internal patterns within it that might have denoted different groups. There were lines of chained prisoners. There were wells around the edge. There were soldiers sitting around campfires, and wagons that looked as if they had come to trade. Was this Sandport? It *seemed* large enough, and it was certainly sandy enough for it.

"It's not supposed to be like this," Nadir said. "Look at the extra tents, look at the wagons. Something is happening here."

"Like a pretender to the throne coming to town?" Merl asked from their wagon.

Erin knew the former bandit had a point. She knew the gathering of a war band when she saw one, and if what she'd been told about the situation in the Southern Kingdom was true, then that meant one of the men had heard of Ravin's demise and decided to take the opportunity to grab power. Here, Erin might have the chance to stop this "Nicholas St. Geste" before he was able to draw the south together again enough to strike at the north.

"We're going down there?" Sarel asked. "There are a *lot* of them."

"Which is why we need a plan to get out of there when this is done," Erin said. "Dern, Nadir, Bertram, Sarel, you're with me. Ceris,

125

Ulf, and Yannis, draw water from the well and guard the way out. Villim, Merl, stay with the horses and be ready if we need to run."

Erin led the way down there. The ones with her were the ones with the best chance of fitting in, while Ceris, Ulf, and Yannis stood out more, but they were good fighters.

Quickly, they were surrounded by tents on every side, and men talking in a variety of accents and dialects of the south. Some of them, she understood, but others passed her by. Men and women gathered around fires, some talking and laughing, some drinking, some playing music. It was strange, seeing them like this rather than in the middle of preparations for battle, seeing any southerners just living their lives.

Erin didn't trust it. She'd seen for herself just how dangerous and duplicitous the warriors of the south could be. Pain flashed through her at the thought of everyone she'd lost to Ravin and the vileness of his kingdom: her mother, her brother Rodry, Odd. She wasn't about to forget them, or the pain, so easily.

"Bertram, Sarel," she said, "sort out supplies."

They nodded and set off through the tents.

"Who rules here?" she asked a man dressed in the armor of a warrior.

He looked at her like she was a fool. "The new emperor. The man who will unite the south: Inedrin!"

Erin frowned. "But that's… I heard it was Nicholas St. Geste."

The man she was speaking with gave her a suspicious look.

"And who told you that?" he demanded. "Who are you? What are you doing here?"

"We came to join the new ruler," Erin said. "Are we in the right place?"

"Inedrin is the new ruler here!" the man said. "He will unify the tribes and conquer the cities. Where are you from, that you haven't heard of him?"

Erin ignored him and backed away, knowing that it was a conversation that wasn't going to do her any good. Instead, she made for the heart of the camp, determined to see this Inedrin for herself.

She moved quietly, keeping her cloak up as she made her way to a fire in the inner circle of them. She, Dern, and Nadir took places around that fire, sipping a drink that tasted sweeter even than the apple brandy that had been served at some of the castle's feasts.

126

Around the fire, men and women were talking and arguing. Mostly, it seemed to be about what would happen next.

"He'll have us take Sandport for sure," one of the women there said, sharpening a blade. "Maybe I'll get to walk the Street of Drifts with one of their menfolk for a prisoner."

"The lines are long enough as it is," one of the men said. "Better just to slaughter them, or what will it do to the price?"

Erin couldn't believe that they were talking so casually about murdering or selling *people*. In one conversation, it confirmed everything she'd known about the south.

"Then we'll go north," the man who'd spoken said. "We need to strike at them before they strike *us*."

"You think the Northern Kingdom is going to attack you?" Erin said with a laugh of disbelief. Nadir put a warning hand on her arm, but Erin ignored it.

"Everyone knows they're going to," the woman said. "How many times have they done it in the past, striking out at us, keeping us scattered and weak?"

"You think the *North* is attacking *you*?" Erin said.

"As they always have," a warrior by the fire said. "For hundreds of years, they have struck over their bridges, or sent spies from their House of Sighs to tear us apart. They know that we are weaker apart. Ravin was the first ruler to overcome that and make us a great nation!"

"You'll see it," the woman said. "They'll send people south, demanding that they pledge loyalty to them, and this young whore of a queen of theirs!"

Erin's temper got the better of her then. Perhaps it had something to do with the drink she'd been sipping steadily since she got to the fire. Perhaps it had something to do with the way these... these *invaders* were talking as if *they* were the ones who had started all of this. Perhaps it was just that, in spite of her efforts, at least some of the anger she felt was still under the surface, waiting. Whatever the reason, she struck out before anyone in her crew could stop her. Her closed fist slammed into the woman's jaw, sending her sprawling.

"Do *not* talk about my sister like that!" she snarled.

"Her sister?" one of the men there said. "What is she..."

Nadir shoved him back toward the fire before he could finish it, and the man cried out as the flames caught his clothes.

"Back!" he said. "We need to get out of here!"

127

A part of Erin wanted to insist that her people stay and fight; that they cut their way through to this Inedrin and end the threat he posed.

Then one of the warriors stepped up beside Dern and thrust a sword into his ribs, the tip protruding from the far side. He was close enough to Erin that she heard his gasp, felt his weight as he stumbled against her. She would have thought that death might have ceased to shock her by now, but the suddenness of this caught her by surprise. With the wrong words, this whole situation had turned into something deadly in less than a minute.

And it was her fault.

Even as Dern died, Erin leapt at his attacker, cutting him down with a quick cut of her spear. Nadir was looking around for enemies, his sword in his hand. Erin knew in that moment that she'd all but condemned the people with her to death. She'd already *killed* Dern with her foolishness. She'd needed to hold her temper, and instead, she'd lashed out.

A part of her told her to ignore all that, cut her way through the danger, get to Inedrin and finish this as she had with Ravin. She knew what that would mean for her people, though. Saving them meant something else, something that she *never* did.

"Back!" she shouted, agreeing with Nadir. "Back into the crowd!"

The two of them fled back into the maze of tents, moving quickly, darting between them. In those first seconds, people moved out of Erin's way, parting to let her through, obviously wanting no part of what was happening.

"They still see it as just a minor fight in the camp," Nadir said. "We need to get out of here before they realize that it's more."

Erin nodded, and she felt fear worming through her. It wasn't fear for herself, but for the people with her. She'd brought them here, and she'd messed up. Now they were all in danger. She hurried through the crowd, pushing people out of her way when she had to. When she spotted Sarel and Bertram, they seemed to understand the danger instinctively, joining up with them and heading for the fringes of the camp.

There was almost a palpable ripple of pursuit behind Erin, traveling out from the spot where she'd struck at the woman who had insulted Lenore. It was a ripple of news as much as of people, a dividing line between the space where they were safe and the space where people had heard that there were northerners in the camp.

128

Erin abandoned all pretense of merely moving at a brisk walk and *ran* through the camp with the others. She knew she wouldn't make it, though. There would be soldiers waiting on the edge, or riders, or…

Something flashed overhead, and it took Erin a moment to recognize the flaming arrows for what they were as they passed. Ceris was there, standing atop the wagon with Villim, firing them at the tents beyond Erin. In the dry heat of the sands, cloth flared and caught with flames almost instantly. Arrows flew back at the cart, but Ceris and the peasant boy didn't give up their positions.

What had been pursuit one moment turned into a frantic effort to keep the camp from burning, people running to the wells, or just running in confusion. Behind Erin, someone called out, but that only made her run faster for the cart, and the horses by it. She turned and thrust with her spear, bringing down a man who got too close, and then she was running again.

Yannis was galloping up to her and Nadir then with a pair of horses. Erin all but leapt into the saddle of one, stabbing down at another of her pursuers even as she turned to flee. She caught up with the wagon in a matter of seconds, where Merl was whipping the horses into a frantic run, and Ceris was still firing arrows back at those pursuing. Erin's heart seemed to freeze as she saw Villim there, clutching at his side, where an arrow protruded.

"The sands!" Nadir yelled. "We can lose them in the sands!"

They galloped for them, and Erin clung to her horse numbly. They were moving fast enough now to leave the people of the encampment behind, still scrabbling for horses while they tried to put out the fires. Even so, Erin knew that she would never be able to move fast enough to elude one thing: the guilt.

She'd done this. Her temper had gotten the better of her again, and now one of her people was dead, another injured. This was her fault.

CHAPTER TWENTY SEVEN

Vars was pretty sure that he'd never worked so hard in his life, or with as many unfriendly stares on his back. He was used to courtiers smiling to his face, whatever they actually thought of him. Now he had sailors who knew who he was and what he'd done. It turned out that they didn't try to hide their dislike.

At least Captain Yula's command kept any of them from acting on that dislike, the way the one who'd attacked him had. Mostly, they kept their distance, or drew Vars into grudging conversation that only opened up as the leagues passed and the moment of the fight started to be forgotten. He was still Vars, but he was Vars the ship hand now, not Vars the murderer.

Simeon didn't seem to care, because he quickly realized that at least some of the lessons master scholars had tried to drum into Vars's head were still there, giving him someone to talk to. Captain Yula didn't care, because one dog of a sailor seemed to be the same as another to her. From the rest, Vars got looks that told him that he couldn't just wipe away who he'd been.

"How much further to the archipelago?" Vars asked Simeon, while the scholar looked out over the waves, apparently sketching the porpoises that darted from them occasionally, following the ship. He looked up at the wispy strands of the clouds above, enjoying the freedom that came with a day like this.

"Possibly ten days," Simeon said. "Such things are hard to quantify when the maps I have are so old."

"Why do you do it?" Vars asked. "Why go traveling the world just to find some lumps of land that might or might not be there? Are you planning on claiming it? Finding gold there?"

The scholar shook his head with a smile. "I'm going just because no one has. Because knowing something is better than not knowing it. Because... well, because I'm a scholar, and if I *don't* check something like this, I'm just a man sitting in a tower, taking the word of dead men for the world."

Vars supposed that he could understand that, although it was certainly never a line of reasoning that he'd found a use for in his life. Maybe if he had, he would have done better.

"I have some concerns about the signs on the sea," Simeon said.

"What do you mean?" Vars asked.

The scholar gestured to the mare's tails of the clouds. "In Treman's *Meteorological Signs*, such things are meant to presage the coming of... storms."

Vars wondered at the hesitation in the other man's voice, and saw him pointing. He wasn't sure what he was looking at for a moment, since all he could see was a dark line on the horizon, not even the width of a finger. It was only as it started to grow that Vars came to understand.

"Storm!" Captain Yula's voice yelled. "Turn starboard, keep ahead of it! Get to your stations, you dogs!"

Vars moved uncertainly to a spot on the deck, and one of the others pointed to a different place, where he stood ready to haul on a rope. Vars risked a glance back, and saw the dark line of the storm rising behind them, so that now it was like a hand rising over the sky, blotting it out. Around Vars, the wind rose, whipping at his clothes and his hair strongly enough that he found that he had to make an effort to stand in place. Simeon's papers scattered, flying across the deck and into the ocean.

"We need to lose sails!" Captain Yula bellowed. "We can't outrun this! Get up the masts and cut sails! Drop the anchor!"

Men started to rush around the deck, hauling on ropes and winding winches. A sailor pushed Vars in the direction of the rigging.

"We have to get the mainsail down, or the wind will capsize us," the man said.

Vars wanted to tell him that *he* should be the one to climb the mast, then, but there was no time for that. There wasn't even time to be afraid, not really, although fear was definitely starting to seep into him, like the rain that was starting to lash into the deck. Gritting his teeth, Vars started to climb.

The rigging was swinging back and forth, and Vars realized that wasn't just down to the wind. The waves around the ship were growing, so that they went from flat to something like field furrows, to something more like hillocks all in the space of a minute.

131

"Climb, damn you!" the sailor who had tried to kill him before snarled, clambering past Vars, toward a spot where the knots holding the mainsail stood, seemingly tightened by the rising wind. Vars saw the man reach toward them…

…and fall, as a blast of wind struck the ship hard enough that Vars had to cling to the rigging with all four limbs to have a chance of staying on it. He saw the man tumble and twist in the air, and the ship was leaning so much by that point that he struck water rather than the deck below.

"Cut the sail, or we're dead!" Captain Yula bellowed up from the deck below. Down there, Vars could see her clinging to the wheel, while water was starting to wash across the deck. It looked slow and languid, yet the force of it was enough to carry more men from the deck. Some seemed to be trying to get the longboat into the water, hoping to survive on it, and Vars saw Simeon bundled into it. Then the ropes holding the boat in place snapped, and it tumbled into the water.

Vars hung there, paralyzed by fear, and the certainty that he would fall if he moved.

"Climb, you dog!" Captain Yula bellowed up.

Somehow, the command was enough to set him in motion. The wind tore at Vars, but he kept climbing, hand over hand up the rigging. He reached the mast, reached the spot where the tangled lines lay. Just looking at it, he knew that there would be no way to unpick a knot like that, so he took out his knife instead.

Another blast of wind almost ripped him from the mast, and Vars cried out with the effort of keeping his hold there. He was sure that he had never been so frightened in his life, and Vars had a whole catalogue of fears to choose from. Still, doing this was the best chance to save his own life, as well as the others'. If he could put a dagger in his own father to do that, he could cut one rope, couldn't he?

He couldn't. Reaching out would mean exposing himself to the wind, and then it would snatch him away, the way the wind and the waves were snatching men from the deck even then, sweeping away their screams even as they swept away their bodies.

"Cut the rope, damn you!" Captain Yula called up. She was wrestling with the ship's wheel now, below.

Somehow, *somehow* Vars managed to do it. He slashed at the rope in a lull between two tearing blasts of wind, and the first cut made it halfway through the rope. Vars dared a second slash, and now the sail fell away, billowing its way down like a dropped blanket.

The wind hit Vars in that moment, smashing the knife from his hand as it nearly ripped him from the rigging. He saw it drop, and knew that would be him in a moment more if he stayed there. He descended the rigging as fast as he could, not caring that it burned his hands now, as he made it down to the deck. He dropped the last little way and tumbled to the deck, feeling his ribs bruise as he did so, and the water washing over him.

It shoved him toward the side of the ship, and the waters beyond. Vars managed to catch himself on the outer rail of the ship, but he could feel his grip slipping, too slick with rainwater by now to ever hold it.

Then Captain Yula was there, her strong grip fastening onto his arm, pulling him back.

"I need your help with the wheel!" she shouted at him. "There's no one else. The others are below, or…"

Or in the ocean.

"Our only hope is to tie ourselves to the wheel," Captain Yula said. "The anchor rope is snapped, so we have to try to guide it, hold it steady so it doesn't sink. Come on!"

She pulled Vars back in the direction of the ship's wheel, the water battering at both of them, threatening to rip them from the deck at any moment. Vars knew he would never have made it there if it had just been him. Instead, the captain's bull-like strength pushed them both on. She shoved him against the wheel, binding him against it with strands of fallen rope so that Vars could feel the bucking and falling of the ship as the waves tossed it this way and that.

"Now you!" Vars called to her.

Captain Yula nodded, moving to the wheel to tie herself there beside him. Together, they could do this. Together, they could hold the ship steady and ride out this storm…

That was when the biggest wave yet hit, washing over the deck, smashing into both of them. Vars felt the ropes that held him tear at him as the strength of the wave threatened to rip him from his place of safety. He heard Captain Yula cry out, but he didn't see the moment when she was plucked from the ship, only her absence when the wave passed. As strong as she was, the ocean was stronger.

133

Vars felt a moment of grief for the woman who had saved him not once, but twice, that she could be gone so quickly and so fully. He wished he could feel that grief more strongly, but there was no room for such feelings, not when the terror filled him so completely. Vars stood there, gripping the wheel while the storm struck the ship, only one thought filling him:

He was going to die.

CHAPTER TWENTY EIGHT

Nicholas St. Geste felt a sense of unease as he stood at one of the windows of the solar room that stood at the top of the Tower of Sand, the traditional home of those who ruled Sandport. It was hard to pin down the cause of that unease when there were so many possibilities.

The city beyond was one source of it. Its streets tangled like the ravings of a madman, buildings and tents alike clustered around the central market that was the only reason anyone *came* here. Spires and towers stood out above white-walled, block-like homes, while squares stood around the dozens of wells that let the city even exist here, at the edges of the desert.

Sandport was inherently a place that created unease for its rulers, whether it was in the sand that constantly needed to be swept from the streets by work gangs, the gangs of a more criminal sort who lurked in the smaller streets, the constant flow of strangers and merchants who could hold any kind of spy, or the endless intrigues and challenges that the noble houses there seemed to think were as natural as breathing. Even the barracks and drill squares of his soldiers created a kind of unease, because there had been enough times in the past that such men had risen up against their rulers. Nicholas had fought soldiers in the dueling ring before, who had thought that their arm was strong enough to let them rule.

This wasn't any of those worries, though. Those were old things, concerns so well known that they were practically like friends. This was something newer.

"How long until the Northern Kingdom invades?" Nicholas asked. He turned back into the room, waiting for an answer. It was a circular room, with wide windows at regular intervals and a table standing at its heart on which Nicholas could set out his plans. Not *all* his plans, of course. Even here, he knew better than to trust people blindly.

He looked around the people in the room one by one, waiting for an answer. Ankari the wise woman stood to one side, a mess of tangled charms and unhealthily powdered skin that disguised the fact that she was a lot younger than she pretended to be.

"The signs all say—" she began, and Nicholas cut her off with a look.

"Less of that," he said. "It's just us here."

He tolerated her, *valued* her, mostly because she *wasn't* the mystic she pretended to be. Nicholas knew how dangerous those with true power could be, and how unpredictable. With Ankari, though, the act gave her a kind of authority, and the network of informants and followers she'd built gave her more clarity on most issues than any spell could. Together, they'd managed to persuade a number of lords to his side simply by telling them that it was written in the stars that they should do so. Nicholas appreciated the level of commitment to a lie that took.

"In truth, my king, we have no news of movement on the borders," Ankari said. "And when the traders come in to have their fortunes read for their next journey, they make no mention of it. Are you *sure* it will happen?"

"It will happen," Nicholas said. How could the hated northerners *not* invade now? They would come, and they would slaughter his people, unless Nicholas stopped them. He turned to the next one there. "Ferrent?"

His chief guardsman was a large man of middling years, skilled with the axe and bow. He kept his head shaved, but his forked beard made up for it, waxed and curling in spirals before his plump belly.

"There's nothing about the Northern Kingdom," he said. "But there's plenty else. Raw Skin gang has taken a well and is threatening to befoul it if people don't pay for the privilege. Seven Hands have been thieving again off the caravans, food mostly. Then there's Inedrin. His camp is closer now."

"I don't care about any of this," Nicholas snapped, and saw the big man look down hurriedly, clearly afraid. "All right, all right. Go to the Seven Hands and employ them as spies. Send them to find out about the other principalities. They're stealing because they're starving, and we can use that. Inedrin… well, our defenses are as good as they'll be. If it comes to it, I'll add his head to the gate beside Oredei's."

"And the Raw Skins?" Ferrent asked.

Nicholas didn't hesitate. "They need to be stopped. Their leaders die. Give the rest the same choice as the Seven Hands. The wells are the heart of this city. I need a message sent that touching them is to invite instant destruction."

136

"I could give any we take alive to your father's master of tortures," Ferrent suggested. "Or maybe the Poisoner. She always likes to—"

"There are to *be* none left alive," Nicholas said, hardening his gaze to make sure that his master of guards got the message. Better to appear impatient for the killing than to let people think he had no stomach for this. "Cut them down where they stand. If you can display them gruesomely afterwards, do it, but not too close to the city. I'll have no disease in Sandport."

He turned to the last figure in the room. Sarit was slender and hardened by the sun, wrapped in the robes that would keep it off, his dark skin marked with white lines of paint that he applied each morning, and that even Nicholas didn't dare ask the meaning of.

"What of you, my friend? What have the tribes heard?"

"Of the Northern Kingdom invading?" Sarit spread his hands. "Little enough. What need have we to worry about folk over the water when we have you city dwellers to harass us?"

"I've ordered my men to leave the tribes allied to me be," Nicholas said. "But I'll tell them again. Come on, Sarit, there has to be *some* news."

The tribesman shrugged. "Perhaps. There was *one* strange thing that they say happened in Inedrin's encampment. A fire that destroyed many tents."

"That will slow his advance, at least," Nicholas said. "But it is not the enemy I fear most."

"It might be," Sarit said. "They say that the fire was started by a group from the Northern Kingdom, asking about leaders, asking about *you*."

"How sure are you about this?" Nicholas asked.

That earned him another shrug of the shoulders. "My people come and go easily enough in the camps."

"Mine can do the same," Ankari said. "Perhaps I can have some go to cast auguries for Inedrin."

"If they could truly do that, I'd have them just cut his throat," Nicholas said, but his attention wasn't on the latest of his so-called rivals for control of the kingdom. Instead, it was on these people who had come to Inedrin's camp, looking for information. He traced his finger over the map on his table, idly running it from the likely site of Inedrin's camp up toward the north. He started to consider what would be needed for an invasion to succeed.

137

"I've been looking in the wrong place," he said softly.

"My king?" Ferrent said with a frown.

"I've been assuming that they will come in a rush," Nicholas said. "That they will pile into Ravin's ships and ride them back to the ports, or that they will rebuild the bridges and march an army over. I assumed that they would be so consumed by their need to destroy us that they would charge in. Instead… they are being cunning."

"There are many ways to be cunning," Sarit said.

"*This* way involves them killing all the leaders who might rise up before they invade," Nicholas said. "A small group like that? Who is to say that it is not one of many, sent to disrupt us, to kill those who pose the most danger?"

He tried to imagine his foes' plans. It was always one of the most important skills that a leader could possess. The more a leader understood what his enemies wanted, the more he could seek to take it away from them, or provide it on his own terms.

These foes seemed to be moving south, looking specifically for leaders. They had already struck at Inedrin, succeeding in damaging his camp even if they had not done the world a favor by simply killing him. They had asked about Nicholas, which meant that they had heard about his attempt to unify the lands around him, and his attempts to resist the invaders.

They would be coming for him now.

It did not spark the fear that it might once have to hear that assassins were coming for him, even assassins sent by as cruel an enemy as the Northern Kingdom. Nicholas had faced assassins before. He had survived more just to rule Sandport than most men would face in a lifetime.

Instead, Nicholas found himself considering the problem the way he might have examined a puzzle box, as something almost detached from the rest of him, there to watch and consider, with a solution waiting if he could only see it.

"What is the biggest problem with assassins?" Nicholas asked the few he trusted.

Sarit snorted. "The part where they kill you is usually considered quite annoying."

"That they come at you out of the dark," Ferrent said, "rather than fighting with honor."

Nicholas smiled, because he could almost have predicted what the two would say. Sarit was all about what was practical, because the desert left no room for more. Ferrent... well, he was tied to city ways. Nicholas looked to Ankari.

"They're almost right, but not quite," he said. "I can stop them killing me. I can stop a man who comes out of the dark. So what's the problem?"

"That you don't know when or where they'll come out of the dark," Ankari said. Of course she got that part of it. "But if you're hoping I can predict that for you, I think I'd actually need to *be* the cunning woman I play at."

"Why predict what you can control?" Nicholas replied, feeling a sense of satisfaction that once again he was the one who saw all of it. "Come on, my friends. We have a trap to prepare."

CHAPTER TWENTY NINE

Renard was drunk. Was "drunk" a big enough word for what he was? he wondered as he leaned against one of Royalsport's many walls. Wait, was this a wall, or was it just a cobbled floor?

Rolling onto his back revealed it to be the latter. The night sky was above him, stretched out in a glittering array of faintly accusatory stars. Renard felt that was particularly unfair. Stars shouldn't be able to accuse people.

"Besides, I'm not guilty of anything!" he yelled at them. They didn't reply. Perhaps it was because they already knew all the things he *was* guilty of. Perhaps, some dim part of his mind suggested, it was because they were stars.

He struggled to his feet. As epic struggles of Renard's life went, it was up there with all the fights with dragons and the armies of the Southern Kingdom. It certainly came as close to defeating him. For some reason, the world didn't want to stay upright at the moment, and it was only with an effort of will that Renard managed to keep it there.

He saw the House of Sighs in the distance, and started to stagger toward it, along the streets of the city. Meredith would be there, and she would shout at him for being a useless drunkard, and probably throw him out of her House again. It would be like old times. He certainly *deserved* the part where she called him useless.

Ordinarily, Renard was pretty sure that the gods hated him, but right now he didn't need their assistance with that. After he'd walked away from the sorcerer's offer, he'd gone off to simply *enjoy* life, the way he always had, but somehow he hadn't managed to find any of the old joy in it. He'd tried stealing from the pockets of passersby, nothing. Eating, wenching, even playing the damnable lute... all of it had turned to ashes in his heart. Even ale, that steadiest of friends, seemed to be failing him in everything except making the world *less* steady.

Whatever he tried, the same thoughts kept returning to him: thoughts of his ancestor so long ago, who had managed to change the world and who had left behind a legacy that now threatened it. He had done so much in his life, while Renard... Renard was a thief.

140

Renard frowned at that. Never before would he have thought of it like that. He'd always taken a certain pride in his profession, and the things he'd managed to do. There had been a certain joy in being able to steal from places that no one else could, and in thumbing his nose at those who tried to catch him. Renard leaned against a wall, and he was pretty sure it *was* a wall this time, trying to make some sense of it all.

As moments for introspection went, it was rather limited by the part where he then needed to throw up. Renard ran for a quiet alley and bent double in the gutter. Great, he couldn't even enjoy ale anymore.

"Help! Help me, someone!"

A woman's voice came from ahead, and Renard could hear the fear there. He leapt, or at least staggered, into action without thinking about it. He found her at the other end of the alley, with two knife-wielding thugs in front of her. Renard cursed and drew his sword, watching the tip dance unsteadily as he raised it.

"Get away from her, or I'll... well, to be honest, I'll probably throw up on you, but I'm pretty sure I'll cut your hearts out somewhere in there too."

The thugs didn't seem impressed by the threat, and frankly, Renard didn't blame them. They came at him then, two big men, and Renard wove aside from the first cut, smashing the hilt of his sword into the man's face as he passed, knocking him flat. One good thing about being this drunk: he couldn't actually feel the fear he probably should have in a moment like this. The other came at him and Renard went for a complex, heroic disarm, the better to impress the young lady who still stood there looking on at the whole affair in horror. He missed, managed to catch the thug's knife arm on his forearm, and headbutted him instead. He went down beside his friend.

"That was... incredible," the young woman said. Renard wasn't sure if there were two of her there because of the drink, or because his head was still ringing from the headbutt. He had to admit that both of her were quite pretty as she leaned up to kiss his cheek. "You saved my life."

"It was nothing," Renard said, and managed to sheathe this sword.

"It was *not* nothing," she replied. "You... you're a hero."

"I am *not* a hero!" Renard said, stepping back from her, and from the confused expression on the woman's face, it was obvious that he'd said it too loud. But what did she expect if she went around saying things like that? Damn it, could a man not even wallow in self-loathing in peace?

"I… I'm sorry," Renard said, and set off away from her. He knew what all this was, of course. He knew *exactly* why he felt so bad, and what he would have to do to make it feel better. That he hated the idea didn't matter, had *never* seemed to matter in his life.

*

"Sorcerer!" Renard bellowed as he walked up to the castle. His drunkenness had receded in the night air to the point where there was only one of it, at least. The gates were shut for the night, two guards standing there staring at him. "Sorcerer! I would speak with you!"

"Go home, you drunk," one of the guards said.

Renard drew himself up to his full height. "I am not a drunk. I am a hero! Whether I want to be or not, apparently."

"Go *home*," the other snapped. "Or you'll be spending the night in the dungeons."

"You can't arrest me," Renard said. "I am a hero of the battle for the city!"

"You're a nuisance, is what you are," the first guard said. "I'm not warning you again!"

Renard laughed at that. "I'm not afraid. I am Renard, master thief and swordsman!"

He drew his sword to emphasize the point, and for some reason both of the guards leveled their spears, starting to shout at him.

"Drop your sword! Drop it *now*!"

It occurred to Renard then that he was about to have a fight with the queen's guards, and he wasn't even entirely sure why. He suspected that Lenore would be annoyed if he cut down her men, too. Unfortunately, things seemed to be progressing quite quickly, one of the guards starting to advance on him with his spear ready to strike.

"And that, I think, is enough."

Renard wasn't sure how Master Grey had gotten there. Perhaps he had appeared in a puff of smoke. More likely, from what he'd seen of the magus, he'd just opened the gate and walked up while Renard hadn't been paying attention. Either way, Renard and the two guards stopped in place.

"I have things from here," Master Grey said to the men.

142

"Yes, Master Grey," one of the men said. They both went back to their posts.

"Renard, walk with me," Master Grey said, leading Renard away from the castle. "I suspect the air will do you some good."

Renard sheathed his sword and fell into step with the sorcerer. "You've done something to me, haven't you?"

"What would I do to you?" Master Grey asked, not looking around as they descended into the noble district.

"Put some curse on me, so that I can't enjoy things, and so that I feel guilty all the time, that's what!" Renard said.

He heard Master Grey chuckle. "I believe that is what the rest of us call a *conscience*, Renard."

"Oh," Renard said, stopping in place. "That."

Master Grey looked over at him. "And what is your conscience prompting you to do?"

Renard took a breath, determined to make the sorcerer wait at least a little longer. "I'm ready to undertake whatever grand quest you have in mind for me," he said at last. "You want someone to do this whole… hero thing, right? Well, I'm ready to be a hero. You need someone to rescue a damsel, fight a monster? I'm your man. Whatever quest you need fulfilled, I'm in. Just tell me what you have in mind."

"Good," Master Grey said as he started walking again. "I need you to steal something for me."

"What?" Renard said. All of this, and he wanted Renard to just *steal* something? "I don't think you heard me. I was offering…"

"To do anything, yes, I know. And *I'm* asking you to do something with skills that you actually *possess*. I sent two young men on a journey. Now, I have learned that one of them may have the amulet you brought to the city. It would be… dangerous, in his hands, so I need you to steal it back. Can you do it, Renard?"

Renard sighed. This, he guessed, was what he got for giving his word to a magus while drunk.

"This wasn't exactly what I had in mind," he said.

Master Grey shrugged. "You aren't exactly what I had in mind either. We work with the tools at hand. Now, will you do it?"

"Yes, all right," Renard said. "I'll do it. I'll steal the amulet back for you."

"Good. And do try not to get killed by the dragon on the way."

143

Renard froze in place, realizing too late that he'd already agreed. "What dragon?"

CHAPTER THIRTY

Devin stared out at the island, connected to the mainland via a bridge that seemed to be formed from pure ice. The island itself seemed to be formed from that ice, so that it stood in a great berg of it, the tip mountainous, only fragments of rock showing beneath it. It took Devin a moment to realize that the remains of a volcano sat under it, frozen solid, pinned in time like a moth to a board.

"It's supposed to be under all that?" Anders asked.

Beside Devin, Sigil was already trotting forward, as if eager to reach their destination.

"I guess so," Devin said. "Come on, we need to get this done with before nightfall, and we still haven't found the dragon."

Anders nodded and the two of them followed in Sigil's wake, down to the expanse of the ice bridge, which proved to be a basalt causeway, buried under layer after layer of it, until it was barely visible beneath.

"We should leave the horses here," Anders suggested. "They won't keep their footing on the ice."

Devin nodded, and together, the two of them started to cross the causeway. Sigil raced ahead of them, surefooted even on the ice. Devin found his feet slipping with every step, though, and even Anders seemed to be concentrating hard so that he didn't fall into the waters below.

Devin felt the moment when his feet gave way, and he barely caught himself in time, grabbing for a spur of ice and clinging to it while his legs dangled over the ocean. He clung on, and felt Anders's hand close over his wrist, pulling him back to safety.

"Thank you," Devin said, as he stood.

"Grip more with your toes as you walk," Anders said.

Devin tried it, and found that he didn't slip quite so much as they kept going toward the frozen volcano. They reached the main body of the island, and Devin found Sigil waiting for him, looking up. Devin frowned and then followed the line of the wolf's gaze up the icy sides of the volcano. It took him a moment, but then he saw the spot where a gap opened up in the ice, only partially covered by bar-like icicles.

145

"There," Devin said, pointing. "A way in."

"So now we have to go *inside* a volcano," Anders said. "That doesn't seem like a great idea, but if it lets us find the dragon…"

"We're going to have to climb," Devin said.

Anders nodded. "I brought ropes. We might have to lift that wolf of yours after us."

Anders was already tying a grapnel to a rope, swinging it round and throwing it up to embed it in the ice. He took out short axes, pitons, everything that might be needed to climb. He took a rope, tying it from him to Devin.

"We'll have to move carefully," Anders said. "Wear whatever gloves you have, make sure of your next handhold before you take it. If we fall here, there will be no help."

He led the way up the wall of ice and rock, and Devin did his best to follow. They set off up the wall together, connected by the length of a single piece of rope, making slow, careful progress. Devin picked his footholds with care, but even so, he felt his grip slipping again and again.

The climb wasn't quite vertical. There were points where it was more like scrambling up a slope, and others where it was almost walking. Still, there were some points when it was hard climbing, with a sheer drop below. It was cold here, in a way it hadn't been back on the mainland. There was something unnatural about this cold, and Devin could feel the edges of magic around it. Sigil scrambled up after them, but there were spots where they had to lift him using ropes, their muscles straining with the effort.

It seemed to take forever before he and Anders reached the level of the opening. The icicles across it seemed as forbidding as steel, but they gave way little by little to the strokes of their hand axes, dropping away like arrows fired from some giant bow. The opening beyond was dark, large enough for him and Anders to stand in side by side. Devin heard Anders whisper a word and a faint light sprang up around them, staying with them as they walked.

The ice around them turned that light into rainbows, refracting it and transforming it. There were more sharp-edged icicles, and Devin had to duck past them, picking his way carefully and avoiding their points. The tunnel wound around until it finally opened out into a space that seemed to be just a tunnel between the outer stone and a wall of ice. It took Devin a moment to realize that actually, the space was cavernous, and it was merely that ice filled it, surrounding something that was hard to make out.

Devin saw it then, and seeing it took his breath away. A dragon sat there, curled up at the heart of it like a cat, except that it was large as a hill, as a castle, large enough that it even made the dragons Devin had seen before look small. Its scales were gray and white, so that it looked like a part of the ice until Devin looked at it from the right angle.

"It's... huge," Anders said. "How are we supposed to do anything about this? How are we supposed to wake it up? Chip it out of the ice with our axes?"

Devin wasn't sure either. He felt at the ice, trying to make sense of it. He could feel the spell there, the way he had when he'd been climbing.

"The ice is part of the spell holding the dragon," Devin said. "It's like... it's like it's here to preserve it."

"So if we change the spell, we might be able to wake up the dragon," Anders guessed.

"Can we do that?" Devin asked.

"Maybe, although the power involved... it will take both of us." Anders didn't look certain about it.

"And then we have to work out how to make a connection to a *dragon*," Devin said. That part seemed even more impossible than just waking it. Better to focus on the first part for the moment.

Devin reached out for Sigil, resting his hand on the wolf's fur, feeling the way the magic of the world came into focus. He could *see* the spell now, and the network of magic that went into it.

"You too," Devin said.

Anders reached out tentatively for Sigil. The wolf growled, but he kept going. Devin heard him gasp as he touched the wolf's fur.

"I get it now," he said.

Devin did too, because with them both touching Sigil like this, he could feel Anders's presence, feel the working of his magic alongside him. It meant that the two of them could work in concert with one another, each adding his power where the other wasn't, working to unpick the spell holding the ice in place.

Devin saw the dragon blink, one great yellow eye closing then opening again. Devin could suddenly feel it, through the ice, and he knew instinctively that waking it would make the spell shatter.

147

"Focus on the dragon," he said to Anders, pouring his efforts into the great beast. He saw muscular legs flex and shift, wings start to open.

Around Devin, blocks and shards of ice started to tumble to the ground. One crashed near them, splintering into a thousand pieces. Devin felt something nick his arm, but he kept going.

"It doesn't exactly look happy at being woken!" Anders shouted out.

Devin saw the dragon open its mouth wide as more blocks of ice fell, turning toward them so that Devin could see all the way down its throat. He felt a moment of terror at that, certain that the creature was about to blast fire at them both, but none came. Instead, the dragon thrashed, and as the spell broke, ice fell and shattered, turning into razor shards before it disappeared.

"We have to control it!" Devin yelled to Anders.

Instead, Anders broke the connection, throwing himself aside as more ice came down.

In an instant, the dragon was free of it, standing amid piles of it that were disappearing faster than any ice had a right to, thrashing and turning, smashing it aside. It stretched out its head toward the ceiling, and *now* flames came, blasting out in a gout that seemed impossibly large even in the now more open space of the cavern. The flames struck the ice, and where they struck, the steam from them was instant.

"Anders, focus!" Devin yelled.

He threw his magic against the dragon, determined to try to control it. If he could just get a clear enough understanding of it, maybe he could find a way to forge a connection to it. If he could just see it well enough...

Devin threw himself to the side as flames passed by him and Sigil just barely. It meant that he tumbled down from his perch into the cavern. He saw Anders and Sigil falling a moment later, all three of them landing in the ice and slush, the softness of it breaking their fall.

The dragon reared over them, wings open wide, the sunlight from above now striking it and making it look almost translucent after so long in this place. Devin grabbed for Sigil's fur again.

"Anders, please! If we don't work together, it will burn us both!"

CHAPTER THIRTY ONE

Anders had stood fast against the last dragon he faced, had fought down his fears and even felt contempt for Devin at not knowing what to do when faced by it. Now though, *he* was the one floundering, standing there staring as the dragon opened its mouth wide.

He threw himself to one side just in time as a lance of heat passed through the space where he'd been. A blast of cold followed it, so that it was all Anders could do to throw up a magical shield around himself, seeing it rime with frost and then crack.

This dragon wasn't like the one back in the city had been. It was huge and ancient, powerful and deadly. Anders had heard of lizards in the Southern Kingdom that grew throughout their lives, until they ended up the size of a dog or a horse. He could only assume that it was the same with dragons, because this one was the same, grown massive over its long period locked within the ice, bloated with power.

"Help me, Anders!" Devin called out, even as he dodged back from a swipe of the dragon's tail. "I can't bond with it alone!"

Didn't he understand? *No one* could hope to bond with this. It was too angry at being woken like this, and too inherently dangerous. Coming here had been a fool's errand, and Anders should have known better than to listen to the sorcerer yet again in his life. He'd put Anders's life in Devin's hands, and Devin's in Anders's, roped together as surely as they had been on the slope outside. That was great, except that here it meant that if either of them failed, the other would die as well.

Could he really trust Devin's skills? Anders had been brought up with every moment of his life dedicated to preparing for this moment. Devin had just learned to do things as he went. How could Anders trust his life to that? He needed to get out of here; he needed to run.

Anders looked around for a way out even as the dragon swiped at him again. He threw himself to the side once more, barely avoiding it as it smashed into a block of ice, shattering it into fragments. Could he clamber up the walls? Could he get back to the entrance they'd come in through? Not without taking long minutes to climb out of there, and

149

there was no way that he would be able to do that while the dragon was still striking out with its claws and its breath, its tail, and its teeth.

"Anders!" Devin yelled out to him. He was on the floor now, the dragon looming over him. Anders wasn't sure what the other boy wanted him to do.

Except that the dragon chose that moment to turn and focus on him again, teeth darting forward to try to engulf him, so that Anders had to dive and roll to keep clear of it. As he did it, he saw the amulet that he'd taken with him from the city tumble from one of his belt pouches, eight gems shining in the light around its central scale. Anders reached out for it reflexively; he didn't want Devin to see anything with so much obvious power coming off it, not when he'd gone to such trouble sneaking it out of the castle. He grabbed it and started to tuck it inside his shirt, out of the way.

The moment his fingers connected with it, he *felt* the dragon's presence. He felt the power there, and the strange, inhuman mind behind it. He threw his power out through the amulet, and in that moment, it was as if he could feel every part of the dragon. It reared up over him, mouth opening to burn him alive.

No! The certainty that it was going to kill him flashed through Anders, and he held out a hand as if it could stop the dragon from killing him.

Then, somehow, it did.

The dragon stopped in place, head weaving back and forth. It stopped thrashing about, then sat back on its haunches, then crouched low as if prostrating itself before him and Devin, its wings back.

Could it be... no, there was no way it was waiting for their orders. Or was there? Had Devin done this? Had his attempts to bond with the dragon worked? Instinctively, Anders knew that wasn't the case, and not just because Devin was still staring at the dragon as if he couldn't quite believe what it was doing. If his magic had worked, he would have looked more certain about all this.

Besides, Master Grey had told them that they would form a bond with the dragon, and this didn't feel like a bond. It felt more like control, as if, for as long as he kept contact with the amulet, Anders could make it do whatever he wanted.

Leave, he ordered it, wanting to test that feeling. *Flee this place.*

For a moment, Anders thought that he'd misjudged it. He knew terror again as the dragon reared up over him, neck stretched out toward the ceiling, flames shooting up again as if in a threat. Ice tumbled around it, crashing into the ground all around Anders.

He saw the dragon's wings spread, the downdraft of them knocking him and Devin alike to the floor as it took to the air. The thunderous rush of air pinned Anders flat, but also gave him a perfect view of it retreating, up through the hole at the top of the volcano's structure, out into the open air beyond.

Anders lay there for several seconds, panting, sure that he should have died, amazed that he hadn't. He saw Devin lying there doing the same, and it occurred to him to finish putting the amulet away beneath his shirt. He didn't want Devin seeing it, or guessing at the power Anders now had.

"Did we... did we do it?" Devin asked, as he struggled up to a sitting position.

Anders went to match him. What was he supposed to say in that moment? Was he supposed to come clean, and tell Devin that Devin'd had nothing to do with it? That might have been satisfying on one level, just letting his rival know that he'd had nothing to do with the way the dragon had run, and that his powers were nothing compared to those Anders now possessed. He didn't, though. This was for *him* to know about, not Devin.

"I don't know," Anders said. "I guess... I guess we must have. Did you feel the moment when I reached out to connect with your power?"

Devin shook his head. That didn't matter. Just the question would make him start thinking about it, so that before long, he would assume that Anders had played his part, rather than thinking about abandoning him.

"It was as if, the moment we were both working together, I could *feel* the dragon there," Anders said. "We connected to it, I'm sure of it."

It didn't matter that all of that was a lie. What mattered was that it gave Devin no reason to suspect the real reason that the dragon had left. Since he was the one with *Loss*, he was still in a position to take the amulet from Anders if he found out about it, and Anders couldn't allow that.

It occurred to Anders then that, if he'd thought, he could simply have commanded the dragon to slay Devin for him. It could have devoured him, and he would have been left with the dragon, with the sword, and with the chance to come out of this as the only remaining

151

chosen one. He could have ridden that dragon back to show Master Grey his success, or had it blast the old fool from existence.

He'd been too shocked to do any of that, though. Maybe next time.

"I don't know," Devin said. "I thought the idea of us pooling our power was that we were supposed to be able to bond with the dragon."

"We stopped it from attacking us," Anders replied. "What more do you want?"

"But it just ran away," Devin said. "I thought the idea was that it would recognize us, communicate with us, not flee."

Anders forced himself to shrug rather than laughing at Devin for not knowing what was going on. How could he have such moments of magical ability, and yet be so blind to what was going on? How could he not feel the power of the amulet?

"Maybe we did something wrong," Anders suggested instead.

Devin nodded almost as soon as he said it, looking suddenly determined. "We obviously haven't perfected our powers yet," he said. "We got part of the way there, but not quite far enough. We need to try again, and this time, we'll get it right."

"When you say 'try again'…" Anders said.

"I mean that we have to go after the dragon," Devin said. "We have to follow it, find it, and try to use our magic on it again. What's the alternative? Leaving it free to terrorize the kingdom?"

"All right," Anders agreed. "But if we're going to do it, we should do it quickly. It will be harder to track the dragon the further away it gets."

He didn't say that he could still feel the dragon's presence via the amulet. He *knew* which way it was going. They would go after it, they would find it again, and this time, Anders wouldn't make the mistake of leaving Devin alive.

CHAPTER THIRTY TWO

The Dance of the Suitors continued around Lenore, as it had for so many days now. Days of feasting, days of dancing, days trying to put off the moment when she would have to finally make a choice. As she had for so long, she had to smile through it, pretending that her thoughts weren't racing, and that her eyes weren't straying to the spot where Finnal was still standing, surrounded by friends and hangers-on.

Guards were watching him too, now, making sure that he didn't leave the castle. Lenore needed him there to make sure that his father brought Aurelle. She wasn't about to give away the only leverage she had in this negotiation. Well, not the *only* leverage. There was still the question of whom she had to marry, and the Dance of the Suitors was starting to wind down. They'd entertained the nobles for long enough, given them rooms to stay in, fed them and given them wine, and now the men were getting restless. They were still taking part in the festivities, but every so often, one of them would look over at her, muttering, obviously wondering when she would get around to making a decision.

She felt sick at the thought that she might actually have to marry Finnal in order to resolve this, and her eyes looked around until she found Lord Hal, who had returned to the party, apparently after taking the time to tour the castle. *He* at least, seemed to be enjoying himself, and Lenore considered asking him to dance again. She also couldn't shake the strange familiarity of his clothes.

Even as she thought about it, Orianne came up to her, bending to whisper in her ear.

"Duke Viris has arrived, my queen. He awaits you at the gates, but will not enter the castle."

Lenore had expected that he might do that. Duke Viris was a wary man.

"Does he have Aurelle with him?"

"Yes, my queen," Orianne said. "Along with enough retainers to fight his way clear of the city if he needs to. We'll not solve this with battle."

153

Then time had run out. The Dance of the Suitors needed to come to an end. Lenore stood, waving her hands for the music to come to a halt.

"My friends!" she called out. "Duke Viris has come to my home, to forge an alliance. That means that the Dance of Suitors must come to an end."

"That means you'll need to pick a husband!" Lord Ness called out. He was clearly drunk by this point. Just one more reason that, however brave and handsome he was, it wasn't going to be him. Lenore had her plan.

"I will," Lenore said. Briefly, she looked over at Finnal. He stared back at her with a tight smile of triumph, knowing what this situation would force her into doing, knowing how few choices she had left in that moment.

She still had *some*, though.

"I have made my decision, and if I am forced to choose a husband, then I will choose the one among you who actually saw me as a person, rather than a prize. Lord Hal, step forward."

The nobleman looked utterly stunned as he moved to the fore of the room. Lenore liked that almost as much as everything else he'd done. The rest there would have taken this simply as their due. Instead, he looked nervous.

"If I must choose a husband, then I choose you," she said. "As the Dance of Suitors requires, I make my offer to you, and ask you to be my husband."

"I… I don't know what to say," Lord Hal said, clearly flustered by the offer and looking around as if he might be seeking a place to run.

"Then take all the time you need to consider your answer," Lenore said. "But I have made my offer, and the Dance of the Suitors is done. So too is the Peace of the Dance. Guards!"

Her men sprang to attention.

"Lord Finnal is no longer under the protection of tradition. Seize him."

"But you can't—" Finnal began.

"I am *queen*!" Lenore shouted back at him, pointing to direct her men. They grabbed Finnal by the arms, and it looked as if a few men might move to help him, their hands moving to their swords.

"This breaks tradition!" Finnal said.

"I have stayed *within* tradition," Lenore said. "And Finnal has sought to manipulate me. Stand with him, and I will name you traitors."

154

The men stepped back, bowing hurriedly.

"You can't do this!" Finnal insisted. "Your spy will die for this! *You* will die for this!"

Lenore stood, taking the sword that Devin had made for her and strapping it at her side.

"Let's go see your father, Finnal," she said. She glanced back over her shoulder as she left the throne room. "Consider my proposal, Lord Hal."

Lenore led the way out into the courtyard of the castle, and found all those who had come for the Dance of Suitors following her. Good, at least that meant that she had the strongest nobles of the kingdom at her back. It didn't necessarily mean that they would all fight for her, but at least they would see what happened today.

The gates to the castle were shut when Lenore reached them, but her guards opened them at a wave of her hand. They ground open to reveal Duke Viris standing there at the head of the ranks of his men. Aurelle was there beside him, her face bruised. Duke Viris had one arm around her, and a knife to her throat.

"Have you accepted my son's offer?" he called.

"No," Lenore called back. "But I have an offer for you. Return Aurelle without further harm and I will return your son the same way. Do that, and you will be permitted to go in peace from my city." She drew the sword Devin had made, moving to Finnal. "Harm her, and I will cut your son down myself."

Duke Viris paused for a moment or two. "My son is protected by the Peace of the Dance."

"He was," Lenore said. "Now he is not."

"She chose another, Father," Finnal called out.

"I'm calling your bluff, Duke Viris," Lenore said. "I think you value your son. If you want him back alive, you'll send Aurelle over to us. Do that, and you get him back. We can even talk. Maybe there is still a place for you in this kingdom."

She didn't like making that offer after all the duke and his son had done, but she knew that this needed to end. If he would accept peace, that would have to be enough.

"Bring my son to me, and I will release your... servant," Duke Viris said.

"And have you kill her as soon as you have him back?" Lenore countered.

155

The duke stood silently for what seemed like a long time, obviously trying to calculate this.

"Does he think that little about you?" Lenore asked Finnal, poking him with the tip of the sword. "He's actually trying to work out if you're worth saving."

"Father!" Finnal called out to him.

"When I was kidnapped, my family came for me at once," Lenore said. "My brother rode into the Southern Kingdom itself. Your father won't even accede to one simple request."

"Please, Father," Finnal called.

Duke Viris looked up from his thinking. "We meet on the ground between our forces," he said. "I will bring your spy, and you will bring my son. We will then return to our sides. You will offer neither myself nor Finnal harm after the exchange. I will leave the city with my men in peace once this is done. Agreed?"

"Agreed," Lenore said, and she could see the way that Finnal smiled as she said it. It was a smile, not of relief, but of a kind of triumph. It didn't matter. She pushed him forward. "Walk. Everyone else, stay back."

They walked forward, Finnal at the point of Lenore's sword, Aurelle before Duke Viris's dagger. They paced forward, and now it seemed that everyone else there was deathly silent, the tension increasing with every step. Lenore felt as if she could hear every creak of wood from archers on the walls, every breath that Finnal took. Duke Viris's men stood there ready, but did not speak or call out, did not take a single step that might have tripped this over into violence.

Lenore kept walking, trying to judge this situation. She could hear Finnal's steps beside her, and didn't like the expression on his face whenever he glanced her way. He didn't look terrified the way he should have, the way Aurelle did. He looked like he knew something she didn't.

Lenore didn't like that. She didn't like the amount of time it had taken Duke Viris to agree, either, suggesting that he had been calculating something, working out some plan. They were getting closer to one another now, but the closer they got, the less comfortable Lenore felt about all this, the more certain she was that all of this was a trap.

Duke Viris was backing himself to be able to grab her, wasn't he? A knife to the throat of Aurelle might just be enough to get her to come out from the protection of her castle, but a knife to Lenore's throat? That might buy him a kingdom. He could drag her away, have a priest remarry her and Finnal, claim the kingdom...

Lenore wasn't sure what it was that made the decision for her, whether it was some look in Duke Viris's eye, some twitch of his hand, some quirk of his expression. Whatever it was, Lenore knew in that moment that this was a trap, and she knew that there was only one way out of this.

She pulled back the sword that Devin had given her, gripped it with both hands, and thrust with it, hard. She drove it through Finnal's chest from behind, and the sharpness of this sword was so much greater than steel that she barely felt the moment when it slid through his flesh, all the way so that it protruded from him, transfixing him.

For a moment, he stood there, and then he toppled, his body tumbling to the hard ground while beyond him, his father could only stare.

CHAPTER THIRTY THREE

Aurelle saw Finnal fall, and she felt Duke Viris stiffen beside her in shock.

"No, my son!"

She understood the scale of the risk Lenore had taken, with both her own life and Aurelle's. They were both out well in front of any friends, alone with a man who might not be known as a fine swordsman, but who had at least been a warrior in his younger days, and who even now held a knife. With her striking down Finnal like this, they might both be killed, but then, weren't the odds good that Duke Viris would have betrayed them anyway?

For now, though, he seemed frozen in place by the death of his son, still trying to work out how to react to what had just happened. Aurelle had a chance, and she of all people had the training to take it.

She twisted away from the knife, getting both of her hands on the knife arm. She felt the tip of it scrape across her collarbone as she did it, but Aurelle ignored the pain. There was no such thing as a perfect way to twist a knife from someone's hand unarmed; inherently, a weapon provided an advantage. The most she could do was try to take advantage of Viris's moment of inattention.

Twisting away from him, she extended his arm as much as she could, then twisted sharply back, driving the knife back in toward him, slamming the point up under Viris's jaw, into his skull. She felt the crunch of the blade against bone as it went in, and jerked the knife again, just to be sure.

"That," she whispered as he died, "is for everything you made me do."

Normally, she felt no satisfaction as she killed beyond a job well done. Now though, *now* Aurelle felt a dark kind of joy creep through her as she wrenched the knife free and watched Viris topple. She turned, as if she might hold off the entirety of Viris's retainers with one knife, but those men were not advancing, not yet. They were too busy standing in silence, as shocked as their lord had been before Aurelle stabbed him.

Finnal wasn't dead. Not yet. He was belly down on the cobbles, crawling toward his father in spite of the wound Lenore's sword had left through his torso. Aurelle looked over to Lenore, barely even needing to ask the question.

"My queen?"

Lenore gave a single, terse nod in response and Aurelle smiled in cruel satisfaction at that. For a moment, she'd been worried that Lenore might be too merciful for a moment like this.

She moved forward and grabbed Finnal's head, wrenching it back to expose his neck.

"You're as vile as your father," she said, and dragged her knife across his throat in a single, satisfying cut.

Even as he died, Lenore was stepping past her, toward the duke's men. Some of them had drawn their swords. A couple had arrows nocked in their bows. Lenore seemed to be ignoring all of it, walking out in front of them with an air of surprising certainty given that she was facing up to row after row of armed men.

"Your lords are dead," Lenore said. "You owe them no more loyalty. More importantly, there's no one left to *pay* you."

Aurelle realized then that Lenore had understood the most important thing about these men: they were all out for what they could get. With Viris and Finnal dead, there was nothing left to receive except an untimely death. Even so, it seemed like a terrible risk to take.

"You could kill me," Lenore said. "But that will earn you nothing except to be hunted by my men in turn. You could fight your way through the city and out to freedom, but for what? To become bandits?"

Aurelle stood tense by her side, ready to defend her from anyone who decided to run forward. The tension there was so great that Aurelle didn't know if there was anything, even Lenore's sense of command, that could stop the violence of battle from breaking over them.

"Put your weapons away," Lenore said. "This is done."

They stood there, and the moment seemed to waver on the edge of violence. If one of them took a step forward, just one, Aurelle knew that the rest would charge forward as one to cut them down. She tensed, her own blade ready to fight back, for all the good it would do.

"Put your weapons *down!*" Lenore said. "Your queen commands it!"

To Aurelle's astonishment, they did it. They sheathed swords and put arrows back in quivers. A few even threw down their weapons and

159

walked away. Aurelle finally dared to breathe a sigh of relief. It was over.

*

"It's not over!"

Lenore sighed as Lord Ness strode beside her through the castle's great hall, trying to explain to her why she should have Viris and Finnal's allies hunted down. She did her best to ignore him.

"Lord Ness," she said with as much patience as she could muster, "I value your counsel, and your skills as a warrior, but please do not presume to tell me how to run my kingdom."

Perhaps before, it wouldn't have worked, but now Lord Ness had seen Lenore cut Finnal down with her own hands. For some reason, there were some men who respected that more than all the diplomacy Lenore could muster.

"Of course not, my queen," he said with a bow. "But what do you plan to do with Duke Viris's men? With their *lands*?"

Oh, so *that* was what this was about.

Lenore raised her voice, so that all the other nobles crowding into earshot could hear her.

"Before you all start an unseemly scramble for Duke Viris's lands, let me say this. They will fall under royal stewardship for now, until I can identify worthy successors, loyal to the crown. If there are those of his blood who are willing to swear fealty, then, once they have shown their loyalty, they will inherit his titles, and the lands will be split between them. They are not a prize to be won at court."

It was a move that would help bring those who had sided with Viris back into the fold. Lenore would also make sure that more than one relation was found, so that the problem of an over-mighty duke didn't come up again, without losing any of the men they could provide to an army.

She looked around to find Orianne. "There will be those among the duke's retainers who do not deserve to live. I know the ones who kidnapped you are dead, but there will be others. Identify them, please."

"Of course, my queen." Her maidservant offered a delicate curtsey at odds with the grimness of her task.

Saying *that* aloud was a different kind of reminder to her nobles: that she was prepared to be fair, and kind, and forgiving, but also that there were limits for all of them. Lenore still had Finnal's blood on her dress. She suspected that helped with that impression, too.

"Now, forgive me," Lenore said. "But I need to talk to my husband-to-be."

She looked around until she found Lord Hal. She went to him and offered her hand. "I need to talk to you. Alone."

She could see how nervous he looked then. It probably involved the fact that she was still holding the sword. Maybe that was a good thing. It was probably better to have him a little nervous for the conversation she was about to have.

She led him through to an empty antechamber, closing the doors behind them. There were chairs there around the wall and Lenore took one of them, happy to sit down after everything that had just happened. The adrenaline that had carried her through the last little while had started to fade now. Hal sat next to her, his face seeming caught between sympathy, nerves, and uncertainty.

"I know," Lenore said.

"I'm not sure what you mean," he said.

"I can recognize my brother's clothes when I see them," Lenore said. "There's no point in pretending, Hal. *Is* that your name?"

She saw Hal deflate a little, but he looked almost relieved at the same time. "No, it's not. My real name... it's Cillian. I'm sorry, I didn't mean for this to get so out of hand. I just came here because I thought that the whole Dance of Suitors thing might be fun."

"*Why* are you wearing my brother's clothes?" Lenore said.

"Would you believe that he gave them to me?" Cillian said. "I was down on the docks, fresh off the ship I was working on, and he came up to me and just... I swear he just gave me all his possessions."

"I believe you," Lenore said. Strangely, she did. It wasn't the kind of thing the Vars she'd known would have done, but he'd seemed... strange when he'd left.

"So... what now?" Cillian asked. "Are you going to have me executed? Are you going to marry me?"

"No, to both of those," Lenore said. She smiled slightly. "What you did actually helped me out. It meant I could make an offer of marriage to someone and know that my lords would never force me to follow it up. If anything, I feel as though I should reward you."

161

"I already have your brother's stuff," Cillian said.

"True," Lenore said. "But I think something more is in order. Lord Cillian is going to go to a very small portion of the lands that were Duke Viris's to rule over them. Nothing fancy, but you will be a lord."

"That... that's too much, my queen," he said.

"Nevertheless," Lenore said. "It is what will happen. I am queen, and I command it."

She stood, because that gave her an idea. She walked out from the antechamber, heading back to the great hall. The nobles were waiting, and watching. She went to the throne and stood before it, setting her sword very deliberately against the side of it.

"Sadly, Lord Hal will not be marrying me," Lenore announced. "He will, however, be helping to administer a portion of Duke Viris's former estates, with the aid of his brother, Lord Cillian."

She added the last part so that Cillian didn't have to spend the rest of his life using a name that wasn't his own.

"Then who will you be marrying?" Lord Ness called out. "The traditions of the kingdom—"

"Master Eames!" Lenore called, and the scholar was there, being supported by his assistant.

"Yes, my queen?"

"Has a queen ever chosen and been turned down?" Lenore asked.

"I would have to check my texts, my queen, but I believe not," Eames said.

"And the choosing ends the Dance of Suitors?"

"Traditionally yes, my queen," Eames said.

"But in this case—" Lord Ness began.

"Enough!" Lenore shouted. "I have played your games of tradition, and I am done with it. I made my choice, the dance is over. All my life, I have been constrained by such things. Now... *I* am queen, and *I* will rule. I will have no king." She rested a hand on the hilt of the sword. "Does *anyone* here want to try to argue with that?"

None did, so Lenore sat on the throne.

"Good, now, let us begin the business of state."

CHAPTER THIRTY FOUR

Erin made her way, grim-faced, through the sands of the wastelands. The peasant boy, Villim, had died in the night from his arrow wound, leaving her with only a small crew around her now. Still they headed south, seeking out Sandport, and the would-be Ravin who waited there.

"The rest of you should turn back," she said to Sarel. The other woman shook her head.

"We knew the dangers when we got into this."

Erin wasn't so sure about that. They'd known that they would be in enemy territory, but to be stuck in the middle of so *many* of their foes, with this heat, and lack of water, and sand... none of them had expected that. Still, they carried on, hoping that they would find the right way.

The heat only increased. It beat down on them, and cracked Erin's lips with thirst. They'd managed to take water at Inedrin's camp, but when they didn't know how far they had to go, it was impossible to know how to ration it properly. All they could do was keep riding, and hope.

Somewhere in it all, they came upon a sight that stood out from all the rest of it: cobbles in the middle of the sand, half covered by it, forming a road. Erin wasn't sure that she'd ever seen anything quite so beautiful. They turned onto it, still heading broadly south, sure that the only place it could lead was Sandport.

They rode for leagues then, until the sun was low in the sky, all without seeing another soul. Then, out of nowhere a single figure stood out on the road ahead.

A woman stood there, old looking, jangling with charms and occasionally whirling in the dying sun in a way that seemed mad, or mystical, or both. Erin approached ahead of the others.

"Hello," she called out. "Are you all right out here? Do you need help?"

The woman laughed. "Why would I need help, when I have the spirits to guide me? They tell me about you, girl. They tell me what you seek."

"Mostly, I'm just trying to find the way to Sandport," Erin said, trying to keep her tone light. If this woman really could see through her disguise, then they were all in danger.

"You will not find Nicholas St. Geste there," the woman replied.

"What do you know about that?" Erin snapped, looking around for danger.

"The spirits tell me many things," the woman said. "For example, they tell me that on nights such as tonight, when the moon is high, the man you seek likes to go to the ruins nearby and give thanks to his ancestors. He tours them in a gilded palanquin and plans his next moves. If you seek him, you will find him there."

"Why tell me this?" Erin demanded. "If you know what I want to do, why help me?"

"They say that you are killing all those who might rise to lead the Southern Kingdom," the woman said.

"I'm trying to stop another Ravin," Erin snapped back. "I'm trying to stop more slaughter."

"A worthy cause," the woman replied. "Do you think you are the only one who shares it?" she pointed. "What you seek is in the ruins. Find it, or don't. The spirits don't care."

Erin cursed, and set off in the direction that the woman pointed.

She rode hard, and the others had to work to keep up with her. Yannis rode up by her side.

"Are you sure this is a good idea?" the nobleman asked. "Do you think these ruins even exist?"

Erin had an answer for that, at least, because she could see stone pillars rising out of the desert ahead of her. The remains of what must once have been buildings stood around them, half covered by the sand. She rode to the edge of those buildings and dismounted.

"We'll leave the horses here. Merl, cover our retreat."

"Yes, your highness," he said.

"The rest of you, with me," Erin said. They bunched up together, moving through the ruins, heading in the direction of the space between those great pillars, each of which looked massive enough that a house could have been set upon it. The remains of what seemed almost like some great stone temple interior stood within that circle, complete with a vast, slab-like altar. The whole place was lit by torches in the falling light, and by that light, Erin could make out exactly what the wise woman on the road had promised: a gilded palanquin, carried by four strong-looking men.

"Take up positions around here," Erin said to the others. "When you see me make my move, you move in."

They nodded and spread out. Erin waited there by the edge of those ruins, watching, letting herself fall into the kind of calmness Odd might have been proud of. She waited until she was sure that there were no guards who were going to interrupt, and then she rushed forward on silent feet.

She was fast and silent enough that for the first few paces the palanquin bearers didn't even react. Even when they did, it was too slow, starting to turn toward the threat she presented far too late. Erin leapt at the palanquin, thrusting with her spear as she jumped into it.

She hit nothing. Instead, she tumbled straight through it. The palanquin was empty.

"Trap!" she yelled to the others. "It's a trap!"

A figure staggered out of the near darkness as the palanquin bearers ran back toward the ruins. Erin recognized Ceris the archer stumbling toward her.

"They were waiting for us… in the… shadows…" she managed, reaching for Erin.

She made it one more step before she fell. There was a dagger sticking from her back. Her eyes were glazing over even as she hit the ground.

Guards poured out of the ruins, forming a circle of steel around Erin even while Erin recoiled from the horror of what was happening. This was a trap, and her people had walked into it at her command. They were dead, because of her.

Anger boiled up in her at that thought, unrelenting, impossible to hold down.

"Nicholas St. Geste, I know you're here!" she bellowed. "Face me, you bastard! One on one! I'll cut your heart out! Or are you too much of a coward even for that?"

A man stepped from the circle. He was… not what Erin expected. He was tall and broad, with deep bronze skin, dark hair falling to his shoulders, and handsome features that seemed only to be emphasized by the torchlight. He wore a dark coat over scale armor, carrying a sword that seemed to curve slightly the wrong way, and a forearm-long dagger. He didn't look much older than her, though he looked every bit as determined.

"You're him?" Erin demanded. "The man who's going to be the new Ravin?"

"And *you're* the invader from the north, here to force us all to be like you," Nicholas said. "I'm going to stop you, invader."

"*You're* going to stop *me*?"

Erin leapt at him, leading with her spear, hoping to catch him off guard. She knew that there was no hope to fight her way free of this place with so many guards there, but at least like this she could rid the world of a man who might be a threat.

He blocked her blow, though, coming back with a snake-fast strike of his sword that Erin barely swayed aside from. She swung her spear low in turn, and he jumped over it, then slashed out with his dagger so that Erin had to give ground.

"You're as fast as your reputation suggests," Nicholas said.

"Well, all I've heard of *you* is about all the people you've killed," Erin shot back. "That ends today!"

In the next few seconds, they rained blows upon one another, yet none of them got through. Her foe was fast for his size, and his strength meant that Erin had to back up as he struck at her again and again. Every parry she made jarred her arms, sapped her strength. Yet her own blows made him move just to stay ahead of them, Erin's fury fueling her attacks now.

"Why won't you *die?*" she snarled.

"You first, invader!"

She knocked the dagger from her enemy's hand and saw it go spinning away into the dark. He struck at her with a great sweep of his sword, and Erin had to throw herself forward to get inside it. He grabbed her spear, and she clamped onto his sword arm, the two of them struggling, fighting, striking with every part of their bodies. They kicked at one another, struck with their knees, barged into one another, as evenly matched as Erin had been with any opponent in her life.

She saw an opening then for a headbutt, one that would hopefully make her enemy loosen his grip enough to stab him. She pulled her head back, jerked it forward... and found Nicholas St. Geste doing exactly the same thing in the same moment. Their heads smashed into one another, and Erin saw stars, blinding pain spreading through her skull.

The last thing she saw before she lost consciousness was Nicholas St. Geste toppling over like a falling tree.

*

When Erin woke, she was in a soft, plush place that seemed to roll around from one side to another as it moved. She was also tied hand and foot, arms bound behind her, legs folded up and tied thigh to ankle, so that struggling against it did nothing. It took her a moment to work out where she was. The palanquin. They were carrying her in the palanquin.

Nicholas St. Geste was there, groaning and rubbing his head like he too was only just regaining consciousness. There was a bruise spreading across his face, and in spite of it, he still somehow remained good-looking. *He* wasn't bound, of course.

He laughed. "I don't think I've ever woken up next to a princess before. I've never been headbutted by one, either."

"Come closer," Erin snarled, "and I'll be happy to repeat the experience."

"I *knew*," he said. "I knew it was you the moment they started talking about a girl with a spear, hunting leaders. And when I saw how furiously you fought, I was certain."

"Good for you," Erin snapped. She struggled against the ropes that held her again.

"Might as well lie still," he said. "If Sarit put you in here with me, he'd be sure you were well tied, and I have no intention of untying you until we reach Sandport. After that... well, we'll see."

"What will we see?" Erin demanded. "Are you going to murder me, like you did my people?"

"Oh no," he said. "You're far too valuable for that. Princess Erin of the Northern Kingdom, I am Nicholas St. Geste, ruler of Sandport, king claimant of the Southern Kingdom, and you... you are my prisoner, to deal with as I wish."

167

CHAPTER THIRTY FIVE

Devin hurried in the wake of the dragon, determined to track it and catch up to it before it went too far. He and Anders just had to hope that it wouldn't fly to the other end of the kingdom on waking, that it had only gone to hunt, or stretch its wings, or something.

"Do you think we'll be able to track it?" Devin asked.

Anders pointed. Ahead of them, Devin could see spots where the ground was smoldering, and others where it had frozen, obviously touched by the dragon's breath.

"I don't think that will be a problem," Anders said. They followed the path of the dragon together, back onto the mainland, collecting their horses and then riding along the route marked out by the ice and flames. It led up over rocky ground, where fissures and chasms stood, so that they had to pick their way between them, leading the horses. Riding them would have been too dangerous when a single misstep would send them tumbling down into one of those gaps in the earth.

"Why did it run?" Devin wondered aloud.

"Maybe it felt the magic we were doing and didn't want to be caught by it," Anders suggested, as they kept moving.

"Maybe," Devin said, although it didn't make much sense to him right then. Surely the magic should have calmed the creature and drawn it in? "When I connected with Sigil, it wasn't like that."

"Your wolf isn't a dragon," Anders pointed out.

"No, but he's still a magical creature," Devin said. "And the power connecting us is the same."

At least, he thought it was the same. Wasn't the fact that he could connect to Sigil supposed to be one of the things that showed he might be able to fulfill the prophecy? Shouldn't that mean that it worked the same way, at least in theory?

They were making their way up an escarpment now, with a drop on one side that seemed to plunge down vertically to a solid ground level below. It meant that Devin had to pick his steps carefully over loose stones, feeling the ground unsteady under his feet.

He kept going, though, because the dragon was there somewhere ahead.

"Are you sure we managed to bond with it?" Devin asked.

"It went away, didn't it?" Anders replied. "Keep following."

"But I didn't *feel* the bond," Devin said. "Normally, I can feel the moment when magic works. It's like something clicks into place. It's like something feels *right*, you know?"

"No," Anders said, and Devin looked over at him in surprise. "That's never what it has felt like for me. Magic has always been one more task to accomplish. It feels precise to me, ordered."

"But you said you felt the connection to the dragon," Devin said.

"That was different," Anders assured him.

Devin sighed and kept walking. "None of this makes sense."

Even so, the only thing to do was to keep going. Once they found the dragon, they could try again, and this time, Devin was determined that he would feel what was happening. He and Anders would throw their magic into the creature, and they would forge the connection that they needed. They would bond with it, and—

Devin stopped short at the sound of a sword being drawn. He looked around at Anders, standing there with his blade in his hand, and Devin's eyes darted to the rocks and fissures around them, assuming that some kind of enemy must be about to leap out to strike at them.

He couldn't see anything, though, and Devin turned back to Anders, staring at him, not understanding.

"Anders, what—"

He was still asking it when Anders struck, not at him, but at Sigil, sword lancing out to spear through the wolf's chest, right through the center of the mark that Devin had named him for. Devin heard Sigil let out a howl of agony as Anders twisted the blade, but that howl was cut short as Anders dragged the sword out.

Devin felt it as if Anders had thrust the blade through *his* chest, instead. Pain flared through him, and grief at the sight of the wolf lying there, still and blood-soaked. Devin felt the loss as pure pain, felt hatred for Anders come with it, but also felt a yawning emptiness. Devin hadn't known just how complete his connection to Sigil had been until it was gone, but now it was, and it felt as if Anders had just torn a hole right through his being.

"Why?" Devin demanded. "*Why?*"

"Because one of us *did* forge a connection to the dragon," Anders said. "And that means that I don't need you, whatever the sorcerer says. Us working together? It's just another one of his lies."

Devin realized then just how comprehensively he'd been tricked. He'd thought that Anders was on his side. He'd thought that, in spite of everything, Anders was beginning to become his friend. Now... now Anders had killed the one creature who was like a piece of Devin, and was still standing there with a sword in his hand.

"I would have let the wolf live if it had been able to tolerate me," Anders said. "Such tools can be useful, and I'm not a monster. I'm not, I'm meant to be a *hero*. But I *can't* give you that connection. I can't let you live either."

"I'll stop you," Devin snarled. "I'll *kill* you."

"No, you won't," Anders said, squaring up before Devin, his blade drawn.

Devin went to draw *Loss*, knowing that at least there, he had the advantage. That was when Anders hit him with a working he'd obviously been preparing all along. Without Sigil there, Devin had no chance to defend against it as a blast of air slammed into his body, strong enough to knock him back even though he tried to brace against it.

He took one step, then a second, and on the second, there was simply no ground to step onto.

His arms pinwheeled as he tried to keep his balance, and Devin felt *Loss* slip from his fingers, toppling into the void behind him. He swung his leg, trying to find purchase, but there was nothing solid for him to find a grip on, only the open air of a fissure, waiting to claim him as he toppled over the edge.

Devin cried out as he fell back, and that cry wasn't just about what was happening to him. It was all of it. It was being betrayed, it was seeing Sigil slaughtered like he was nothing but an inconvenience to Anders, it was being caught so utterly unawares that he couldn't even fight back.

Above all of it, though, there was the certainty that the kingdom was in danger because of this moment. If he could have found the dragon, and bonded with it, Devin could have found a way to save them all, but as it was, there was only the falling, seeming to hang in space forever as the air rushed up around him.

Devin found himself thinking of Lenore, of her face, of her smile, of the moment when they had managed to kiss, just briefly. It hadn't been enough, could *never* be enough, and now it wouldn't be anything more. Just like that, all the possibilities that could have been were swept away, leaving only the falling, the emptiness…

…and the impact.

The ground struck Devin with the force of a hammer to every part of his body, so that for a moment the impact was too great even for the pain to get through as Devin rolled and bounced down what turned out to be a slope, tumbling like a rag doll down deeper into the fissure, toward its base.

Devin felt his head strike something as he fell, the impact sickening, the pain sudden and sharp, filling his skull, eclipsing even the impacts that slammed into the rest of his body. He tumbled and fell, and eventually came to a rest.

Devin struggled to rise, knowing that he couldn't stop, couldn't just give in with Anders still up there. He had to find a way to rise, even though his body was refusing to right then, had to find a way to get back and face up to Anders. If he didn't, the whole kingdom might be in danger; *Lenore* might be in danger. He couldn't give in, not like that. Groaning with the effort, Devin started to crawl.

He looked up, seeing the shadow of Anders somewhere up there above him. He needed to climb up, needed to find a way to fight back, but his body wouldn't let him. The pain from where his head had been struck was growing, threatening to consume all of him, impossible to push back down.

Devin's last thoughts before he slumped back to the earth and the darkness claimed him were of Sigil.

CHAPTER THIRTY SIX

Vars was quite surprised to find that he wasn't dead. After the storm, after the impact of the ship on rocks that he hadn't been able to even begin to steer away from, he had been sure that death was the only possibility. His finely honed capacity for fear had been screaming at him all the ways that it might be possible to die, and yet none of them had touched him.

He would have felt happier about it if he weren't currently hanging at an odd angle, kept in place by the ropes that bound him to the ship's wheel. The *Azure Hound* itself was currently listing badly, leaning over on rocks that poked up like jagged teeth in the mouth-like enclosure of a circular cove. A beach lay ahead, with a path leading up through cliffs of white chalk, but for now, that was all that Vars could see.

He'd see more of it soon though, just as soon as he got free of this wheel. He'd been lucky, been the one to survive when the others almost certainly hadn't. He'd landed… somewhere, and he could find a way to live here, and even to thrive. He would be running wherever this land was…

…if only he could get free of these damned ropes. The only problem was that Captain Yula seemed to have tied these particularly tightly, and the saltwater had made them shrink tighter still. Vars thought that he'd learned a thing or two about knots in his brief time as a sailor, but his fingers couldn't begin to unpick these.

He wrenched at the ropes instead, trying to pull free of the wheel through simple force. The wood groaned and creaked, but it showed no sign of giving way. Vars sagged against it, feeling exhaustion seeping into his bones.

He was thirsty, he was hot, and it seemed that here, the sun was hotter than usual, beating down with relentless force. Vars could feel his skin starting to burn in the heat, his lips already cracked with the lack of moisture, his eyes having to half close against the glare of it.

He was going to die, wasn't he? He'd thought that he'd been the lucky one, the one who was special and got to survive this, but no, it just meant that he was trapped here alone on the deck of the ship, dangling like a scarecrow while the sun slowly cooked him. Lenore had sent him into exile thinking it would be the merciful option. Now, it seemed like he was going to get a fate that might satisfy even Erin's bloodlust.

Vars threw himself against the ropes again and again, burning up his strength with the effort of trying to get free even as the sun slowly leached the moisture out of him. He sagged against the wheel again, but he knew that resting wasn't going to give him the strength he needed. Nothing would.

"Hello up there. Should I come back? Only you seem a little preoccupied right now."

Vars looked around, straining as hard as he could to look far enough. There, approaching barefoot across the rocks, was a dainty young girl, slender and small, probably no more than ten years old, picking her way from rock to rock the way someone might pick out the steps of a dance. She wore layers of gossamer that wove together to form a gown, covered in layers of dirt that she didn't seem to care about. She smiled over at Vars.

"You don't look very comfortable up there," she said.

"That's because I'm *not*," Vars said. "I need help!"

"Looks like it," the little girl said. She at least stepped closer, so that it didn't hurt Vars's neck so much to turn and look at her.

"What's your name?" Vars said.

"I was told I should never give my name away to strangers, in case they take it and use it to fill me with nightmares," the girl said. "But you can call me Vey, if it helps. What's your name?"

"Vars," Vars replied. "Please, just go get help, your parents or something!"

"I don't have any parents now," Vey said. "And there isn't anyone on the island except me. Just me."

She spun in an elegant twirl, apparently happy with the world. Then again, she wasn't the one hanging tied to a ship's wheel.

"Just you?" Vars said.

Vey nodded. "This is my island. All mine. I can do whatever I want here."

"Does what you want include helping to get me down from here?" Vars asked.

173

Vey looked at him with that strange kind of mock seriousness small children seemed to do so well. Erin had been particularly good at it when they'd been younger.

"I don't know," she said. "What are you going to give me for letting you go?"

"I don't know," Vars said. He looked around. "This ship? The things on it?"

"Are they really yours, though?" Vey asked. "Besides, I could just wait until the sun bakes you like an apple, then they'd all be mine anyway. What's *yours*?"

Vars had to admit that this girl had a point, not to mention a ruthless streak. What *was* his?

"I don't have anything," he said. "I gave it all away. I don't have anything to give you."

"You could give me your fealty," the girl said, and smiled up at him. "Did I say that right?"

"You did," Vars said. "What, you want me to become your vassal? Your servant?"

She nodded enthusiastically. "We could have such fun. And I'd untie you. But you have to say it first. You have to *promise*."

"All right, all right," Vars said. "I promise. I give you my fealty. Just get me down!"

"Okay," the girl said, and waved a hand almost idly. The ropes that held Vars seemed to part from him like living things, and he only realized the danger of doing that at such an angle as he started to slide down the sloping deck of the ship, tumbling out into space with a cry.

He hit the water before the rocks with a crash that knocked the air from his body. His feet hit sandy rock, and he pushed off, breaking the surface with a spluttering cry. Vars dragged himself up onto those rocks, lying there for several seconds at the little girl's bare feet.

Only they weren't bare anymore. Instead, they were clad in elegant green and gray leather boots, laced up the front with something that seemed to be a strand of vine. Looking up further, Vars saw the strangely pristine hem of a dress that seemed to be woven from flower petals and leaves, clinging to long, slender legs that were not those of a little girl.

Vars looked up, and *kept* looking up. The woman there would have been taller than him, even if he had been standing. She was slender and willowy, long limbed and so pale-skinned that she almost seemed to glow with it. Her eyes were the deep green of a forest, and seemed to flicker with a kind of madness that Vars couldn't place. Those of her features he could see were delicate and beautiful, with hints of the girl that had been there before in the curve of her jaw, the upturn of her nose. Most of those features, though, were hidden behind a mask of curling leaves.

Vars stared at her. "You... you're... who are you?"

"Now what did I tell you about names?" she asked. "Still, you can call me Verdant. And this is Void."

A man walked down onto the beach, and it was as if Vars's mind simply refused to accept him until he got close. He wore a long robe, and *his* mask was blank where the woman's was woven from greenery.

"You should probably get up, Vars," she said. There was something about her words that seemed to flow straight into his heart, pushing him to move. "Void will want to talk to you."

Vars did it, still staring at her. How could he *not* stare at her? He understood what was happening here, but it was the kind of explanation that made no sense in itself, that didn't really *explain* anything.

"This is sorcery," he said.

"Hmm, a talent for stating the obvious. I'm not sure if I like that in my vassals," Verdant said.

"Your vassal?" Vars repeated, and then realized just what he'd sworn to this woman when she'd been a little girl. "No, that isn't... I didn't mean..."

"But you said it," the man, Void, said. "You gave your word to Verdant, and now she will hold you to it."

Vars felt terror start to rise inside him, and it was a different fear from the one he'd felt during the storm, but it was at least as strong.

"Oh, don't worry, Vars. If we'd wanted you dead, we would have simply drowned you in the storm with the others," Void said.

Verdant ran a finger along Vars's jaw. "That would be a waste. We're going to have so much fun."

Somehow, that was more frightening than the rest of it.

"What are you planning to do with me?" Vars asked. "I'm nobody anymore. I can't help you."

"Oh, I'm sure you can," Verdant said. "I'm sure we'll be able to do *something* with you."

Vars swallowed in fear.

"Don't worry, Vars," Void said. "You're very important. We have plans for you, Vars. Big plans."

CHAPTER THIRTY SEVEN

Greave had never ridden quite as hard as he did toward Geertsport. His horse thundered beneath him, its hooves kicking up sparks from the cobbles of the road. Behind him, Peris and Meagan struggled to keep up, the swordsman sitting high in the saddle as he rode, the peasant woman clinging to her horse as if she feared that it might buck her at any moment.

"Slow down, my prince," Peris called.

Greave didn't slow, though, not when Nerra was still out there somewhere ahead. He'd worked out the path the dragon was taking, but now he needed to travel that path as fast as possible, needed to get to the place he was going before his sister could leave. He hurried along the road toward the coastal town, and it was only when Greave caught sight of it that he slowed his horse to a walk.

He could see the damage there, obviously wrought by fire, buildings burned, structures flattened where they might otherwise have stood tall. His heart stopped in his chest. Was he too late already?

No, he realized as he looked out at it, this was old damage that had simply yet to be repaired. This was a hangover from some earlier attack. Did that mean that they were heading to the wrong place? No, Greave decided. He'd gotten this right, he was sure of it. Nerra, or the creature claiming to be her, had all but *told* people which way he should go.

There was a patch of ground ahead, shaded by trees on both sides, and with rocks rising up between them. The road curved between the two, and as he got closer, Greave saw that several trees had fallen, as if pushed over by the passage of a creature that was...

"Wow," Meagan said. "This thing's *huge*."

It was. Just based on the trees that had fallen, Greave guessed that the thing that had done it had to be larger than a house, and stronger than a dozen oxen.

"How is a man supposed to fight a thing like that?" Peris asked, resting his hand on his sword as if contemplating exactly how little damage it might do to something of that size.

The sight of it should have been terrifying, but it actually gave Greave hope. One look at the trees told him that they'd been knocked down recently, the broken wood still green, but with no signs of new growth. The dragon was close by.

"We need to move these trees," Greave said, pointing to the fallen trunks. "At least enough to get through."

He started toward them, looking around for something that he might use for a lever and a fulcrum. There might only be three of them, but Greave was sure that with a basic knowledge of mechanics, they would be able to move them.

"Start clearing the brush," he said. He took out a rope. "I'll try to find something we can use as an anchor point for a pulley."

He stepped from the path, looking for a suitable tree around which to wind it. He needed something with smooth enough bark that it wouldn't damage the rope, slender enough to wind around multiple times, yet strong enough to hold against the effort required.

Greave was still looking when a voice whispered to him on the wind.

"Greave."

"Nerra?" Greave recognized his sister's voice instantly. "Nerra, are you there?"

He hadn't dared to believe that it might actually be her. He'd *hoped,* but if the world had shown them all anything in the last few months, it was that hopes could easily be dashed. Now, though, that voice hung in the air, familiar and tantalizing.

"Greave, I'm over here."

Nerra's voice seemed to be coming from deeper in the trees, and Greave followed her voice, trying to track it, trying to understand why his sister wasn't just coming out to meet with him.

He continued to follow, but the problem with doing that was that Nerra had always been better in forests than him. She'd spent so much time outdoors that she could easily stay ahead of him. The only question was why.

"I'm not following any longer, Nerra," Greave said. He turned back toward the road. "If you *are* Nerra."

If this was really his sister, she wouldn't keep playing games with him. Greave started back toward the road, and he was in sight of it when Nerra called him back.

"Greave, wait!"

Greave didn't look back, though, because his sister could come out to him if she wanted to speak with him.

"I have your cure, Nerra," Greave said. He kept walking toward the spot where Meagan and Peris were working to move the trees. "I want to *help* you, but you have to come out into the open."

"Greave!" Nerra called. "I'm trying to *save* you!"

There was a shadow above the trees then, vast and dark and deadly looking. Greave couldn't see all of it through the trees, but even so, the glimpses of dark scales and claws he caught made terror rise inside him. The dragon seemed to hang there in the air, vast wings beating slowly as it swooped in low, and even as Greave opened his mouth to shout a warning, the dragon opened *its* mouth, too.

Peris and Meagan obviously sensed some of the danger, because they had started to turn toward the threat when the dragon washed flames over them, white hot and focused, enough to turn the fallen trees into a bonfire with them atop it.

"No!" Greave cried out, but he could barely hear it over their screams, his two companions turned into human candles with what seemed like no effort. They screamed their agony to the air around them, and then the flames were too hot even for that, stealing away the breath that they might have used to cry out, leaving them staggering and writhing as their skin blackened, their clothes caught fire. The flames were so hot that Peris's armor started to melt, the metal turning liquid as Greave watched, no defense against an attack of that magnitude. Greave could only watch their deaths in horror, the moment when they tumbled to the ground as charred remnants left seared into his brain.

Then the dragon was past, the wash of its wingbeats blowing at the flames consuming the trees, its dark form retreating into the sky. Greave ran out onto the road, to the spot where his companions lay, no more than blackened lumps on the ground there.

"Why?" Greave shouted, turning back toward where he'd last heard Nerra. He knew the trap for what it was now. It seemed so obvious, looking back. Greave had read enough books on tactics to know what trees left across a road meant.

The thing that stepped from the forest wasn't his sister, wasn't anything human at all. It was taller than Nerra had been, and scaled, with iridescent blue running across its flesh. Its features were lizard-like and hungry, while its hands had claws. It wore a kind of robe of

179

rough cloth, and a lizard's tail poked out from beneath it. There was something about the look in her eyes, though, some hint of recognition there between them that told Greave that this *was* her, however little it looked like her.

"Nerra?"

"It's me, Greave," she said, and it was still her voice. That struck to the heart of him, more surely than those claws ever could have.

"You're… what happened to you?" Greave asked.

"I became what I was always meant to," Nerra said. "I became Perfected. I was Chosen by the dragon queen herself."

"What are you talking about?" Greave asked. "Nerra, you had the scale sickness."

"It wasn't a sickness. It was a transformation," Nerra said. She looked him over. "What are you *doing* here, Greave? It wasn't supposed to be *you* who came here. The trap wasn't meant for you."

"You're behind this trap?" Greave said, but he knew it had to be true. Why else would Nerra be here if not for this? Even so, he couldn't bring himself to believe it. How could his sister ever have begun to do this? "Nerra, this isn't you."

"You don't know who I am, Greave," Nerra said. "And you still haven't answered my question. What are you doing here?"

Greave realized that he'd almost forgotten his purpose in doing this. He reached into a belt pouch, taking out the cure that he'd so carefully crafted.

"I made this," he said, holding it out to her. "I traveled the kingdom. I found the recipe in the Great Library of Astare. It… it's a cure for the scale sickness. You could be who you were, Nerra. You could change back."

Nerra reached out to take it delicately between two claws, holding it up to the light as if to examine it.

"You actually did it?" Nerra said. She held it there. Then, carefully, precisely, she put the vial away somewhere in the folds of her robes.

"I told you before, Greave, this isn't a sickness. All my life, people treated me as if I were something to be shunned, something to fix. Now, I know the truth: I am more perfect than any human-thing can be. I am joined to Shadr the dragon queen herself. I am exactly what I need to be."

Greave knew in that moment that his sister was gone. She had become a monster. There was no way to help her.

CHAPTER THIRTY EIGHT

Nerra couldn't believe that her brother was standing in front of her, that he was here, actually here. She wanted to tell him so many things, wanted to express her surprise that he'd come this far for her.

"What are you doing here?" Nerra said. "You shouldn't *be* here."

"I came to try to help you," Greave said. "Now I see... now I see that there *is* no helping you."

Nerra thought about the vial he had given her. He could never understand that she had never been meant to be human. She had always been destined to be this. She was needed in the war that was coming. She knew the role she had to play. In all the attacks, she'd been the only thing holding back Shadr.

Holding me back? Shadr sent to her. *You think you're holding me back, little princess?*

"I'm trying to make what's coming better," Nerra said, and she wasn't sure if she was saying it to Shadr or to her brother.

"How is it better to side with *dragons*?" Greave asked. Shadr's thoughts echoed his almost exactly.

Would you choose humanity over your true kind, my Chosen?

"It's not like that," Nerra said. "Humanity and dragons don't have to be at war. They could find a way to coexist. When I first found Alith—"

Do not think of that one! Shadr sent, and Nerra could feel the anger there. *You are mine, not that of some lesser dragon!*

Nerra flinched back with the force of that, and Greave must have thought that it was about him. It wasn't, though, and Nerra knew that she had to get him out of there, because this wasn't safe for him. She'd only barely saved his life by calling to him, but she couldn't guarantee that twice.

"You've done what you came to do, Greave," Nerra said, putting a hand on his shoulder. "You've given me your 'cure.' You've succeeded in whatever quest this was. Go home."

"Come with me," Greave said. "Take the cure and come back."

181

Nerra shook her head. "I can't. You need to go, Greave. Carry back a warning about what's coming. Tell them that the dragons will descend on the kingdom, and that their armies cannot stand. Tell them—"

This is not what we discussed, Shadr sent. *The idea was to lure the amulet bearer here and finish him.*

This isn't the amulet bearer, Nerra replied. *He's my brother.*

I thought that if we burned their lands, the amulet bearer would come, Shadr sent. *Instead, a human-thing who doesn't matter has come to us.*

"You need to go," Nerra said to Greave. "You need to go *now*."

Why feel so much for him, my Chosen? He is not like you, could never be like you. He is a chain, tying you to a former life that was never truly yours. Be rid of him.

"Be rid of him?" Nerra said, and realized that she'd spoken the words aloud.

Greave was backing away now, a frown on his face. "Nerra."

You need to kill him, Nerra, Shadr commanded her, and it was definitely a command. Nerra could feel the weight of the dragon's will on her, pushing her to act. Nerra found herself taking a step toward Greave before she'd even thought. She held herself in place only with an effort of will, fighting back against the tide of rage and bloodlust that threatened to overwhelm her.

"Run, Greave," she snarled, the words coming out as something inhuman. "Run while you still can."

You have to do this, Shadr said. *You have to shed these last limits of humanity. You think that you are holding me back? No, that cannot be permitted. Do this!*

Nerra pressed her claws into her palms, crying out as they drew blood. "No, I won't. I won't kill him. He's not the amulet bearer. He doesn't need to die."

He needs to die if I say he does! Shadr roared in Nerra's head, and Nerra's hands swiped at Greave almost before she could stop them. He was far enough away now that Nerra missed, and she was grateful for that. She flung herself back from her brother, so that she wouldn't be able to strike out at him anymore.

"No, I won't hurt him!" Nerra yelled out. "This is evil. This is cruel."

182

Perhaps, Shadr said, and Nerra felt a note of something like compassion there. *I am not unkind to those who are mine. So I will not make you do this.*

"Thank you," Nerra breathed. "Thank you, my queen."

I will do it, instead.

"No!" Nerra shouted, but already, the shadow of the dragon was passing overhead. She looked up, and Shadr was there, having wheeled around, coming back for another attack.

Remember afterwards that you chose this. You could have made this quick.

"Run, Greave!" Nerra yelled. "Run, or she'll kill you!"

Her brother stared at Nerra as if he still couldn't quite understand what was happening. Then he turned, running for his horse, leaping into the saddle and turning it back so that it could run along the road. He spurred it into a gallop, and the terror of the horse seemed to propel it to greater speed still.

Nerra saw the danger in it at once, though, because Shadr was gaining on her brother, the dragon's wings beating almost languidly as they propelled her forward faster than any horse could gallop.

"No!" Nerra called out. "Into the trees!"

At this distance, though, there was no way for her brother to hear, or react in time. He kept galloping forward, even while Shadr blasted the ground in front of his horse with shadow, making it stop and rear with terror, Greave barely clinging to its back.

Then Shadr landed in front of him, rearing up on her hind legs. Her tail whipped around, slamming into Greave's horse, and even at this distance, Nerra heard the crack of bone, the scream of the horse as it toppled.

Greave fell with it, and Nerra saw his leg briefly caught beneath the horse as it fell. He managed to roll clear as the horse bucked and thrashed, but that just left him crawling along the road.

Nerra started to run toward him, her Perfected form letting her do it faster than any human could have. Even so, she was too slow. She saw Shadr start toward him, footsteps thunderous as she stalked him.

She reached the horse first, and her great jaws opened, darting down to clamp shut on the thrashing animal. Those jaws crunched through flesh and bone, cutting off the horse's cries of agony. She lifted the bloody carcass and tossed it into the air, jaws opening wide to

183

swallow it, crunching and cracking coming as the dragon queen devoured the dead horse.

All the while, Greave was backing away, crawling with one leg dragging as if broken, clearly hoping that he might be able to get to the trees before Shadr's attention returned to him. Nerra could feel that attention on him, though, could feel through their link that Shadr was tracking him as efficiently as a cat might a mouse. Nerra sped up, hoping that she could get there in time to intervene and help her brother.

It only meant that she got there just in the moment when the dragon struck.

Greave had his sword out by then. He'd never been a fighter, but Nerra could guess what he was doing, his brain running through everything he'd ever read about dragons, trying to recall if this or that tome held some secret weak spot that might let him slay one. Even as Shadr rose over him, he struck out, the point of his blade aimed at what he must have thought was a softer patch of scales, or a vital organ.

He struck, and the blade kicked up sparks as it hit Shadr's scales. Perhaps the strike might have worked on a young dragon, too weak to fight back, but as it was, it merely skittered from the hard armor of the dragon queen's hide. Shadr struck back then, as delicately as a surgeon, one foreclaw coming down like a falling spear, plunging into Greave and transfixing him.

"No!" Nerra screamed, but Shadr wasn't listening. Instead, the dragon lifted Greave, still thrashing, still impaled on that claw, hoisting him up to eye level, to mouth level.

She blasted him then, with both shadow and fire, the two combining into something stronger that made Greave scream in agony as Shadr killed him. It blackened his flesh and flayed it from him. Then, just like the horse, her jaws opened wide.

"Please, no," Nerra begged. "Not that."

They are no different from animals, Shadr replied. *And will be treated as such.*

She bit down on Greave then, once, again, tearing chunks of flesh from him the way a noble at a feat might have torn at a chicken leg. She tossed his body into the air, opened her mouth, and caught it, crunching down on it, spraying blood as she consumed him.

Nerra fell to her knees in agonized grief, the dragon staring down at her. She ached with the loss of her brother, but she couldn't even feel that grief properly, because Shadr wouldn't let her. The dragon's presence pressed in on her, obliterating everything else.

This is the fate of all humanity, she promised. *And you... you do* not *hold me* back! *You do not have the power! You are mine, not theirs!*

CHAPTER THIRTY NINE

Renard enumerated the problems of being sent on a quest by a wizard as he rode, following a map Master Grey had given him to what looked suspiciously like an island made out of pure ice.

First, there was the lack of drink, since sobriety was not a look that suited Renard *at all*. Second, there was the prospect of hideous death at the hands of a dragon, or the boy who had the amulet. Third, there was the awkwardness of having to ride across an entire kingdom. Fourth, it meant that he'd had to leave Meredith behind in the city, and whatever her protestations that he was useless and had no place in her House, he'd been sure he'd been just on the cusp of getting through to her. Fifth… he struggled to think of a fifth, but was sure that something would come up shortly. Probably bandits.

Renard sighed. All this, because he hadn't been feeling sufficiently heroic. It was irritating what things like a conscience could do to a man. And drink, of course. The drink had definitely had a role to play in him being here. Still, he couldn't blame it for all of this. Not when he hadn't had a drop all morning.

He would be at the coast soon, at least. Once he reached that Renard would legitimately be able to say that he'd gone as far as the magus's map showed him, and would then be able to turn around and find a tavern, or a brothel, or both. Just a little further, over this next rise, and Renard would be free of all heroic obligations, able to…

"Oh," Renard said as he crested the rise. "All the gods damn it."

Two things caught his attention at more or less the same time. The first was an island linked to the mainland by a causeway, only this one wasn't ice covered like the drawing on the map. There were chunks of ice that had obviously toppled from it, but instead of a giant island of ice, a volcano sat there, open at the top. It had to be the same place, but something had changed, something on a level that could only mean magic. Renard was starting to get very tired of magic by this point.

The second thing was the trail of flame-blackened and ice-touched spots leading up through a series of rocky escarpments, through partly burned trees and on out of sight. As trails went, it was one that a blind man could follow, obviously showing the route that a dragon had taken. Renard didn't have to think too long to decide which direction Devin and Anders would have gone; he just had to think of what would be the heroic thing to do. Put like that, it was *obvious* they would have gone after a creature that had the potential to eat them both.

Renard set off in their wake, and the ground rose and fell around him, fissures in the rocky earth making it increasingly difficult to navigate. Only the trail set out ahead of him drew him on.

He could be wrong, of course. The two young men could be waiting back at the volcano, while he rode off in the wake of a dragon. Renard might find himself, once again, staring right down the throat of one of those things, and that was an experience he'd already had more than enough of. Still, he kept going, while the ground around him grew ever more broken. After a while, Renard had to dismount and keep going on foot, leading his horse by the reins.

He found the body of the wolf first, larger than most, shaggy furred and with a curious marking in the middle of its chest. Though he'd never met it, Renard knew all about Devin's wolf from the stories about the fight against the invasion. Those had cast it as a magnificent beast, bringing down foes with relentless jaws, tamed by magic. Now, it lay there in death, blood covering it from a wound that looked to Renard like it had been made by a sword.

Renard tried to calculate all the ways that could have happened. Bandits? No, because this wasn't the kind of ground for a good ambush. An accident? Not when the wound was so precise and clear edged. What then?

Renard was still contemplating that when he heard scraping sounds coming from one of the fissures nearby. Renard drew a long knife on instinct, ready for danger. He crept forward on silent feet, picking his way without a sound in spite of the loose stone of the ground around him. He made his way to the edge, ready for someone, or some*thing*, to fling itself up at him.

He found himself looking down at a young man in dirt-stained clothes trying to climb the sides of the fissure without success. It probably didn't help that one of his ankles looked twisted and couldn't bear his weight.

"Are you Devin, or Anders?" Renard asked, because it seemed inconceivable that this could be anyone else.

187

"Devin," the young man said, looking shocked that anyone would know his name. "And you…"

"I'm Renard," Renard said with a hint of pride. "Master thief, swordsman, hero of the siege of Royalsport."

Devin shrugged, like he'd not heard of Renard, which was slightly galling. Still, it couldn't be helped.

"Master Grey sent me," Renard went on, by way of explanation. "He thinks your friend Anders stole an amulet that has the potential to be incredibly dangerous."

"He's not my friend," Devin growled up from the bottom of the fissure. "He attacked me. My wolf… he killed Sigil."

That fit with what Renard had seen. That was good. Even now, it was probably a good idea to be wary.

"Can you help me out of here?" Devin asked.

"I have a rope in one of my saddlebags. If you wrap it round yourself, I can probably haul you up. Wait here a moment."

Renard went and fetched it, fastening it around a spur of rock and testing it with his weight. He threw it down to Devin, who caught the end and tied it around him. Renard saw him lift a scabbard holding what looked like a finely worked sword.

"Okay, I'm ready," Devin called up.

Renard started to pull the rope up, and even with Devin helping by trying to climb, it was hard work. Renard was used to lifting nothing more demanding than his own weight, or perhaps a few jewels. He dug his heels into the ground, pulling the rope up hand over hand until Devin crested the ridge of the fissure, throwing his sword up ahead of him. When he did, the first thing he did was to go over to the body of the wolf, kneeling beside it, laying a hand on its still head. Renard could see the grief there, and wished that he could give Devin more time.

As it was, Renard had to lay a hand on his shoulder.

"I'm sorry," he said. "But we have to go. If Anders has the amulet as Master Grey suspects…"

"He said that the two of us would work together to fulfill the prophecy," Devin said. "He said that we'd go to the island and wake a dragon. He lied to me about… well, everything. I'm not sure how much more I can trust him."

"Who said anything about *trusting* him?" Renard replied. "Since I started getting involved with magic, I've been lied to, attacked, manipulated, and almost drained of every scrap of life I have."

"Then why not walk away?" Devin asked.

"You know why," Renard said. "The same reason you came here. Probably the same reason you tried trusting Anders: it's the right thing to do. It's not even heroic, it's just the thing you know you need to do."

Devin let out a shuddering breath and Renard kept going.

"The amulet Anders is carrying is dangerous," he said. "I've felt the power in it. Someone like that shouldn't have it, which means we need to find a way to stop him. Since I know nothing about magic, that means I need your help, and I guess, after all this, you have your own reasons for wanting to find him."

Devin nodded then. "I do."

Renard offered him his arm, helping the young man back to his feet. Then, together, they set off in the direction of the dragon trail that would lead them to Anders. Renard just had to hope that the two of them together would be enough, or the whole world was going to suffer for it.

NOW AVAILABLE!

DREAM OF DRAGONS
(Age of the Sorcerers—Book Eight)

"Has all the ingredients for an instant success: plots, counterplots, mystery, valiant knights, and blossoming relationships replete with broken hearts, deception and betrayal. It will keep you entertained for hours, and will satisfy all ages. Recommended for the permanent library of all fantasy readers."
--Books and Movie Reviews, Roberto Mattos (re The Sorcerer's Ring)

"The beginnings of something remarkable are there."
--San Francisco Book Review (re A Quest of Heroes)

From #1 bestseller Morgan Rice, author of A Quest of Heroes (over 1,300 five star reviews) comes a startlingly new fantasy series. DREAM OF DRAGONS is book #8—and the finale—in Age of the Sorcerers. The series begins with book #1 (REALM OF DRAGONS), a #1 bestseller with over 400 five-star reviews—and a free download!

In DREAM OF DRAGONS (the series finale), the great war between dragons and humans finally unfolds. The entirety of the kingdom is threatened, with the dragons' aim set for Royalsport. A prophecy will come to fruition, while a new menace in the south threatens to tip the balance of power, and Queen Lenore must defend her capital as best she can under dire circumstances.

Will she prove herself worthy of the throne?

Will Royalsport survive?

And will Lenore and Devin finally be together?

AGE OF THE SORCERERS weaves an epic sage of love, of passion, of sibling rivalry; of rogues and hidden treasure; of monks and warriors; of honor and glory, and of betrayal, fate and destiny. It is a tale you will not put down until the early hours, one that will transport you to another world and have you fall in in love with characters you will never forget. It appeals to all ages and genders.

Book #8 is the series finale!

"A spirited fantasy ….Only the beginning of what promises to be an epic young adult series."
--Midwest Book Review (re A Quest of Heroes)

"Action-packed …. Rice's writing is solid and the premise intriguing."
--Publishers Weekly (re A Quest of Heroes)

BOOKS BY MORGAN RICE

AGE OF THE SORCERERS
REALM OF DRAGONS (Book #1)
THRONE OF DRAGONS (Book #2)
BORN OF DRAGONS (Book #3)
RING OF DRAGONS (Book #4)
CROWN OF DRAGONS (Book #5)
DUSK OF DRAGONS (Book #6)
SHIELD OF DRAGONS (Book #7)
DREAM OF DRAGONS (Book #8)

OLIVER BLUE AND THE SCHOOL FOR SEERS
THE MAGIC FACTORY (Book #1)
THE ORB OF KANDRA (Book #2)
THE OBSIDIANS (Book #3)
THE SCEPTOR OF FIRE (Book #4)

THE INVASION CHRONICLES
TRANSMISSION (Book #1)
ARRIVAL (Book #2)
ASCENT (Book #3)
RETURN (Book #4)

THE WAY OF STEEL
ONLY THE WORTHY (Book #1)
ONLY THE VALIANT (Book #2)
ONLY THE DESTINED (Book #3)
ONLY THE BOLD (Book #4)

A THRONE FOR SISTERS
A THRONE FOR SISTERS (Book #1)
A COURT FOR THIEVES (Book #2)
A SONG FOR ORPHANS (Book #3)
A DIRGE FOR PRINCES (Book #4)
A JEWEL FOR ROYALS (BOOK #5)
A KISS FOR QUEENS (BOOK #6)
A CROWN FOR ASSASSINS (Book #7)

A CLASP FOR HEIRS (Book #8)

OF CROWNS AND GLORY
SLAVE, WARRIOR, QUEEN (Book #1)
ROGUE, PRISONER, PRINCESS (Book #2)
KNIGHT, HEIR, PRINCE (Book #3)
REBEL, PAWN, KING (Book #4)
SOLDIER, BROTHER, SORCERER (Book #5)
HERO, TRAITOR, DAUGHTER (Book #6)
RULER, RIVAL, EXILE (Book #7)
VICTOR, VANQUISHED, SON (Book #8)

KINGS AND SORCERERS
RISE OF THE DRAGONS (Book #1)
RISE OF THE VALIANT (Book #2)
THE WEIGHT OF HONOR (Book #3)
A FORGE OF VALOR (Book #4)
A REALM OF SHADOWS (Book #5)
NIGHT OF THE BOLD (Book #6)

THE SORCERER'S RING
A QUEST OF HEROES (Book #1)
A MARCH OF KINGS (Book #2)
A FATE OF DRAGONS (Book #3)
A CRY OF HONOR (Book #4)
A VOW OF GLORY (Book #5)
A CHARGE OF VALOR (Book #6)
A RITE OF SWORDS (Book #7)
A GRANT OF ARMS (Book #8)
A SKY OF SPELLS (Book #9)
A SEA OF SHIELDS (Book #10)
A REIGN OF STEEL (Book #11)
A LAND OF FIRE (Book #12)
A RULE OF QUEENS (Book #13)
AN OATH OF BROTHERS (Book #14)
A DREAM OF MORTALS (Book #15)
A JOUST OF KNIGHTS (Book #16)
THE GIFT OF BATTLE (Book #17)

THE SURVIVAL TRILOGY
ARENA ONE: SLAVERSUNNERS (Book #1)
ARENA TWO (Book #2)
ARENA THREE (Book #3)

VAMPIRE, FALLEN
BEFORE DAWN (Book #1)

THE VAMPIRE JOURNALS
TURNED (Book #1)
LOVED (Book #2)
BETRAYED (Book #3)
DESTINED (Book #4)
DESIRED (Book #5)
BETROTHED (Book #6)
VOWED (Book #7)
FOUND (Book #8)
RESURRECTED (Book #9)
CRAVED (Book #10)
FATED (Book #11)
OBSESSED (Book #12)

About Morgan Rice

Morgan Rice is the #1 bestselling and USA Today bestselling author of the epic fantasy series THE SORCERER'S RING, comprising seventeen books; of the #1 bestselling series THE VAMPIRE JOURNALS, comprising twelve books; of the #1 bestselling series THE SURVIVAL TRILOGY, a post-apocalyptic thriller comprising three books; of the epic fantasy series KINGS AND SORCERERS, comprising six books; of the epic fantasy series OF CROWNS AND GLORY, comprising eight books; of the epic fantasy series A THRONE FOR SISTERS, comprising eight books; of the new science fiction series THE INVASION CHRONICLES, comprising four books; of the fantasy series OLIVER BLUE AND THE SCHOOL FOR SEERS, comprising four books; of the fantasy series THE WAY OF STEEL, comprising four books; and of the new fantasy series AGE OF THE SORCERERS, comprising eight books. Morgan's books are available in audio and print editions, and translations are available in over 25 languages.

Morgan loves to hear from you, so please feel free to visit www.morganricebooks.com to join the email list, receive a free book, receive free giveaways, download the free app, get the latest exclusive news, connect on Facebook and Twitter, and stay in touch!

Made in the USA
Las Vegas, NV
14 April 2023